KAT and MEG
CONQUER the WORLD

KAT
and
MEG
CONQUER
the WORLD

ANNA PRIEMAZA

HARPER TEEN
An Imprint of HarperCollinsPublishers

HarperTeen is an imprint of HarperCollins Publishers.

ISBN 978-0-06-256080-3

Typography by Torborg Davern
17 18 19 20 21   PC/LSCH   10 9 8 7 6 5 4 3 2 1
❖
First Edition

To every best friend I've ever had

KAT and MEG
CONQUER the WORLD

KAT

HELL IS NOT BRIMSTONE AND SCORCHED FLESH; HELL IS BEING A HIGH school freshman for the second time. Hordes of cocky, confident upperclassmen swarm through the hallway behind me on their way to the cafeteria, jostling my backpack or my shoulder like I'm nothing. Because I am nothing to them. Just a freshman. An insignificant particle who can't get her locker open fast enough to move out of the way of the lunchtime rush.

I yank at my lock once, twice, three times, before it finally clicks apart and I can swing open the forest-green metal door to use as a shield. In Legends of the Stone, I don't bother using a shield, since enemies never get close enough for me to need one. But I need one here. I hide behind it, finally safe from the wandering elbows and careless shoulders, as I slide off my backpack and start to line up my textbooks on the top shelf.

I've made it to Friday, but Friday's not over yet. I count my breaths as I try to block out all the chatter behind me.

One mathematics . . . two science . . . three Ancient Civilizations . . .

Being a noob freshman again would be easier if it was because I had failed all my courses. That would mean it was my own idiotic fault. But I'm not a freshman again because I failed. I'm a freshman again because Alberta and Ontario hate each other. Which is worse than if I had failed, because it's so entirely out of my control.

"High school should start in grade nine," says Ontario.

"No way, loser, it should start in grade ten," says Alberta, for no reason other than to be spiteful.

And who suffers as a result? Innocent students like me, dragged through the crossfire by my parents, who thought it was a brilliant idea to move from Ontario to Alberta just before my grade ten year.

My English text drops into my backpack with a loud thud, and I hold my breath, hoping the noise doesn't draw anyone's attention. But the throng behind me is already thinning, and I'm still a nothing, thank goodness. I let my breath out slowly. Grab my other textbooks and my lunch and slide them more carefully into my bag.

I suppose my parents should be left out of it. They're just trying to look out for Granddad. And he really does need looking after. His skin is so thin and papery these days that when he leaned in to hug me after we arrived, I thought the zipper of my hoodie might catch on a wrinkle and tear away an entire gray sheath of it. But when I drew myself away, it was still intact; no recesses of red flesh contrasted against his colorless skin like he's a wereboar that's been sliced open with a legendary sword. Thankfully. I hope I die before I get that old, because I don't think I could handle worrying about my skin peeling off like paint from an abandoned barn.

I click my lock shut, swing my backpack on, and turn to face the almost-empty hallway. My throat constricts. Now what? There's no way I'm going to the bustling cafeteria, with its fluorescent lights and jabbering students and judging eyes. I don't know anyone, so anywhere I sat, I'd be an isolated doe, an easy kill for a hungry wolf pack. Their stares would tear me apart, and within seconds, my bloody carcass would be spread across the floor. Not literally, of course. But I'm still not doing it.

For the last few days, I've eaten outside, in a forgotten corner of the school—back against the cold, coarse brick, face to the sun's soothing heat.

But today the rain's coming down so fast the sky's practically melting, so outside isn't an option. I have nowhere to go. I force myself to go anyway. To wander down the hallway, one step after another. To hurry past the couple making out in the back stairwell and past the group of girls who chatter away like they've known one another since kindergarten. Because they probably have.

I pass a girls' washroom. I could eat in there, out of the way. But I don't really want to munch on my sandwich to the soundtrack of toilets flushing. Besides, the washroom may sound solitary, but there are always people in there.

So not the washroom. But then, where? I'm running out of ideas.

I hear, instead of feel, my breathing quickening into short, uneven spurts. *Get it under control, Kat,* I chide myself. *Just breathe. One wolverine . . . two toilet stalls . . . three . . . three what . . . three wild mushroom soup . . .*

Mom made me see a counselor in Ontario after I had one of my panic attacks in the canned vegetables aisle of the grocery store. The store manager had to call my mom to come get me. I'd have been painfully embarrassed if I wasn't too busy focusing on my inability to breathe.

The counselor was useless, mostly, so I'd never admit to her that the breathing exercises she taught me actually help.

"Try breathing," she said. "That's right, nice and slowly. Count them in your head. One elephant . . . two elephant . . . three—"

"Why elephants?" I interrupted, crinkling my nose. I'm not sure why it bothered me, because I do like elephants.

"It doesn't have to be elephants, Katherine." She always said Katherine, even though I had specifically told her it was Kat. "It's just a placeholder word to slow down the counting. You can put in whatever you want."

Four cucumber . . . five Alberta . . . six Pythagorean theorem . . .

My breathing has slowed. Thank goodness. The last thing I want is to have a full-blown panic attack in the middle of the hallway during my very first week at a new school. Talk about something to attract the wolves.

I need to get out of this hallway. I just have to get somewhere. Anywhere. Please.

As if in answer to my silent plea, just to my left a door opens and a safe haven materializes out of nowhere—the library. With computers. I force myself not to run. One step. Two steps. Ten steps. Eleven. Then I am in a seat and wiggling the mouse. Wake up, computer.

The screen flickers to life. I log on to the internet.

It's not going to work. Of course it's not going to work. But I can't not try.

My fingers automatically tap out the web address, click download. I watch the progress bar slowly fill.

The other computers are empty. If it was possible to download and install and log in, wouldn't all the computers be in use? Wouldn't everyone want to be in here?

But the file finishes downloading. And installing. And I'm entering my username, tapping out my password. Inputting our server details.

Then I am blinking at the screen, at the shimmering fantasy

world hovering in front of me. Legends of the Stone. LotS. It actually worked. At my Ontario school, the game was blocked. Along with pretty much every other good thing the internet has to offer. You could look up the scientific names for algae or the middle name of the first prime minister and that was about it.

I take two steps forward—or at least my fingers do. The flowers I planted last week on the sandy floor of my underwater castle wink at me, as vibrant and dazzling as any real-life meadow of blossoms. I pull out my bow and ready an arrow. If a wolf attacked me here, I would kill it. If an entire pack of wolves attacked me here, I would kill them all.

No one else is online on our server, so a rift raid probably isn't going to happen. But I can work on my underwater castle. Or search the badlands for packs of baddies who've wandered up from the rifts.

A real-life sound startles me, and I glance up. A freckle-faced librarian sits at her desk, coughing delicately into the crook of her elbow. As she finishes, her eyes meet mine and my chest constricts. The game isn't blocked, but I don't know the rules. Maybe I'm not allowed to—I stop myself before I panic. From where she's sitting, in front of me and to the right, she can't possibly see my screen.

In game, I steady my bow hand. In real life, I smile at the librarian. She smiles back, then glazes over, looks down at her papers. I am safe.

MEG

"TEN HIGH FIVES!"

"What?" Lindsey doesn't look up from rummaging in the bottom of her locker. Instead of crouching at floor level like I would, she leans over with her butt sticking out toward the chattery rush of passing students—probably on purpose.

"I got ten high fives," I say. "That's better than the eight from this morning, though I might have lost count because I thought I saw a guy wearing a LumberLegs shirt, but he wasn't, or maybe he was and I went running after the wrong guy. I'm not sure. I'm pretty sure it was ten, though."

I lean out into the hallway—farther than Lindsey's butt—and stick my hand in the air. "High five!" I shout. Two white girls pass by in almost-matching jeans and cardigans, too lost in their conversation to notice, but the Filipino guy behind them grins through his mouthful of braces and smacks his hand against mine so enthusiastically that he forgets to aim and hits my wrist. The brown flushes a little red.

"Eleven," I say, giving my arm a shake as I lean back against the wall of lockers. "Holy tiddlywinks, I love high school." There are so many more people here than in my tiny junior high. And it's Friday, so they're all happy.

"Have you seen my lip gloss? I can't find it and my lips are so—what are you wearing?"

I glance down at the lime-green leggings and black coverall

shorts I found at Value Village. "It's retro. And I'll have you know that this shade of green complements my *particular* kind of brown." I flash her my arm and put it against my legging. "See?"

Lindsey crinkles her tiny pink nose. "It's weird." She pushes a strand of her red hair behind her ear.

"You're weird."

She frowns. "You took your meds today, right?" she asks, then disappears back into the depths of her locker without waiting for an answer.

She's always asking me if I've remembered to take my meds, like she thinks they're some magic pill that'll cure me of me. Ugh, blah, and sigh. I think I was better off in the spring, when I hung out with those girls who were obsessed with making friendship bracelets. Then again, maybe not. I'm pretty sure it wasn't just my ADHD that made me bored out of my mind within the first ten minutes. Just thinking about it makes me want to do jumping jacks. I stick my hand back out into the thinning river of people and snag a slap from a too-tan white guy in sweatpants and a hoodie.

Fact: guys high-five more than girls. I mean, I haven't actually been keeping track or anything, but I'm pretty sure it's true.

Lindsey's face is *still* buried in her locker. I don't know why I bothered to trek all the way over here between afternoon classes. If high school had just started one week earlier, I could be two halls over, hanging out with Bradley Dennis's posse instead.

"His loss," I say.

"Whose what?" Lindsey finally resurfaces.

"Brad's."

Her expression softens for just a moment. "He's a jerk. He shouldn't have broken up with you. Can you throw this out for me?" She deposits a crumpled piece of paper into my hand.

The bell rings for the next period right then, and Lindsey swears. "I've got to go." She kisses the air at me, then turns and scurries off down the hall.

I smooth the crumpled paper against my leg, then fold it and feed it through the slot in her locker door before heading off to my science class.

Brad's friends all chose him over me, which is ridiculous because I was closer to most of them than he was, even though I'd only known them for a couple of months and he's known them for years. Although maybe we weren't as close as I thought, because the last time I tried to get them to do the chicken dance with me, a couple of the guys just rolled their eyes instead of laughing their heads off as we strutted and bucked like at the beginning of the summer. Ugh. Good riddance to all of them.

I should really find some new friends, though. I'm not going back to those friendship bracelet girls. They got all annoyed when I started spending so much time with Brad, as if they couldn't believe that I'd find my *boyfriend* more interesting than friendship bracelets. Good riddance to them, too.

Thank goodness none of them are in this class. I put my

head down on my desk, resting it on my arms for just a moment before popping back up again. There are approximately a bajillion people in this classroom, and I could make friends with any of them. There aren't any other black kids, but that's no surprise. My classes are scattered with Filipino and Chinese and East Indian kids, but other black people—not so much.

The Asian guy in the back corner is wearing a Legends of the Stone T-shirt, which is awesome. It has one of those ginormous rabbit creatures fighting a filthworm, and the cartoony art style makes them look even more hilarious than they do in the game, but the shirt would be even funnier if it had LumberLegs on it, too. If he doesn't watch LumberLegs, it might not be worth befriending him. I'm not putting up with another lecture about how I'm not a true Legends of the Stone fan if I only watch other people play and don't actually play it myself.

That's one good thing about He-Who-Must-Not-Be-Named splitting up with Mom. His rule was I couldn't watch YouTube until my homework was done, but in the one year and four months since he left, Mom's only enforced that rule maybe three times. So screw you, Stephen. All right, so I used his name—it's not like he's the world's most powerful wizard and he's going to abracadabra me out of existence. His only magical power is leaving.

"Megan?" Mr. Carter asks, and I snap my head forward. Mr. Carter's eyes are hidden behind the reflective glare of his thick-rimmed glasses, but his chin is pointing directly at me, expertly. No, expectantly. I have no idea what the question was.

If I was still in junior high, I would say, "Sorry, ADHD got the better of me," because everyone at Britannia Junior knew that about me and because when you're officially diagnosed, teachers have to make concessions. It's the law or something.

But high school is going to be different. I'm not going to be known for that.

"I'm sorry, sir, but I seem to have missed the precise nature of your question."

Mr. Carter raises his eyebrows, and I wait for the usual sigh, but instead the corner of his mouth twitches upward in an almost smile. "I asked if my instructions were clear."

His instructions? What instructions? Gee, thanks, Mr. Carter. That was helpful. "Perfectly clear." I smile at him, flashing my pearly whites, which really should be quite white since I've been plastering them with whitening strips for the past month, at least whenever I remember.

"So no questions?"

"Not from me." Perfect grin. I should be in a toothpaste commercial.

"Great. Thank you, Ms. Winters. Anyone else . . . No? Then I'm going to give you the last ten minutes of class to sort yourselves into pairs. Choose partners wisely, as there'll be no switching. Ready, set—pick!"

Partners? Great! I love partners. Maybe I *will* take a risk with that Legends of the Stone guy.

But no, he's already talking to the scrawny white guy sitting next to him. Ang and Jenni, the two Filipino girls in the front row, will of course be pairing off, since they've been attached at the hip for as long as I've known them. And the two girls next to me are apparently BFFs already, because they've got their heads together, giggling in a way that makes me think they're not talking about science. Though, wait, I think I saw them holding hands yesterday, so they're probably dating.

I could ask the goth girl two rows ahead, Alexis, but when I hung out with her at Folk Fest this summer, she spent the entire time smoking pot, and she's one of those people who gets super boring when she smokes. Like all mellow and crap. I am not ending up with her.

And I am not sitting here like a friendless outcast while others pair off all around me.

I whirl around. The pink-shirted, blond-ponytailed white girl sitting right behind me glances down at her desk, then to the side, then back at me. She bites her bottom lip.

I flash her my pearly-white grin. "Hi, I'm Meg. Want to be partners?"

KAT

THE GIRL—MEG, I GUESS—COCKS HER HEAD AT ME, WAITING FOR MY RESPONSE. One of her black corkscrew curls falls in front of her dark-skinned face, and she shakes it out of the way while somehow maintaining eye contact. Her grin is a little too broad. I shift back in my chair just an inch.

Here's the thing: this science project isn't like some grade five thing where you make a volcano and everyone cheers when the red-dyed vinegar and baking soda explode and you get a gold star just for participating. We're supposed to work on it for most of the year and then present it at a schoolwide competition at the beginning of March. It's worth 30 percent of our entire science mark.

And grade ten marks matter for getting into university. And getting into university matters for the rest of life. And the rest of life is a really long time to be a jobless, homeless bum.

So I can't partner with just anyone.

But here's the other thing: I don't know anyone in this class. I don't know anyone in this whole school. What am I supposed to do—interview her?

One introvert . . . two unemployed . . .

"Um, sure," I say.

"Great. Give me your phone." She sticks out her hand, palm up.

"What?"

"So I can put my contact info in. Oh, I guess I need yours, too." She draws back her hand and fishes her own phone out of her pocket. Its case is green and sparkly. She taps at the screen a few times, then looks up at me. "What's your number? Oh, and your name, duh."

"Oh, um, Kat. Kat Daley."

"Okay, Kat Daley. You want mine?"

My phone is in my backpack, on silent. I'm not sure what the rules are about having them out during class time. Tonight, I'm reading the student manual.

"Um, just write it here." I push my planner across the desk. She holds her phone in her left hand as she scribbles down her name, phone number, email address, and even her street address with her right. "Can I have your email password, too?" I think about joking, but don't.

She hands back my planner and returns to her phone. "Okay, now you."

I feel weird giving my info to this stranger, but I can't really say that when she just gave me all of hers.

Once she's entered it, she plunks her phone down on her desk—in full view of Mr. Carter, which means either I'm worrying needlessly or she's not worrying enough—and grins at me. Less manically this time. "So," she says, "what are we partnering for?"

"What do you mean?"

"I zoned out for a bit. What are we partners for? Labs or something?"

I regret everything.

KAT

"HOW WAS YOUR DAY?" MOM ASKS SECONDS AFTER I WALK IN THE DOOR, in her usual fifties-sitcom way.

Peachy. I had to explain to my new science fair partner what a science fair is. Thank goodness we have a few weeks to turn in our topic choice, and until March for the final project. Hopefully that's enough time to just do it all myself like I did last year, if need be. I should probably get started this weekend. Or tonight. I should get started tonight. *One boring volcano . . . two chemical reactions . . . three sound barrier . . .*

Mom waits cheerfully for my answer. I don't bother to

complain about being forced to move to this alien province or about the fact that I'm going to fail science. I know how that conversation would go.

"Why did we have to move here? Why couldn't Granddad come to stay with us?" I would whine, like a three-year-old.

"Granddad has lived here his entire life. We couldn't ask him to move across the country."

"Well, I've lived in Ottawa *my* entire life."

And then she would stare at me until I caved and admitted that Granddad's "entire life" is more significant than my "entire life" and that of course we should have moved here.

Mom doesn't need words to win arguments. And I don't need words to lose them. "It was fine," I tell her.

"That good, huh?" She glides across the kitchen and wraps her arms around me, practically smothering me. I lean into her for just a moment, letting her warmth surround me like a living, breathing afghan. She smells of apples and cinnamon, and the scent lingers in my nose when I finally pull away.

"Pies?" It's a safe guess. When Mom's not writing math textbooks, she's usually lost in a cloud of flour and brown sugar.

"Mm-hmm." She reaches across the counter to a mound covered by a checkered dishcloth and, with a flourish, reveals a circle of golden perfection.

"Is this one for us?" I lean forward and inhale deeply. Mom's worst trait—worse even than her love of warbling ancient pop songs in the shower—is that she sometimes makes baked goods and then gives them away to other people. Like old folks' homes and homeless shelters. Which makes it even worse, because I can't feel sad about it since that would make me a horrible person.

"Depends on whether you and your dad behave yourselves." With another flourish, she covers the pie back up.

"Mom! That's just cruel. I should report you."

"Good luck with that, dear."

I can't think of a single clever thing to say in response, so I just hoist my backpack off the floor and onto the table with a thud. A pity-me-for-all-the-work-I-have-to-do-and-give-me-some-pie thud. Sadly, after years of working in the textbook industry, Mom is immune to the textbook thud. She scurries about the kitchen, wiping down counters, without so much as a sympathetic glance in my direction.

I yank my math text out of my bag. "Hey, you didn't write this, did you?" Her name isn't in the front, but she ghostwrites sometimes, so that proves nothing.

"Let me see." She leafs through a few pages at the front, then the back, before shaking her head. "Not one of mine. Why?"

"I started reading ahead into the next chapter on the bus, since there was nothing else to do." Well, nothing but worry that I'd catch whatever was making the guy across the aisle cough and cough and cough, and then I'd pass it on to Granddad, and he'd cough so hard that his fragile bones would collapse in on themselves like a toppled house of cards. I hate public transit. "A couple of sections don't make any sense."

"I can look at it later, if you like. I've got to start chopping veggies."

I should probably offer to help, but I need to decompress with something funny if I'm going to survive family dinner. Technically, almost every dinner of my life has been family dinner, but since we left Luke behind in Toronto for university and replaced him with Granddad, dinners have been different. Granddad eats slowly. And I can't always tell if he's joking. And I have to keep my elbows off the table; I don't know if Granddad cares about that, but he might, so it's best to be safe.

"We'll be done by seven, right? Luke's supposed to call." On Friday evenings we play LotS together. That's the way it's always been. Except for last week, when he was too busy to play for the first time ever. "Frosh stuff," he said.

He said he could play tonight, though. He promised.

"That's perfect," Mom says. "We can all chat with Luke."

"Right. Of course."

One rutabaga . . . two old folks' home . . . three legendary sword . . .

"Kat?"

"Mm-hmm?" *. . . four rift raid . . .*

"We'll just chat with Luke for a few minutes. Then you can politely excuse yourself and slip off to play your game with him."

I love my mom.

MEG

OUR EMPTY HOUSE IS SO QUIET I CAN HEAR SOMETHING BANGING ABOUT IN the wind on the back porch from all the way up in my room. The stillness makes my earlobes itch. I drop my backpack on the rug and kick at my laptop on the floor, hoping it will magically turn on and blast some music into the silence, but it just groans.

When Mom and the halflings get home, the place'll start whirring with noise, but it'll still be boring. I've got to find a party or something to go to tonight. I should have asked that skinny-as-a-twig white girl who sits next to me in math class. She looks like she'd know where the good parties are at.

I flick on my phone. Lindsey is usually pretty up on party news, and she's the last person in my call log, so I hit the call button, then put it on speakerphone and sprawl on my bed.

"Hi, Meg." Lindsey sighs. She's been doing that a lot lately.

"I'm so happy to talk to you, too!" I practically chirp.

"Sorry, I just—I can't decide whether I should pack my straightener or my curling iron. What do you think?"

I lean over the side of the bed so my own mass of curls hangs to the floor. Even when Lindsey uses a curling iron, her limp red hair looks straight compared to mine. "I don't know. Straightener." I reach for my laptop and turn it on. LumberLegs's gorgeous face grins out at me.

"Did you put me on speakerphone again? You know I can't hear you when you do that."

I swing around and grab my phone off the bed, dropping it onto the floor beside my laptop. "No." I blow Legs a kiss. "Hey, what party are we going to tonight?"

"I can't. I told you, I'm going to my aunt and uncle's for the weekend. My aunt's taking me to a fashion show."

I'm pretty sure she told me no such thing, but she seems hangry, so I'm not correcting her. "Right, well, do you know about any parties tonight? You're okay with me going to one without you, right?" I'm pretty sure she would be, but we haven't been hanging out long enough for me to know for sure. One of the girls in this summer's crowd got mad when I did that.

"Meg, no, I don't. And I don't care what you do this weekend, either."

I want to spit something snarky back at her, but I know she doesn't mean that the way it sounds. At least, I hope she doesn't. I'm not ready for this friendship to be over yet. Not so soon.

There's a long silence on the line, broken up only by muffled clattery noises. Probably Lindsey throwing her straightener *and* curler into her suitcase; she's the type of person who would take both.

My laptop beeps at me that it needs to be plugged in soon, and I'd just switch to my tablet, but I have no idea where it is right now, so instead I rest the top of my head on the floor as I look under the bed for the cord. "Hey, did I tell you there are rumors LotSCON might be in Canada this year?" I ask as cheerily as I can.

"LotS—oh, that game you're always rambling about? I don't know. Probably. Look, I've got to go. I'll see you around, okay?"

"Yeah, su—" The line clicks dead.

I slap my beeping laptop closed, roll over, and stare up at the ceiling, where a tiny spider happens to be skittering across the expanse of white like it's on a mission. I grab my pillow and whip it into the air. It zooms across the room and lands with a clatter and thud in my closet, completely missing the ceiling. Probably for the best.

Maybe I shouldn't go out this evening. Maybe I should just lie here and watch my new eight-legged roommate make himself at home.

My phone rings, and I jolt upright. It might be Lindsey calling back. I snatch my phone off the floor.

"Evil McNastypants," reports the screen. I blink at it for a moment before remembering I renamed him that, then jab at the ignore button. The last time he called, I had him labeled just "Jerk."

I open my contacts, pull him up, stab at the edit button, then rename him again. "Stephen-the-Leaver." It almost rhymes, but doesn't, which is disappointing, but I can't think of anything better right this minute, so it'll have to do.

The voice-mail message notification pops up just as I hit save, and I delete the stupid thing without listening to it.

Right, it's his weekend with the halflings. I can't be here when he shows up. He might ask me to join them again.

If he wanted me to join them, maybe he should have sought custody of me, too, instead of telling the judge that I'm not his real daughter. I saw the papers in Mom's desk. He didn't ask for custody or even for any time with me at all.

I'm too ADHD, too stupid, too not-his-own-blood for him to care about me.

I flick through my phone contacts again. Maxx, who I went to junior high with, would probably know where there's a party tonight, but he doesn't answer when I call. Neither does good old Greggles, who works down the street at the 7-Eleven. Finally I give in and call pot-smoking, boring Alexis, who of course has a party to invite me to. Praise Her Majesty the Queen.

I've been to parties with Alexis's friends before, and like Alexis, they're all potheads who sit around doing nothing, but at least I can do nothing somewhere else instead of here. I grab a pen and scribble down the address on the back of my hand, then run the pen over it a few more times.

A car door slams outside just as I'm hanging up the phone. Mom and the halflings.

More doors slam, and then I sit up as the frizzy-haired bundle that is three-year-old Kenzie barrels into my room, onto my bed, and into my lap, still-shoe-covered toes smashing into my knees as she throws her arms around my neck. Halfling #1.

"I just magicked you into a goober," she says. Her natural black curls, which puff out of four little ponytails, blend with my own.

"Why thank you, Kenzie dear. I've always wanted to be a goober." I pull off her pink Mary Janes and throw them onto the floor, and she rolls off my lap and starts jumping on the bed in her stocking feet, her only-slightly-ripped pink dress flapping up and down with each jump.

"Hi, Meg." Nolan's quiet voice drifts in from the doorway, where he stands with his backpack hanging off one shoulder and his tiny glasses slipping down his freckled, dark-brown nose. Halfling #2. He pushes his glasses up with a single finger. At six years old, he is already pure nerd. In the best way.

"Come here," I say, and he sets his backpack down carefully in the hallway before plodding across the room. As soon as he gets close enough, I scoop him up into a bear hug, and then Kenzie launches herself on top of us, and we are a jumble of arms and legs and Kenzie-giggles.

My half siblings. The miniature-sized spawn of my mother and Stephen-the-Leaver. Nolan with skin just a shade lighter than earth brown, like our mother's. Kenzie with skin just a shade darker, like our respective fathers. And mine. I should ask them if they're packed for tonight. Should ask them what they're all doing this weekend—if he's taking them out for pizza like last time.

But I can't bring myself to ask any of that.

"You guys want to watch LumberLegs with me?" I ask instead once we disintegrate. No, dis*entangle*. Mom always says that if I took more time to think before I talked, I wouldn't mess up words so much. But how can I take time to think before I think? I point at my laptop. Kenzie crinkles up her nose and flees from the room. Nolan blinks up at me with a look that says, "I don't really want to, but I will if you want me to."

"Get out," I say, smacking him on the bum with Kenzie's shoe. "Go play with your books or whatever." He smiles gratefully at me and ambles away.

No one ever wants to watch LumberLegs with me.

My friend Larissa, from my friend group before the friendship bracelet girls (or maybe the one before that), introduced me to LumberLegs around the time Stephen-the-Leaver left. She kept telling me about this YouTuber who does play-throughs of this super-popular video game, Legends of the Stone—aka LotS—and posts the videos, and it sounded dull as heck, but then she showed me this video where Legs is trying to reach this golden crown but is so terrible at jumping that he constantly lets out these ridiculous screams that are more squeals of terror than roars of frustration as he plummets into the lava below. By the end of it we were both laughing so hard I peed myself just a little and had to spend the rest of the evening with my legs daintily crossed.

I started watching all the time, but apparently my preference for losing myself in Legs's hilariousness over actually playing the game meant I wasn't a *real* LotS fan, so she made a character for me and then couldn't understand why it bothered me that the brown of the character's skin was so much lighter than mine. She called me picky and went off on her "not a real fan" lecture again, so I called her racist or something and that was the end of that friendship. But I kept LumberLegs, so it was a fair trade.

I pull my laptop closer and roll over onto my stomach.

I don't get why no one ever wants to watch with me. Lumber-Legs is hilarious and thoughtful and has like five million subscribers. Plus he's drop-dead gorgeous, so even if they're not into games and hilarity, at least there's that. Since he's a guy who plays video games for a living, you might expect him to be pale and pimply, with greasy hair and glasses, but he has sleek black hair, sharp green eyes, and a perpetual five o'clock shadow. I think he's white, but he could be mixed, like maybe his grandpa is East Indian or something. Each week he does FaceCam Fridays, and I curl up on my bed with my laptop and laugh my pants off. Not literally, of course. Other girls don't get it, though. The one time at a sleepover when I convinced everyone to watch the lava video, only one girl laughed the way I did, and she moved away three weeks later.

I wink at Legs on the screen, then grab my mascara and green shadow from off the floor beside Kenzie's shoes and start smoothing on my makeup while Legs fights a venomous wereboar. There's no time to do anything with my hair, so I fight the curls back into a ponytail. My cousins have gotten their hair relaxed since they were maybe three years old, but Mom has ranted so many times about the years it took for the frizzy straightness to grow out when she decided to stop relaxing it and go natural, and I don't have that kind of patience. Besides, I like my curls. I just wish they weren't so much work.

By the time Mom calls me down for supper, I am fully decked out and ready to go.

"Is that what you're wearing?" Mom asks when I waltz into the kitchen, though she can't really complain. I'm decent by anyone's standards. Strappy black dress that reaches more than halfway to my knees, lime-green leggings, my favorite black cardigan with big purple buttons that cloaks my shoulders and arms, and my green high-top Converses. I can take the cardigan off when I get to the party.

"No, Mom, you're imagining it. I'm actually wearing a penguin suit." I grab a dough dumpling off the table. "I'll see you later."

Mom sets the leftover saltfish she just pulled out of the microwave on the counter and wipes her forehead with her sleeve. Kenzie and Nolan's cartoon fills the kitchen with a punchy beat, even though they're watching it all the way in the other room. "You're leaving already?" Mom asks. "I made supper."

"Yeah, it's after six. I need to leave before he gets here!"

"Meg," Mom sighs, but without conviction. She hates him, too. When they first split up, just the mention of his name could start her ranting for hours. Now she doesn't bother to rant anymore. She's already said it all. She wipes at her face again. Her makeup is wearing off, and the bags under her eyes are starting to show through. I'd throw her the concealer in my purse, but we can't share makeup like we do hair stuff, since mine's a darker shade of brown than hers.

"I'll be home by midnight," I promise. My usual curfew.

"And no city buses alone after ten."

"Yeah, yeah."

"Meg."

"And no city buses alone after ten, I got it." I throw an air kiss at Kenzie and Nolan in the other room, then wave my dumpling good-bye and slip out the door. I'm out of here.

KAT

"KAT, CAN YOU GRAB THE FRONT DOOR, PLEASE?" MOM CALLS DOWNSTAIRS TO me. "I just heard the car." I hit pause. Normally I hate answering the door—and the telephone—but I have a sudden need to see Granddad, to know for sure that time hasn't caught up to him and stopped his heart. I close the LumberLegs video I was watching and take the stairs two at a time.

When I open the door, my still living Granddad is taking his final wobbly step up onto the front porch. "Hello, Katharina," he says. He's always called me that, for as long as I can remember.

"Hi," I say quietly as I open the door nice and wide for him. I wanted to see him, but now that I have, I've no idea what to say.

Mom says that Granddad is recovering much faster than they expected him to after the hip replacement, but I find that hard to believe. He is definitely wobbling as he takes one slow step after another through the door.

I look out the door behind him instead of at him. "Where's Dad?" According to Mom, Dad took Granddad to his appointment, then to grab a few groceries.

"Your dad's still at the car. I beat him here with my superhuman speed." He grins, but the joke tastes sour to me. Like an emaciated child in Africa joking about having too much food to eat.

I lean carefully toward him. After school, I purposely changed into my softest pants and my fluffiest knit sweater, no zippers. It's really more of a pat than a hug that I give him, but it's still close enough to feel the jutting boniness of his shoulders. If his skin did tear off, perhaps there would be no oozing flesh underneath, only brittle bone. Like a shadowdragon—all skeleton and shadow.

Dad arrives in the front door then, blue-plaid-shirted arms laden with cloth grocery bags. "Kat, my favorite daughter!" He holds the grocery bags out to me. I roll my eyes, then take half of them.

It's been an exhausting week, and all I want to do is disappear downstairs to the computer and work on my castle until Luke comes on and we can do a rift raid. But first I have to survive family dinner.

"How was school today?" Dad asks once we're all sitting at the table. He adjusts his tie. He never takes it off until after dinner.

"Yes, Kat, how was school?" Mom passes me the roast turnip with a raised eyebrow that says, "I notice you don't have any of this delicious vegetable on your plate."

"Fine, I guess." I scoop a spoonful of diced turnip onto my

plate. Definitely not my favorite, but I'm not going to argue with Mom's raised eyebrow, especially with Granddad sitting there watching me. I mean, he's not watching me right this minute, but I'm sure if I started arguing with Mom, he would.

"Any major events?" Dad's forkful of mashed potatoes hovers in front of his mouth. "Meteors? Apocalypses? Math tests?"

I don't really want to talk about my clueless new science fair partner, but it's either that or explaining how I almost ate my lunch in a washroom. "We had to choose partners for our science fair projects."

"Oh? And who's yours?" Mom asks.

"This girl Meg." I want to sneak a peek at my phone to see what time it is and whether Luke will be calling soon, but that's sure to earn a lecture from Mom or Dad, and then what would Granddad think of me?

"Is she nice?" Mom likes to ask questions more than she likes to eat.

I shrug again. "She didn't know what a science fair was."

"Well, maybe she didn't have to do a project last year."

Yeah. Because this isn't her second time being a freshman. I take a biteful of potatoes.

"So what are you going to do for your project?" Dad asks.

"I don't know. I was looking up some ideas this afternoon, but nothing popped out at me." Last year, my partner and I did ours on how fast helium balloons deflated in different temperatures and why. I barely knew my partner, despite having gone to school with her since kindergarten, but fortunately, school wasn't her forte and she was content to just let me do most of the work, so we didn't actually have to spend much time together. We got an A, but I don't think my analysis section was quite up to snuff, because we only came in eighth. This year's will be better. Assuming this Meg girl doesn't ruin it.

"Oh, you shouldn't look something up, sweetie." Mom again. "It'll feel too rote. Make up something creative."

"Like what?"

"We've got some interesting new materials we're experimenting with at work," Dad says. He's an engineer of some sort. Mechanical, maybe? I've never been able to figure out exactly what he does, only that his company is apparently just as happy to have him doing it here as in Ottawa. "Don't know if I could get clearance for you to run tests on it, though."

"Why don't you test how effective human urine is as a fertilizer?"

If anyone else said it, my response would be "Eeeeewwwwww!" accompanied by a scrunched-up nose. But my two-hundred-year-old granddad stares at me, bifocals perched on the tip of his bony nose, likely awaiting a more sophisticated response.

Fortunately, Mom saves me. "Dad," she says, smacking him on the arm a lot harder than she should, considering that just falling down was all it took to break his hip. "Kat isn't going to pee on a bunch of plants for her school science project."

"Maybe not. But it would be a real showstopper." I can't tell if he is grinning at me or if the wrinkles in his cheeks are so deep that they yank at the corners of his mouth.

I have no idea what to say to that. My fingers itch to check my phone. I pull it out of my pocket and wrap my fingers tightly around it. "I do like the idea of plants," I finally say.

"Can't go wrong with plants," Dad chimes in. "They're time-less."

"So's urine," Granddad says.

My phone vibrates beneath my fingertips with a message, and I push back my chair to look at it before I can stop myself. Maybe Luke's ready to play and I can be excused and escape to safety. After they all have a chance to talk to him, of course. Ugh. I unlock the screen and check my messages.

Can't play tonight. Sry. Next week?

"Kat? Is it Luke? Can you ask him to call your dad's cell? We can put him on speakerphone for a bit before you go off to play." Mom's words wrap themselves around my chest and squeeze the air right out of my lungs. How do I tell her that Luke doesn't have time for us? That he doesn't have time for me?

One turnip . . . two university . . .

"Don't be silly, Laura." Granddad's voice cuts off my count-ing. "It's Friday night. They don't want to talk to us old fogies. Let them go do their thing."

When I look up, Mom and Granddad are locked in a staring match. Dad is eating the last of his potatoes, either oblivious or just refusing to get involved.

Mom sighs. "All right. You're right, Dad. Go ahead, Kat. But tell Luke he'd better call us later this weekend."

I grip my phone tightly, unsure what to say. Is it a lie to disappear downstairs without telling them that Luke's abandoned me? Is it even worth disappearing downstairs if Luke's abandoned me?

Luke's the one who got the server set up and makes sure it's running 24/7. And recruited people to play on it through the LotS forums. And organizes our rift raids. And knows everyone by name as well as by username.

But that doesn't mean we need him. I don't need to know real names to play with people. Usernames are enough.

And I can always just work on my underwater castle alone. Again.

One jelly bean . . . two underwater windows . . .

"Go," Granddad pronounces. He literally waves me away, flapping his hand in the air like one of Mom's dishcloths. "Those animated creatures aren't going to kill themselves. Go have fun."

So I do.

LEGENDS OF THE STONE

KittyKat has logged on.
[]Sythlight: Hi
KittyKat: hi
Moriah: Hi
HereAfter: hey

[]Sythlight has discovered a legendary weapon.

KittyKat: sweet, which one?

[]Sythlight: Battle-ax of Lorenzo

[]Sythlight: Shadowbeast spawned right outside my
    door. Practically gave me a heart attack.

KittyKat: yikes

[]Sythlight: Yeah

KittyKat has entered the waterlands.

KittyKat: there's water pouring into my tower!!!

[]Sythlight: That's what you get for building it
    underwater. ;)

KittyKat: our world's never been so unstable before

KittyKat: rifts are usually under control

[]Sythlight: Yeah, Lucien hasn't planned a rift raid in a
    while.

KittyKat: yeah, he's been busy :(

[]Sythlight: Two new rifts spawned outside town. One
    in the drylands and one in the badlands.

KittyKat: that'd do it

[]Sythlight: Want to do a raid?

KittyKat: sure

KittyKat: moriah, hereafter, you up for one?

HereAfter: Sorry about to log off

Moriah: me too

Moriah: good night everyone

HereAfter: bye

[]Sythlight: Ciao

Moriah has logged off.

HereAfter has logged off.

KittyKat: have a good night

[]Sythlight has entered the badlands.

KittyKat: well, so much for that idea

[]Sythlight: Badlands rift is small. Might be able to do it
with just 2.

KittyKat: really?

[]Sythlight: When the 2 are us, definitely. We'll be done
in 5 minutes. ;)

KittyKat: ha ha yeah ok. but only if I can be the archer

[]Sythlight: We could both be archers.

KittyKat: that'd be suicide! >:O

[]Sythlight: But hilarious.

KittyKat: lol it's ok. you be the archer. I'll tank.

[]Sythlight: jk jk. It's fine. You be the archer.

KittyKat: you sure?

[]Sythlight: Yep. I prefer tank anyway.

[]Sythlight: Still no VoiceChat?

KittyKat: no. no mic. sorry

[]Sythlight: No problem. Typing's fine. Ready?

KittyKat has entered the badlands.

KittyKat: yep, let's do this

3

KAT

THE TREADMILL CREAKS AS I MOUNT IT. I HAVE GOT TO CONVINCE MOM and Dad to buy a new one. In Ottawa, I used to just run outside, but even though the streets are numbered here, I'm not confident that I won't get lost. Plus, from what I've heard about Edmonton weather, winter will probably be here in a matter of days. The leaves have already started falling from the trees. And not a slow, colorful striptease like in Ontario, but a sudden, down-to-business discarding of a plain dress onto the floor.

My phone dings. It's Mom.

We're stopping for groceries after dinner this eve. Need anything?

She, Dad, and Granddad have gone to some conference for the afternoon, then out for supper. Their absence leaves me with the house magnificently to myself. And since I finished all my homework this morning—teachers always start the school year off easy, trying to win us over before destroying our souls—that means I get to spend my whole Saturday afternoon and evening with LotS and LumberLegs. Glorious.

I do a mental inventory of our cupboards, then slow the treadmill to a walk so I can type.

Yeast. I think we're almost out.

Tomorrow, maybe I'll make a loaf of bread. I haven't done that since we left Ottawa.

I increase the treadmill's speed and lose myself in my breathing. *One dog . . . two cat . . . three fast . . . four faster . . .*

After my run, I'm going to work on my underwater castle. It took us a couple of hours, but Sythlight and I managed to close up two whole rifts last night, so that should make the world more stable—no more damaged castles or shadowbeasts spawning in safe zones. For now. But I still have to fix up the gaping hole in my castle tower.

The doorbell rings, echoing hollowly down the stairs, and the castle in my head shatters from the noise. Outside, real-life noise. I hold my breath and slow the treadmill—not to stop it, but just to quiet it. Make it sound like no one's home. The only people I know in this whole city—Mom, Dad, and Granddad—are all out for the day. Which means it's a stranger at the door. Not even the promise of Girl Guide cookies could get me to talk to a stranger right now. Even a ten-year-old stranger.

My phone dings again. Probably Mom wondering if there's a brand of yeast I prefer.

You home?

Not Mom. I slow the treadmill even more.

Who is this?

Another ding, a moment later.

Meg. your brilliant science partner. If you're home let me in it's cold out here

I stop the treadmill abruptly. Not Girl Guide cookies. But still a stranger. Knowing her name doesn't make her not a stranger.

The doorbell rings again. My throat tightens.

Why is she here?

I focus on my breathing.

One chocolate mint . . . two . . . two . . . two . . . I can't get my—breathing—under—control—

Ding.

I thought we could work on our science thing

She thought she could just show up and work on our science thing? Without calling ahead to make plans?

I already have plans. I'm going to go to the water cave to collect more coral rock, then use it to patch up the hole in my castle. Then I have to fix the water damage in the hall, and then

I'll finally be able to organize my armory, which I've been dying to do forever. I need a big block of time to do that, so I can log and chart everything in a spreadsheet and decide how best to sort it. And then watching Legs this evening. I have the entire rest of my day planned and full of glorious awesomeness.

I can't just leave her standing there, though.

Two helium balloons . . . three peeing on plants . . .

I hop off the treadmill, take the steps two at a time, then unlock the front door and swing it open.

Meg is halfway down the sidewalk, striding away from the house, but she must hear the door open because she whirls around to face me. "Oh, I thought you weren't home," she calls out.

So I could have just waited and she'd have left? Crap, screwed that one up!

"Sorry, I was working out," I say, still breathing hard, though not from the exercise.

She drops the skateboard she's holding, hops onto it, starts speeding toward the front step, then kicks back or something and thrusts herself and the board into the air. She almost lands on the top step, but then her skateboard goes skittering out from under her, and she bashes her knee into the porch column. I lurch forward to help her, but before I can even reach out my hand, she's already back on her feet, grinning. "Still working on that one." She rubs her knee, still grinning, then scoops up her skateboard. "Okay if I bring this in? Don't want it to get stolen."

I blink at her. "You skateboard?"

"I've been trying it out. Stephen-the-Leaver gave this to my brother, and he didn't want it, and I don't believe in trashing things just because they're from Stephen-the-Leaver. I mean, why should I deprive myself just because he's a jerk? Anyway, I was just trying some jumps at the park down the street—it's got some good benches for it—and I realized I was near your house and I thought I'd see if you were home, because I have this really cool idea for our science thing. You free?"

"No!" I want to yell at her. "I'm not free. You can't just show up here and expect me to be available! I have plans. That armory won't sort itself."

I guess our science project won't do itself either, though. And she's voluntarily offering to work on it. That was something my last partner never did.

"You said you have an idea?" I ask.

She grins. "Sure do. Just thought of it."

It would be nice to have the brainstorming done and not have to worry about that part anymore. Maybe we could have our topic ready to submit to Mr. Carter by Monday—a couple of weeks early. I'd have to change my afternoon plans, though. I hate changing plans.

I take a deep breath and do my best to smile at her. "I guess now's fine. I just have something on at five, so I have to make sure we're done by then." I kick myself as soon as the words leave my mouth. Five is two entire hours away. I should have lied and said it was at four. Or even in half an hour. Now I have no excuse to evacuate if things get awkward. "Come on in."

She steps inside and leans the skateboard against the hallway wall. She's not wearing a coat, but she strips off her fingerless orange mittens and tosses them onto a nearby chair. Then she follows me into the living room.

I gesture toward the couch, but she either doesn't notice or chooses to ignore me, because instead she wanders over to the wall of shelves. This is why I hate spending time with people. It's like when I started playing The Sims and didn't realize you could turn off free will. I kept telling my Sim to go to the bathroom, but she kept ignoring me and playing on the computer and dancing and eating until eventually she just peed on the floor.

I mean, what exactly am I supposed to do now? Sit down on the chair like I had planned? Join her by the shelves? I haven't even offered her a drink yet, which makes me a terrible host.

One lemonade . . . two chocolate milk . . .

Right, just offer her a drink. That's something I can do. "Do you want—"

"Okay, so I was thinking about this, and what if we threw cantaloupes off the roof? I mean, not just threw them. My six-year-old brother could do that. He's technically my half brother. Nolan and Kenzie. I call them the halflings. Of course Nolan never would throw cantaloupe. He's a goody-goody. Who's this?"

"I—um—what?" Is she talking about science?

She points toward the shelf. I've been backing away toward the kitchen to get us drinks, so I have to step toward her and lean to the side to see which picture frame she's pointing at. "Oh, that's my brother, Luke."

"Is he around? He's cute."

"No. Toronto. University." For the first time the words are a relief instead of a knife in my gut. The last thing I need is for her to start flirting with my brother.

"Too bad." She sets the photo down and continues her survey of the wall. "I know the cantaloupe thing sounds simple, but you can take something that a toddler could do and make it complex, right? And epic. We could totally do that with the cantaloupe. This guy's adorable."

"What? My granddad?" I've given up on my quest to get drinks—keeping up with this girl requires my full attention— so this time I can easily see which picture she's looking at. I try to see the adorableness she mentioned, but all I see is the rosy skin that's since gone gray, the white hair that covered his head, the cheeks that hadn't yet sunk into his face. I look away from the picture.

"Is that who this is? Yeah, I love the bow tie. And those eyebrows. Have you ever seen eyebrows like that before?"

"Well, sure, I mean, he lives here." At least his eyebrows haven't changed.

"Okay, yeah, obviously on your granddad himself. But I meant other than that. I bet you haven't."

"I—" I break off and bite my lip. How did we end up talking about eyebrows? This is not what I let her come in and ruin my afternoon plans for. "You were saying something about cantaloupe?"

"Have you read this book?" she asks. I shake my head without even looking at the cover, and she slides it back onto the shelf, then picks up another. "Okay, yeah, with the cantaloupe, we could get some fancy equipment and test the force of impact depending on what we throw it at—grass or concrete or wood or whatever. Or maybe . . . what's it called . . . that speed thing . . . velocity? Depending on the weather. Like would a cantaloupe drop slower on a windy day?"

"Did you find that idea on the internet?" It didn't come up in any of my searches.

"Nope, in my brain." She taps her forehead, then shrugs. "We don't have to do that. I don't know where we'd get the equipment for it anyway. Can I borrow this? It looks good." She holds up the book she's been thumbing through.

"Um—I—I guess so?" I don't mean for it to come out as a question.

"You have any ideas?"

"For our science fair project?"

"Yeah, what else?"

"A couple." As I start to explain the ideas I've researched, she finally flops down on the couch to listen, feet tucked up under her. I've Googled a lot, but I can't decide if I like any of the topics I've found. There's this paper you can use to separate out the different chemicals in a liquid—we could use that to determine the ingredients of different types of pop. Or test tooth decay in a variety of different liquids over time, though I'm not sure where we'd get the teeth. Or we could use cutworms to test the durability of different breeds of grass.

Meg follows along with the first two, asking questions and nodding her head. But in the middle of my explanation of cutworms, she yawns unapologetically and gets to her feet.

"I need a break. How about a house tour?" She marches out of the room before I can protest, and I have to hop up and sprint after her. She stops when she reaches the stairs—half a staircase up, half a staircase down. "Up or down?"

I wasn't expecting to give her a house tour. I mean, I wasn't expecting her to be here at all. "Um, down, I guess."

She grabs the banisters and launches herself over all seven stairs, landing with a thud at the bottom.

I don't usually swear, but a curse pops out of me.

She laughs. "You should give it a try."

"No, thank you." I take the stairs one at a time, holding carefully to the railing.

Downstairs, Meg keeps chattering away, examining my dad's shelf of knickknacks. Some people who talk a lot are know-it-alls, but Meg's ramblings are more random than lecture-y, like she never learned the difference between thinking and talking.

"Where's this from?" She lifts a striped wooden mask with short, stubby antlers. I should tell her to put it down, but to be honest, I wouldn't mind if she broke it. I wouldn't be surprised if its leering grin appeared some night in my nightmares. It's terrifying.

"South Africa."

"Oh, cool. Have you been there?"

"No." My parents and Luke went last summer. I refused to fly—planes are claustrophobic metal cages of gravity-defying death—so I spent those three weeks at my aunt's farm in southern Ontario instead. Dad wanted to force me to go, but Mom talked him out of it. I overheard them talking one night.

"She's only fourteen." Dad.

"That's old enough." Mom.

"She's going to regret it."

"Then she regrets it. And if she does, maybe that will be enough to push her out of her comfort zone next time."

On the first half of the trip, they went on an elephant safari, paddled in dugout canoes, and ate peanut stew. On the second half of the trip, they all got so dreadfully sick that Dad refused to eat solid food for at least a month after they got back. I didn't regret staying behind.

I show Meg my mom's office, the rec room, then the kitchen and bathroom back on the main floor. She prattles away throughout, picking up and asking about little odds and ends everywhere.

Upstairs, she stops to study a picture in the hallway. "Your parents still together?"

I nod.

"That's nice. My dad left when I was four, then promptly died in a car accident three months later. So, frozen in a perpetual state of having just left us."

"I'm sorry." I have to say more than that. I search my frazzled brain. "Maybe he would've come back, though. If he had lived, I mean."

"Maybe, but probably not. What's in here?" She points to the closest door.

"My room." I swing open the door and gesture for her to enter. She steps inside. Then she squeals like a piglet.

MEG

THERE IS A LUMBERLEGS POSTER ON THE WALL. A LUMBERLEGS POSTER! HIS LotS character, with its tree-stump legs and teasing grin, winks at me as he tumbles off the side of a cliff and hurtles toward a pool of lava below. Even his in-game persona makes me want to giggle. I leap up onto the bed and kiss his perfect face.

Then I turn to grin at Kat. "I can't believe you like Lumber-Legs! This is fate." This is the moment—I have found my new best friend. Thank goodness, because Lindsey hasn't responded to any of my texts since she hung up last night, and I'm starting to wonder if she ever will again. But that doesn't matter now. Kat and I can swoon over Legs's FaceCam together, and she can come to LotSCON with me, and we can both be awesome, just like Legs always says.

Kat pulls at the sleeves of her pink knit sweater so they cover her hands. "You know who LumberLegs is?" Apparently she's never found anyone to watch with either. Maybe Legs's millions of subscribers are actually all bots except for me, Kat, and that girl who moved away. Oh, and my old friend Larissa, but she likes the game more than she likes Legs, so she doesn't count.

"Know who he is?" I say. "I'm going to marry him! He's hilarious. You can be one of my bridesmaids. How do you feel about turquoise for dresses?"

"I . . . what?"

"I'm joking, don't worry. I'm not a creepy stalker. He *is* awesome, though. Hey, you're not going to move away anytime soon, are you?"

She blinks at me a few times, then shakes her head. "We just got here." She looks unusually small, like she's shrunk to Nolan's size, or even Kenzie's. Probably doesn't help that she's standing on the floor, while I'm still standing on the bed.

I plop down, landing on my butt on the mattress. "Excellent. Hey, Legs is livestreaming tonight, right? We should totally watch it. We could walk down to the corner store and get enough salt-and-vinegar chips and Rolos to survive an apocalypse, then pig out while we watch it. What do you say?"

Kat just stares at me.

KAT

MEG GRINS EXPECTANTLY AT ME, HER SMILE SO WIDE THAT IT PUFFS OUT her cheeks and turns her oval face round.

She wants to watch a LumberLegs livestream. Together. With salt-and-vinegar chips and Rolos.

One asparagus . . . two introvert . . .

I am not good at making decisions, at least not without a good pro-con list. If I reached for a pen and paper right now, though, I'm pretty sure she would classify me as a freak. I do a quick tally in my head instead.

REASONS I SHOULD SAY NO TO MEG:

1. The first thing that popped into my head was that, if she watched LotS with me, I could make Luke feel like I've replaced him. Which I'm pretty sure makes me a sociopath (the kind that lies and manipulates people, not the kind that murders prostitutes and buries them in a farmer's field).

2. She's probably one of those people who talks the whole way through movies and videos, as if her own thoughts were more important.

3. I told her I have a thing at five, so I have a perfect out.

REASONS I SHOULD SAY YES TO MEG:

1. I can make Luke feel like I've replaced him.

2. The box under my bed that already has both salt-and-vinegar chips and Rolos in it.

3. The livestream *is* the thing I was going to do at five.

I kneel down, push aside my blankets, and reach into the darkness for the box.

───────────────── MEG ─────────────────

IT'S JUST A PLAIN BLACK BOX, BUT THE SOLEMN WAY KAT RETRIEVES IT FROM under the bed makes it look like ancient treasure. Like a treasure chest dug out of a spot marked *X* by a one-eyed pirate or a box of valuable old antiques brought down from a dusty attic, or best of all, a loot box heaved from the depths of the waterlands in LotS.

I flip open the lid.

"O! M! G! Is this your stash?"

"I bought this more for the Kit Kats, not the Rolos." Kat points her thumb toward the bag of mini chocolate bars.

"Kit Kats? No way. You can't really prefer Kit Kats to Rolos!"

"Kit Kat has my name in it."

"Oh. Touché." I tear open the bag and pull out one Kit Kat and one Rolo, studying the block letters on each wrapper. "There's no bar with 'Meg' in the name. That hardly seems fair."

She nibbles on her bottom lip for a moment before responding. "They could rename Mr. Big the Megabar."

"I'm totally going to write to them and suggest that!" I toss her the Kit Kat, then rip open the Rolo, popping all the little pieces into my mouth at once before reaching into the box for another. "This is perfect. I'll eat the Rolos, you eat the Kit Kats— it's meant to be."

She opens her mouth as if to argue, then doesn't, which is just as well, because there is nothing she could say or do that could convince me that this isn't a sign.

"Hey, have you seen the Legs video where he falls in lava over and over trying to get the crown?" I ask.

"Episode two of his Speed Run Fails videos? Of course. Who hasn't?" The corners of her mouth twitch upward just a little, which I think is her equivalent of a huge grin.

"Want to watch it now?"

She looks down at the Kit Kat in her hand. "What about our project?"

"Oh . . . uh . . . right. When's that due again?" I lift up the bag of salt-and-vinegar chips, revealing a disordered jumble of caramels, Pixy Stix, and other deliciousness at the bottom of the box.

"Well, the final project isn't due until March—"

"Lizard balls, we've got loads of time. Why are we even thinking about this now?" I snatch a caramel. Not my favorite, but better than the bag of dried fruit lying pathetically in the corner.

She blinks at me. "You were the one who—never mind. But we can't just do the whole thing in March. Our topic's due in three weeks. Then our proposal, and then we have to complete the experiments by the beginning of February, which means we might have to start it soon if it's something that takes place over time, and—"

"But our topic's not due for three weeks?" I can't get the caramel wrapper off, and I don't think I've ever tried dried fruit, actually. I drop the caramel back in the box, grab the bag, and pull out a soft, white, doughnut-shaped thing.

"Just under three weeks, actually, so—"

"So we've got tons of time." The doughnut-shaped thing is chewy, but not gross. Kind of sweet, actually. "And since Legs doesn't livestream every weekend, we should do a Legs-a-thon tonight, then the science project next weekend. Or during the week, or whatever."

I hold out the bag to her and she pulls out a peach-colored mound, which she studies just like the Kit Kat she still hasn't eaten. "I guess I could use a bit more time to do research," she says. She pops the peach thing in her mouth.

"Great," I say, picking up the epic black box of snacky goodness. "Lead on to your computer."

"Well . . ." She pauses, either to chew or to make a decision or both. "I was going to watch on the big screen in the basement. So we could do that."

"Even better!" I say. Then I march out of the room with my new BFF right behind me.

■　■　■

Having the Legs video up on the big screen is pure perfection. Normally I'm stuck watching Legs on my tiny laptop or my tablet in my room while Kenzie monopolizes the TV with her Cheery Muffincakes or whatever that show's called. But down here in Kat's basement, his cartoony face is big and beautiful.

And it's not just any episode that Kat puts on. She goes right to the exact episode of his speed runs series that we were talking about, without having to search for it in her video history for a million years like I always have to.

As I settle onto the floor, grabbing a handful of chocolate bars and tossing half of them to Kat on the couch behind me, Legs starts his descent into the rift, leaping from stone to ledge to the wobbly bridge that he immediately tumbles off of, falling into the lava below with a high-pitched scream. "FAIL" scrawls across the screen in big red letters. A deep, echoey, announcer-y version of Legs's voice reads out the word, accompanied by the ridiculous animation of Legs's real face crying cartoon tears that I had as my screen saver for a while. I giggle and glance back at Kat, who is scrunching up her lips like she's trying not to smile.

By the time Legs falls in lava for the bajillionth time, I'm laughing like a hyena and Kat is full-on grinning.

On his bajillion-and-first attempt, Legs finally manages to make it onto the ledge, across the bridge, through the shadowy spiky things, up the vanishing platforms, and, with a whoop of victory, reaches for the crown—as the final platform vanishes and he plunges with a scream of agony into the bottomless lava pool.

"EPIC FAIL," says the announcer. And the screen. And me.

I turn to Kat, who stands abruptly, her grinning face turning to all business. "We should make pizza. I've got a frozen one. I'll put it in before the livestream starts." Then she rushes off toward the stairs. I trot after her into the kitchen, where I grab a pizza out of the freezer and start unwrapping it while she turns on the oven.

"Okay," I say as I set it down on the metal tray she's pulled out, "one thing I've never understood is how Legs knows when a rift is a speed run rift and when it's just a normal rift full of monsters. They look the same from the outside."

Her eyes widen as she takes the tray from me and sets it on the stove. "It's a mod," she says like it's obvious.

"A what?"

"A mod."

I blink at her.

"You know, it's not part of the original game. It's a modification someone's made. You download it and it turns normal rifts into speed runs instead." She glances at the oven, which is still preheating.

"But everyone does speed runs."

"Because everyone uses the mod. Or goes on servers that use it. Legs made it popular. Or maybe it made him popular. I don't know. Probably both."

As we wait for the oven to warm up, she rambles about mods and whether it's better to have them server-side or on some other side and why she likes to watch some and play others. It's the most she's talked all afternoon.

We watch another video, and then the pizza is ready, and then it's time for the livestream and Legs's real, huggable face joins his cartoony in-game one on the big screen, so big we can see every twitch of his dark, dancing eyebrows when he's joking, and every clench of his square jaw when he's passionately serious.

He's doing a rift raid with some friends, and when a wingling swoops out of nowhere, Legs and I both shriek, and Kat and Legs's friends all laugh, but not meanly.

Kat uses a plate, and I use a napkin, and by the time we discard them on the coffee table beside the leftover pizza, the raid is over and Legs has moved on to Legs Advice Hour—a name that makes me giggle because it always prompts someone to throw questions about leg shaving into the chat. (And yes, I'll admit it, sometimes that someone is me.) In game, Legs heads to the greenlands, where he'll work on his base as he takes questions from the chat—never the leg-shaving questions, though—and gives brilliantly sage advice. He has bases in all the different areas of the map, but the greenlands one he's heading to is my favorite; it has all these different-colored staircases that shoot into the sky and up to these misshapen, precariously balanced towers.

The first question he takes this time is about how to ask a girl out, and he rambles in his usual kind way about being brave and taking risks and treating people with respect as he chops down trees for wood to build a balcony for the red tower.

"Thanks for the question, man," he says. Then he looks directly at the screen as I join him in saying, "Be awesome!"

"I love that," I say, sighing, as I slip off the armrest where I've been sitting and onto the main part of the couch beside Kat.

"He says it to everyone," Kat says, looking down at the chat log on the tablet in her lap.

"Because he wants everyone to be awesome. Here, hand me the tablet."

Her grip on it tightens like a reflex, then loosens. "Why?"

"So we can ask a question." I snatch the tablet out of her lap and settle it onto my own. "What do you want to ask?"

She shakes her head. "Nothing. I don't have any questions."

"It doesn't have to be a real question. Last time I asked about how to woo my band partner. I don't even play an instrument."

She grabs a pillow and sets it in her lap like she misses having the tablet there. "That was you?"

"Good one, right? That was the first time he answered one of mine. I whooped so loud Mom thought I tripped and fell or something. So what should we ask? Maybe something about a bully? He's pretty good at giving advice about that, though he's better with the love stuff, don't you think?"

She chews on her bottom lip. It's astonishing that it isn't chapped and bloody by now, considering how often she does that. "What if he answers our fake question instead of someone's real one? That doesn't seem right."

I stop typing. "Okay, fair point. So we can ask a real question, then. What should we ask? Got any problems?"

She hugs the pillow to her chest and looks down. "No. Do you?"

The question shouldn't throw me, since I came up with it in the first place, but it does. I glance at the chat, with its endless questions and jokes and ridiculousness scrolling by.

Last night's party was just as much of a snore-fest as I thought it would be. Lindsey still hasn't texted me. In fact, I haven't gotten a single text from anyone the entire time I've been here. Brad used to text me all the time, but he broke up with me when I thought things were going great, and now his friends don't text me either. And my stepdad—the only dad I've known—doesn't want me because I'm not his real kid.

What could I possibly ask in this chat? *Dear LumberLegs, is it my ADHD that's scaring everyone away?*

I force myself to grin at Kat. "Nope, me neither," I say. "So, no questions, then." Instead, I start typing into the chat box: *TO THE RIFT!*

Kat leans over to look. "Meg! You can't!" She grabs the tablet from me before I can press enter.

I stare at her. "You've never started a chat spam before?"

"No! They're horrible."

"They're not horrible. They're power." I grin as maniacally as I can. "Go on, do it. Press enter."

"No," she says, though she sounds less certain. "I'm not going to—"

"Do it. Do it, do it, do it."

"I—fine!" She hesitates, her finger hovering over the touch keyboard, then she jams it into the enter button.

TO THE RIFT! appears in the chat.

And then, a split second later, the chat is filled with it as thousands of other viewers echo our battle cry—one of Legs's most famous lines.

TO THE RIFT!!!!

TO THE RIFT!

to the rift

TO THE RIFT

to the RIFTTT

TO TEH RFIT

TO THE RIFT!

On-screen, Legs rolls his eyes. "Guys, not again." He glares right at us, but his green eyes are sparkling.

I grin at Kat. "See. Power."

"Shut up," she says. Then she thrusts the tablet back at me, grabs a slice of cold pizza, and stares straight ahead at the TV screen. But the corners of her mouth are curved upward.

"To the rift!" I shout out loud to the room. Kat just shakes her head.

KAT

ON MONDAY AT LUNCH, MEG APPEARS OUT OF NOWHERE AND FALLS INTO
stride beside me as I head to my locker. "You going to the caf?"
she asks.

I wasn't planning on going to the cafeteria. I was going to
spend my lunch in the library, playing LotS. But here's the thing:
food isn't allowed in the library. Which means I'd have to scarf
down bites of my sandwich in the hallway and hope I didn't stand
out as that freak girl who eats like a friendless, famished hobo.

But here's the other thing: Meg didn't explicitly ask to eat
with me. She might just be making small talk. Or she might just

want to walk together, and then once we step inside the door, she'll wave a cheery good-bye, leaving me standing alone on a cliff, staring at not just a pack of wolves, but the entire extended-family reunion. A horde. And no bow or arrows anywhere in sight.

"I'm thinking about it." It's the most ambiguous, noncommittal answer I can conjure up.

"Great. You getting your lunch from your locker? I have to grab mine. What's your locker number? I can meet you there in a minute."

That's a lot of work to go to just to walk with someone and then ditch them. *One cantaloupe . . . two be brave . . .*

"It's five ninety-two."

"By the science labs? Got it. See you in a jiff."

I don't particularly like this plan—waiting alone in the hallway for an indeterminate amount of time like some hopeful, jilted loser—but she scurries off before I can suggest we meet at her locker instead. I needn't have worried, though. I've barely lined my textbooks up on the top shelf before Meg is back, panting over my shoulder.

"Did you run?"

"I—uh—" She breaks off awkwardly, and when I look at her, her mouth hangs open a bit—though whether from trying to catch her breath or something else, I can't tell. "Is that weird?" The question is part challenge, part worry. Part brave gladiator, part scared child.

All those glinting wolf eyes would have leered at her as she went flailing by. Yes, it's weird. But also brave. "No," I say. "It's not."

"I'm trying to be more normal," she says. Maybe I should adopt that as my life mantra.

I needn't have worried about the cafeteria either. Meg plops down at the nearest empty table and starts gabbing away to me about the livestream, reliving all the funniest moments, before I'm even sitting. Her chatter lasts through every slow-chewed bite of my sandwich and at least partway through my apple, and it's distracting enough that it makes this whole sitting-in-the-cafeteria thing okay. Or mostly okay. Okay enough that I can handle it.

As I start on the baby carrots, though, her voice fades away, and I look up to see her surveying the room.

I follow her gaze around the place—the lunch line, the back windows, the throngs of people filling the cafeteria's long tables. Nowhere in particular, it seems.

"Hey, do you know that guy over there? I keep seeing him around. The way he clenches his jaw when he's thinking reminds me of Legs." Her voice is airy, as if she's trying to whisper but forgot to turn down the volume knob.

"Which one?" There are at least a hundred guys in here.

"Over there. Floppy brown hair, red shirt. White, but kind of tan. Boxers usually showing, though you can't see that from here."

That doesn't help at all, but considering that I know the names of approximately two people in this entire school, the chances are that I don't know him. So many people, and I don't know any of them. I shake my head.

"I call him Boxer Boy. Because of the boxers thing. I mean, not to his face. I don't actually know him. I think he's a grade above us. But he's got a jawline just like LumberLegs, so I bet he's as hilarious as Legs. Well, no one's as hilarious as Legs, but I bet he's close. If I can't marry Legs, Boxer Boy would definitely do."

I scan the room again, searching for red shirts. Literal red shirts, not *Star Trek* crew members destined to die. There are so many people. So many annoyances attacking my brain. The prattling strangers, the fluorescent lights, the ever-present aroma of nacho cheese. *One disco ball . . . two migraine . . . three stampede . . .*

I was wrong; I can't handle this. "Want to go to the library to work on our science project?" I ask, a little too abruptly.

Her head snaps back to me. "Oh hell no! Are you kidding me? It's like a cardinal sin to do homework at lunchtime. The only homework I'll do at lunchtime is history, and that's not really homework, it's just reading random books about epic and weird stuff."

"Well, when are we supposed to do it then? We still need a topic."

"You can come over to my house this weekend. You said yourself that we have lots of time."

I've never said that—she's the one who repeated it as she settled into our home like she owned it—but the bustle of the cafeteria and the daunting thought of going to Meg's unfamiliar house and the smell of that plastic cheese are all too loud and jumbled in my head to say that. *Four unexplored territory . . . five fluorescent lights . . . six science project . . .*

"Fine. Any chance you want to get out of here and go for a walk then?"

"Yes!" she practically shouts, and leaps to her feet, then sits right back down again. "Sorry, it's just—no one ever wants to go for a walk at lunch. They just sit around blabbing on and on."

I don't bother pointing out the irony in her statement. "Well, let's go then," I say, rising. I gather the remains of my lunch. I should finish the baby carrots to prevent heart disease and eyesight deterioration, but sometimes I chew and chew and chew carrots to mulch in my mouth and still can't figure out how to swallow them. I head toward the door, and Meg scurries after me and snatches the bag of carrots out of my hand. She pops one into her mouth like a gumdrop. "Don't choke on that," I warn her. "I don't know the Heimlich."

"Can't I just throw myself over a chair or something?"

Okay, I lied—I do know the Heimlich, at least in theory. But we're almost out of this noisy place, and I'm not stopping to explain.

I shrug and Meg pops another carrot in her mouth as we make it out the door.

We spend the rest of the lunch hour wandering about the school yard, walking laps around the football field and parking lot. Or at least, I walk. Meg's walk is more of a saunter—sometimes forward, sometimes backward facing me, sometimes almost skipping around me like those whirling green shells in MarioKart.

It's admittedly not the worst way to spend lunch. Better than being in the caf. Maybe tomorrow I'll eat my lunch outside before going to the library to play LotS.

But at the end of lunch, Meg walks with me to my locker, then says, "See you tomorrow! Same time, same space! No, place. You know what I mean." Then she's off running down the hall.

So . . . I guess this is a thing now. Which shouldn't make me smile, but for some reason it does.

LEGENDS OF THE STONE

[]Sythlight has entered the waterlands.

KittyKat: I like your new cloak

[]Sythlight: Thanks. I designed it myself.

KittyKat: really? how?

[]Sythlight: You can upload your own textures to the online profile. Not many people do it because it's uber complex.

KittyKat: well it looks amazing. I <3 the black hood.

[]Sythlight: Thanks. I did one with a red hood too . . . couldn't decide which looked better. Want to give me your opinion? www.blog.sythlight.com/art

[]Sythlight: So what do you think?

[]Sythlight has entered the barrenlands.

[]Sythlight: Found another rift.

[]Sythlight: You still there?

KittyKat: sorry, got distracted by all the stuff on your page. this artwork is incredible. I love the painting with the rocks and the darkening sky and the little duckling. it feels lonely. in a good way.

[]Sythlight: Thanks . . . I think. I did up that one for my final project last year.

KittyKat: I love it. what are you working on now?

[]Sythlight: For art class? Nothing. My dad thinks that since I'm a senior, I should be taking all "serious" classes to increase my chances of getting into university.

KittyKat: aren't your grade ten and eleven classes more important? since they won't even see this year's marks until after you're accepted?

[]Sythlight has entered the waterlands.

[]Sythlight: Don't tell my dad that. He'll figure out some way to create a time machine, go back in time, and retroactively remove me from grade ten and eleven art. Then, poof, that painting will disappear into nonexistence.

KittyKat: nooooooooooo! not the painting! not

nonexistence!

[]Sythlight: lol

[]Sythlight: waterling behind you

KittyKat: thanks

[]Sythlight: So which do you like better?

KittyKat: what?

[]Sythlight: The hoods . . . black or red?

KittyKat: oh right

KittyKat: black

KittyKat: the red is good too, but the black is
particularly . . . I don't know . . . . . . dark?

[]Sythlight: Profound. :P

KittyKat: shut up. I'm not an artist. how am I supposed
to know what to say about artwork?

[]Sythlight: You don't draw or do crafty stuff or
anything?

KittyKat: nope, I can barely draw a circle

[]Sythlight: lol. You have other hobbies then?

KittyKat: yes. gaming. duh.

[]Sythlight: Ha ha. Guess we should do some of that,
then, eh?

KittyKat: yes. stop distracting me with your airy
aristocratic painterly ways. to the rift!

KittyKat has entered the barrenlands.

[]Sythlight: To the rift!

[]Sythlight has entered the barrenlands.

KAT

GRANDDAD'S FAVORITE GAME IS CHESS. WHICH IS A PROBLEM. NOT BECAUSE I don't know how to play—I do—or because Granddad is beating me—he is, but only barely—but because we shouldn't really be playing at all. I can hear my mother's interrogation already.

"So, what did you do to help Granddad clean out his old house this week, darling daughter?"

"Um, well, I let him beat me at chess. To get his morale up, you know?"

"Katherine Putnam Daley," she'll say with a sigh, "you're supposed to be packing and cleaning, not playing chess." My parents want to get Granddad's house ready to put on the market, since he lives with us now, but Granddad won't let anyone work on it unless he's there to supervise. Somehow I got put on the rotation, so I'm stuck here for the evening in this house whose insides are being stripped away until not even memories can live here. Alone with Granddad in this half-empty shell of a place.

When he asked me to play, I thought of saying, "No, sorry. You sit there and tell me which of your treasured belongings we should throw in the trash so we can sell this house full of a lifetime of memories and you can prepare for your impending death." Really, what else could I say except, "Okay"?

I glance around Granddad's tiny living room while he thinks

about his next move. The kitchen's been packed up entirely, leaving only a skeleton, but the living room still looks the same as it did when we visited a couple of years ago. The same as it did every time we drove out to visit before that. A worn, flowered couch. An entire wall of jam-packed bookshelves. A piano that I've never seen anyone play. And atop the piano, a framed photo of child-sized Luke and me, dressed in matching red shirts and black pants, sitting in front of a Christmas tree.

That was the year Granddad gave me a doll for Christmas. She had long, dirty-blond hair, just like my own, and she came with not one but three different dresses, and two pairs of shoes. I've always loved dolls—tiny, perfect humans who don't try to talk to me or yell or expect me to be anything I'm not—but she was my favorite. She still sits on a shelf beside my bed.

The best part wasn't that first Christmas, but every birthday and Christmas for almost a decade, when Granddad gave me outfit after outfit for her. I think the first was a frilly bubble-gum-pink tutu and a sequined top. After opening the gift, I escaped up to my room, where I dressed my doll, then dragged a fluffy pink skirt out of my own closet. In my birthday photo, the two of us—my doll and me—matched.

I sometimes wonder if my mom had a chat with Granddad about gender stereotyping, because after that there was a real mishmash—navy overalls and a jean jacket, a silky black evening dress, doctor's scrubs with a mini stethoscope, shorts and a soccer jersey.

Luke got something different from Granddad every time—a video game, roller skates, some levitating magnets, a Hardy Boys book—like Granddad's feelings for him were always changing. My gift from Granddad was always predictable, and always perfect. As I opened each package and carefully smoothed out the outfit inside, I was conscious—in the way that one is conscious that the sun will rise tomorrow—that Granddad loved me best.

I study him now as he considers the chessboard—head poking out of his sweater-vest like a turtle's out of its shell, eyebrows bushy with almost as much hair as he has left on his head. His jaw rises and falls as if he is chewing a wad of tobacco, though I'm pretty sure his mouth is empty.

When I was younger, I thought the reason I was too scared to talk to Granddad was because I only saw him a couple of times a year. But now I see him every day, and I still never know what to say.

That's not quite right. I know what I want to say, I just don't say it. My heart thumps loud enough to drown out the words in my head. I want to ask him about the doll clothes, where he got them, how he came up with the idea, but I don't. I can't.

One pink tutu . . . two corduroy jacket . . .

No, that's enough. I'm being ridiculous.

"Granddad, where did you get all those doll outfits you gave me?" I replay the words in my head. Yes, the sentence was coherent. Yes, the words made sense.

"My friend Margaret," he replies, looking up at me. "She lived next door. I told her the plan when I bought the doll, and she was excited to help. Measured the doll before I wrapped it up so she could make sure the outfits would fit her. She loved to sew. I'd tell her my idea and we'd go fabric shopping together. Though really, beyond the initial idea for each outfit, I had very little say." He chuckles hoarsely.

"Why did you stop?" I ask, though I don't really mean to. I already know the answer. It's obvious—I got older. Of course he would stop.

That's not what he says, though. "She died," he says simply. "A few years ago. Heart attack."

"Oh. I'm sorry." I shouldn't have asked. I should have picked up on the past tense. *Lived* next door. *Loved* to sew.

He nods and leans over the board, going back to planning his next move.

"What's it like being so old that friends dying is *normal*?" I ask, not out loud—only in my head.

"Tiring," he answers, not out loud or in my head, but in the way his shoulders fold in on themselves like a pleated paper fan. I want to hug him, but I don't. I can't.

Maybe I should get Mom to find me a new counselor.

Granddad reaches out and nudges a pawn forward one square. "Your turn."

I hate doorbells. I mean, I guess they're useful. But I hate standing on a porch, having just pressed that little white button, unsure whether the bell even rang. Hate having to decide whether it's better to stand stupidly in the Saturday-afternoon cold and wait or to press it again and risk being that obnoxious jerk who rings the bell over and over because they don't hear the people inside shouting, "I'm coming, I'm coming!"

I'm about to become that obnoxious jerk when the door is flung open, revealing a tiny bespectacled boy wearing a miniature black suit jacket. Freckles dot his dark-brown skin, and I feel stupid for not realizing until this moment that black people can have freckles.

"Um—oh—I'm here to see Meg," I tell him. "We have plans. To work on our science project." You'd think I'd be less awkward with kids than adults, but I'm not. If Meg had been willing to work on our project during lunch hours, we could have avoided this uncomfortableness altogether.

He holds out his hand. "May I take your coat, mam-le-zelle?" His voice is quiet, but so confident that I wonder if I've been pronouncing mademoiselle wrong my whole life.

"Um, sure, okay." I step inside, happy to be out of the wind that tormented me all the way here. Mom and Dad weren't free to drive me, and I hate the bus. I slide off my brown jacket and set it gently in his hand, releasing it slowly so its weight doesn't drag him to the ground.

A loud thud announces Meg's arrival at the bottom of the nearby stairs. "Hi. You got that, Nolan? He likes to play butler."

"Butler?"

"Yep. Think he saw it in an Archie comic or something. He's

been doing it all week. Keeps his suit jacket by the front door and makes us all call him Jeeves."

"Oh. Well, thanks, Jeeves." Nolan grins at me as he reaches on his tiptoes for a hanger. "Is he going to be—"

"He's fine. Mom normally likes to greet my friends, but she's got to get a thing to the accountant by Monday or something like that, so she's glued to her computer downstairs, and I'm pretty sure we'll get the glare of death if we interrupt her. C'mon, let's go to my room."

Meg's room is like a forgotten museum storeroom, cluttered with knickknacks and piles of books and layers of dust. Since I was about six, Mom has refused to let me have dessert unless my room's clean. Meg's mom clearly doesn't have the same rule. She picks up the lime-green bra lying on her bed and tosses it into the corner before plopping herself down on the patchwork comforter.

A tank on a side table houses a turtle. He rests on a rock, head poking out of the water, eyes open but not moving.

"What's his name?" I ask.

Meg scrunches up her entire face, as if she can't quite remember. "Snappy," she says at last.

"Hi, Snappy," I coo at the little guy. He still doesn't move.

A tiny bundle of purple charges into the room and onto Meg's lap, and Meg kisses her head. Meg's sister's hair is a mass of natural, flyaway curls, just like Meg's. "I still like the cantaloupe idea," Meg says as she starts braiding the girl's curls together. "We could throw them off my roof, right here. I go out there sometimes. The sidewalk is right below it, so we could drop them onto that."

"Who's going to pay for all the cantaloupes?"

Meg is still midbraid, but the girl on her lap pulls away, thuds to the floor, then skips over to me. She hugs my leg, kisses my jean-covered kneecap, then rushes out of the room with a giggle before I even have time to feel uncomfortable about the tiny stranger who was attached to my leg and now isn't.

Meg doesn't even blink. "My mom will buy them," she says. "She'll give me anything if I just ask her on the right weekend."

Right weekend? I'm not sure I want to know. I'm definitely not going to ask. "Okay," I say instead. "But then who's going to clean up the mess?"

"We can—" she starts, then pauses. "Okay, point taken. But we have to come up with something, right? We could just tell Mr. Carter we're doing the cantaloupe and change it later."

"Maybe we should tell him we're doing the grass durability one."

"Ugh, that's so boring." She pitches backward onto the bed, sprawling out starfish-style. She has a desk along one wall, with a twirly, orange-cushioned chair and a laptop right there in her own room. And one, two . . . five LumberLegs posters. *Five* of them. Two of Legs doing speed runs, one of him fighting the filthworms with a boot, one of him beside his barrenlands castle, and one simple one with his character's head and the words "BE AWESOME" in big bubble letters.

"You have a lot of posters," I say, because I'm great at stating the obvious.

Meg pushes her shoulders into her mattress in what I think is supposed to be a shrug. "I got them after Stephen-the-Leaver left. He would have made me get just one or two, but screw you, Stephen. You can't tell me what to do."

I have no idea what to say to that, so I turn the chair to face her, then perch on the edge. Meg sits up with a start. "Do you play LotS?" she asks. "Like, not just watching Legs's videos, but actually playing?"

"Of course. Don't you?"

She shakes her head vehemently. "I prefer funny over scary."

"You find LotS scary? You're kidding me." In the short time I've known her, I've seen Meg dive down multiple flights of stairs, run through the hall without worrying about staring wolf eyes, and attempt to leap—unsuccessfully—onto our front step with her skateboard. I could probably manage that sort of thing in game, but she managed it *in real life*.

"No, I'm not. I scream every time a wingling attacks." True, she did squeal when one ambushed LumberLegs during the livestream. But winglings are rare and not that hard to kill.

"You could try a speed run," I suggest, though I'm not getting my hopes up that she actually will. "You don't usually have to fight in those."

"Can I make my own character?" she asks.

"Of course. What else would you do?"

"An excellent question. Okay, let's do it," she says, getting to her feet.

"What, now?"

"Of course!" She reaches over my shoulder and taps a button on the laptop to rouse it.

I should object, probably. We're going to have to decide on a science project eventually. But we still have almost two weeks before it's due, and I've done all the rest of my homework for the weekend, so I can always spend tomorrow afternoon researching more ideas, and what if she changes her mind later? I swivel my chair to face the screen.

Meg must have at least tried to play the game once before, because it's already downloaded on her laptop, so I just have to update it and it's ready to go.

When I get to the character creation screen, Meg practically pushes me out of the chair, as if she's still worried that I wouldn't let her make her own character for some weird reason. I cede the chair to her, settling on her bed instead.

I start explaining her options—the character classes, the color choices, the starting abilities. "I spent an hour making my elf warrior," I say. She has pale skin and pink hair and an epic battle scar that stretches all the way from her right eyebrow to her left cheek.

She ignores my comments, goes straight to the skin color

menu, and scrolls down to the browns. "Blah," she says, crinkling her nose.

I'm unsure what she's upset about until she holds her arm up to the screen, and then I get it. There are three brown options, but none of them really match the rich brown of Meg's skin—one's much darker, one's much lighter, and one's really more like tanned white skin than brown. "Are games usually like this?" I ask. Meg laughs humorlessly. "This is actually better than usual. Usually the choice is 'Do I want to play that one black character or not?'"

"That sucks," I say, which feels wholly inadequate.

"You got that right." She frowns at the screen for a moment longer, then sits up and scrolls away from the skin color options. "All right," she says, voice cheery again, as if shaking off systemic racism is something she's practiced so often that she's already an expert. "If I can't make me, let's go fantasy. Can't I just—yes, here." She clicks the randomize button in the bottom right corner over and over, and her character morphs from a blue dragon-lord to a brown elf and everything in between. Then she stops abruptly. A squat dwarf knight with purple skin and bright-green hair glares out at us. "Perfect!"

I point toward the screen. "Okay, so if you want to customize—"

"Nah. Look how badass she is!"

She does look pretty fierce. "Well, you should at least—" But she hits the start button before I can suggest she choose a non-randomized starting ability or try out the different cloaks.

I sigh and Meg grins; then we play musical chairs again as I set up the speed run. It's easier to go onto a public server that has speed runs set up server-side than to download the mod and set it up client-side like I've got at home, and Meg is hovering way too close, ready to take over the instant I've got a speed run started, so I log her on to one of the popular servers.

Legs has it set up client-side, too, but I've seen other You-Tubers go onto this server. Being on it myself feels way more hectic than in their videos, though, with elves and dragonlords and dwarves scurrying past me and the chat log flying by so fast I can't even read it and walk at the same time.

"You're too slow. I've got this," Meg says, and I have to leap out of the seat to avoid her sitting down right in my lap. By the time I've settled back on the bed, she's already found the server's speed-run menu.

"I think they're divided by—" I break off as she clicks on one in the middle. And then she's in a speed run. The lava bubbles up around her, and the first platform is just a sprint-jump away. "It's *w* for forward," I say. "Space to jump."

Her character lunges forward, and she slams the space bar, leaping over the fiery gap. Almost over. Not really over at all. Her dwarf erupts into flames, and the screen reports, "You died," in case that's not obvious from the cartoony, charred body the camera pans out to show. Meg jabs the respawn button, and she's back at the beginning.

"You have to—" I start to say, but she's already off again. This time she tries to move slower, taps the space bar way too late, and walks right off the platform into the lava.

I laugh. I can't help it.

"It's not funny," she says. She grimaces, and then her shoulders slump. "Apparently I'm crap at this. Like everything."

I shake my head, and my cheeks flush hot at the words I know I'm about to say. "Epic fail," I practically whisper, because quoting LumberLegs videos is a thing I usually do only in my head or online, not out loud.

The words hover between us, as if the heavy air has trapped them and refuses to send them on their way. Meg stares at her dwarf's scorched corpse. I can't see her face. Maybe I've gone too far.

But then she straightens and turns to me with a grin. "Epic fail!" she shouts, in a surprisingly good impression of Legs's deep announcer voice.

I stifle the idiotic grin that's trying to push its way onto my face. "Your timer is still running," I say, pointing at the screen, and she swivels back around. And dies again. I could suggest she switch over to a much easier run, but I don't. She could pout again, but she doesn't. Instead, we both giggle.

Many deaths and cries of "epic fail" later, the screen reports her final time—forty-one minutes, eighteen seconds—and my stomach hurts from laughing.

MEG

DESPITE MY PROTESTS THAT NONINTERESTING HOMEWORK SHOULD NEVER BE done at lunchtime, Kat and I banter all week about our science project, as Kat continually insists on some boring grass thing, ignoring all my much flashier—and much better— suggestions. At last, in the middle of Thursday night, a new idea comes to me in a swirl of brilliance. I dream of my speed run. I become my purple dwarf self and try to run it, but I keep missing the final step and plunging into the lava below, and my armor gets heavier and heavier as it gets coated with more and more soot and ash, and when I finally land the jump, my eyes fly open and I know exactly what we should do for our science project. I flick on the light, grab my cell, and tap out a series of texts.

> We shld do speed runs in LotS
> Use them to test reaction times
> Maybe after eating sugar? And before the sugar? And a
> little while later?
> Or maybe coffee?
> It's perfect cuz the computer will time it for us
> And we can use the same map every time
> An easier one than the one I did
> What do u think?

This idea is awesome. Kat can't possibly shut it down like she did with all my others, which admittedly were nowhere near as good as this one. I cup the phone in my hand, staring at the screen, waiting for it to roar with a response. I've got Kat's ringtone currently set to Chewbacca's cry from Star Wars.

"Come on, Kat," I whisper. "Wake up." I don't know how she can be sleeping when I'm having an Aristotle-apple moment! Or was it Einstein? Newton? Hercules? It can't be Hercules, because there was that Disney movie about him and I don't think there was an apple falling in it. If the apple guy was Canadian, I'd probably know. I should get a book about him, and one about Hercules, too.

I crinkle my nose in disgust at the silent phone, set it on my side table, and flick out the light. In the distance, a car alarm blares. The window by my bed breathes frosty air into the room, like Kenzie's favorite Disney princess, Elsa, is turning the world to ice. Winter is coming. I wrap the covers tight around my shoulders.

I have just found a comfortable resting place on my lumpy pillow, preparing to drift back into the imaginary land of sleep, when the Wookiee roar comes. I snatch up my phone, counterarguments ready to fly off my tongue—or out my fingers—then let my battle-ready face dissolve into a grin as I read her text.

I wish I'd thought of that.

5

MEG

I MUST HAVE ACCIDENTALLY TURNED OFF MY ALARM DURING MY middle-of-the-night texting, because I wake up late Friday morning, which makes me miss my usual bus, which makes me late for math class, which makes my math teacher, Mrs. Brown, decide that I need to spend my lunch hour in her office going over problems that make less than zero sense. Which means I don't get to talk to Kat in person until science class, when I slip into the seat in front of her and beam. "It's perfect, right? You think it's perfect?"

She clicks her pen over and over like she's anxious or maybe just thinking, but she nods. "It's definitely better than helium balloons."

I have no idea what she's talking about, but I don't care. "Awesome. We can tell Mr. Carter today, then."

She stops clicking abruptly. "We can't tell him today. We need to do more research." She starts clicking again.

"No way. Someone else might steal the idea."

"No one's going to—"

"LotS is basically the most popular game in the universe," I point out. "Anyone could think of it. We've got to get our idea in first. Today." I don't know how she can even think when she's clicking her pen like that. It's like a chicken pecking on your brain.

"But—"

"Shh, class is starting," I say, pointing to Mr. Carter, who's started writing on the board. "And give me that." I snatch the pen-chicken out of her hand, tap her on the forehead with it, then grin at her before turning around to try to pay attention to whatever weird diagram Mr. Carter is drawing. Our idea is brilliant, and our project is going to be amazing. Even Kat can't deny it.

At the end of what has to be the longest science class in the history of time, I grab Kat's arm and pull her across the room. "Mr. Carter!" I say when we're almost at his desk. "We have our science fair project idea."

He looks down at us—everyone looks down at me, but he's taller even than Kat—and beams. "A whole week early. That's great. Let's hear it."

"You know the video game LotS? Legends of the Stone, I mean? Well, there are these things in it called speed runs. It's a mod, and they're timed and stuff—Kat can probably explain it better than I can."

Kat chews her lip, and for a moment I'm worried she might back out or change her mind or something, but then she clears her throat and rattles off this perfect explanation of how we can have people eat sugar and then test the impact on their reaction times using LotS speed runs, because they're timed and we can choose an easy one to use on everyone for consistency, and Mr. Carter nods along because it all sounds epic. I mean, as epic as a science project can get.

When Kat finishes, Mr. Carter gives us an actual thumbs-up. "That sounds great, ladies. Edgy and modern, but still scientific. I like it. And a whole week early. Good job." Then he babbles on about questionnaires and testing and other random things that we're supposed to keep in mind or something, and then Kat and I are finished and heading out the door.

"So when do you want to start working on the proposal?" Kat asks as we step into the hall.

"The proposal?"

"Yeah. You heard Mr. Carter. It's due in a few weeks. We should get started right away, since we'll need to do some research on sugar and reaction times before we can write it."

I shake my head. "No way. No. Way. We just handed in our idea. And Mr. Carter loved it. Now we get a break."

She purses her lips but doesn't say anything.

"We're a whole week early!" I say.

"Fine," she says, sighing. "We can take a one-week break. But then we need to really knuckle down."

"Aye aye, Cap'n," I say, saluting her. In a week I'll find some other way to distract her from this science project obsession. For now, we're free. And brilliant.

My giddiness at our brilliance only lasts a few days, but Mr. Carter reenergizes it all over again when he lets us skip deadline day—the Thursday science class when the rest of our classmates have to hand in their topics and get approval. If I'd known handing things in early could result in being excused from class, I would've switched to being a keener nerd a long time ago.

Although I guess I'm already kind of a keener nerd in history, since I've been bringing in books about space travel and how the pyramids were built—some people think aliens!—and other random things to discuss with my teacher. But that stuff is interesting, so it's different. Stephen-the-Leaver would say it still counts, but *he* doesn't count, so it doesn't matter what he'd say.

We spend our free period in the library, and Kat must be as happy as I am about the break, because she plays LotS the whole time and doesn't even mention our science project once. I switch back and forth between playing LotS and shopping for new nerd accessories. Well, window shopping, since Mom'd probably have a fit if I used her credit card to buy glasses when I don't actually need them. But I bet I'd look baller with glasses. Especially if they had bright-green frames.

When school ends on Friday, I race down the hallway, still on a high, speedy as a cheetah, or a race car, or a rocket, whichever is fastest, which is probably the rocket because it can fly and the others can't. Flying cheetahs would be awesome, though.

I whip around the corner and slam on the brakes.

"Do you go everywhere at top speed?" It's the boy I pointed out to Kat in the caf, with the floppy brown hair and the jaw like LumberLegs. The white guy whose eyes I keep meeting across the cafeteria. Boxer Boy. His face is only a foot away from mine. His bushy eyebrows are a shade darker than his shaggy brown hair; I wonder if he dyes it—the hair, not the eyebrows, though I suppose it technically could be either. He reaches out his hand to steady me, but his hand just grazes my arm before falling back to his side. His boxers are blue plaid today.

"Top speed?" I say. "This is slow for the Flash." I back up just a little so I'm no longer cross-eyed when I look at him.

"Are you implying that you're a superhero?"

"Have you ever been attacked by a supervillain?"

He cocks his head as if to consider it. I knew it; he *is* funny. "No," he says, "I don't think I have."

"Exactly. You're welcome."

He grins. There's a small patch of darkness along his chin that must be five-o'clock shadow. And another one on his cheek. If he tried to grow a beard, it would probably come out all scattered, like some parts forgot to grow.

"I'm Meg, by the way. When I'm Peter Parkering it, I mean."

He runs a hand through his floppy hair, still grinning. "Well, hi, Meg, I'm—"

"No, don't tell me!" I spit out. Boxer Boy, his name is Boxer Boy. If he tells me his real name, I'll have to start calling him that instead, which is boring.

"What? Why?" His grin is gone but his eyes are still warm—brown like chocolate.

If I explain, he might think I'm weird, and then I'll lose that warmth, too. I guess I can't call him Boxer Boy forever. "I—never mind. It's ridiculous. Go ahead."

Boxer Boy raises one of his dark eyebrows, which I hope means I've intrigued him, not spooked him.

"Grayson," he says. "My name is Grayson." He glances at the phone in his hand. "Unfortunately, I have to go. I'm late for archery practice."

"Archery? Like with bows and arrows and stuff?" I've never thought of archery as an actual thing people do—maybe at those festivals with the court jesters and Robin Hoods and stuff, not in real life—but it's suddenly on my bucket list. I've never written out my bucket list (does anyone in the world actually have a written bucket list?), but if I did, it would probably fill a book. Things like skydiving, yodeling, yo-yoing, climbing Mount Everest, riding a hot-air balloon, riding a camel, riding an elephant, riding a dolphin, marrying LumberLegs, of course, and now archery.

"Yeah," Grayson says. "I've only been doing it for a couple of years, so I'm not that great. There's this ten-year-old at the range who's always giving me tips."

"How do you keep your pants from falling down?" The question just pops out of me. For one long, frozen moment, the words hover in the air between us like wintry puffs of breath.

Then, thankfully, he laughs. "Invisible suspenders. Standard issue." He backs away down the hall, still looking at me. "Catch you around, Flash," he says.

"Only if you can catch up with me," I call after him.

He grins broadly as he waves and disappears out the side door.

I'm still floating on his dreamy grin when I arrive home from school to find Kenzie dragging her pink suitcase down the stairs, one thud after another. My own grin falls off my face.

I grab her suitcase from her hand and march it over to the door. "Don't you have stuff at your dad's place? I thought you didn't have to pack anything." I try to keep the bitterness out of my voice. It's not her fault she has an entire life over there, and I've never even seen where Stephen-the-Leaver lives now. Not her fault he's still her dad, but not mine.

"I have to take my ponies!" Kenzie snaps open her plastic case to reveal a huge, jumbled pile of hair and plastic hooves.

"Doesn't your dad have ponies?"

She snatches one out of the suitcase. "He doesn't have Rainbow Dash!"

If that's reason enough for her to take them all, I'm not arguing with her. "Well, have fun," I say, with as much enthusiasm as I can muster, which admittedly isn't much.

Kenzie looks up at me with wide eyes, like she's worried my frustration might be her fault.

I plaster a grin back across my face. "You're going to have an epic time," I say. "Now go watch your show until he gets here."

She scampers off, abandoning her open suitcase, as if she can't get away from my terrible acting fast enough.

I head toward the stairs to disappear into my room, but Mom pops her head out of the kitchen before I reach them. "Meg—" She breaks off and studies me. Her curls puff out of her ponytail like mine. She hasn't had time to style them today either. She tries again. "Meg, maybe you should go with them tonight." The corners of her eyes crinkle, like it physically pains her to say it. She'd rather none of us ever saw Stephen-the-Leaver again.

"I'm not invited," I say.

She fiddles with the beads on her necklace. "He said you were welcome to come along anytime."

"I don't need his pity invite," I almost say, but don't. He doesn't want me. That much is clear. "Well, I already have plans tonight," I say. "Kat's coming over."

"Oh!" Mom says. She should get mad at me for not asking first, maybe, but she just looks relieved.

I've had enough of this conversation. "I'll be upstairs," I say, then whirl around and bound up the stairs two at a time.

In my room, I plop down on my stomach on my bed, pull out my phone, and text Kat.

Come over tonight.

While I wait for her response, I pull out my laptop and find Legs's channel. My phone roars just as I find the new FaceCam Friday video.

I'm not great with spontaneous.

Right. She likes plans and schedules. I sigh, then type my response.

Come after supper then. That gives you a couple of hours.

I want her to come now. I want something fun and epic and amazing to do now. But later is better than never. I roll over onto my back, not bothering to push my hair away from my head or neck. Some days, it gets so big it could be its own pillow. You know, if I wanted it to end up totally squashed and lopsided.

My phone is silent. What the heck is taking her so long? She needs to come over. *I* need her to come over. I refuse to let tonight be blah.

I grab my phone and start typing again.

We can work on our project proposal.

Okay, so maybe tonight will be a little blah. But at least I won't be blah and by myself. It's not long before Kat's answer arrives.

OK. I can be there at 7.

Perfect. Well, mostly perfect. Perfect enough. I text back to confirm, then sit up and grab my laptop.

Even on the highest volume, Legs's FaceCam Friday video isn't loud enough to drown out the sound of Stephen-the-Leaver's car in the driveway. Or the sound of Kenzie's giggled greeting and Nolan's serious one. Or the sound of the front door closing and the car pulling away. Nothing is ever loud enough to drown out the sound of Stephen-the-Leaver leaving.

KAT

THIS IS NOT ME. I DON'T GO OVER TO CLASSMATES' HOUSES ON JUST A COUPLE of hours' notice. I don't go over to classmates' houses, period. Except Meg's, apparently, because here I am standing on her front step. Again. Ringing her doorbell. Again. But she said we could work on the proposal. Which we really need to get done. How could I say no to that?

One control factors . . . two spontaneity . . .

Meg's mother greets me at the door instead of the miniature butler, who is nowhere to be seen. "Meg's upstairs. You remember where her room is?" she asks as she hangs up my coat. I nod.

I ascend the long staircase, trudge down the long hall.

Seven schedules . . . eight hermit . . .

Meg's room is empty—maybe she's in the bathroom?—so I wander over to the terrarium. The turtle is motionless again but sitting on a different rock this time.

"Hi, Snappy," I say.

"It's Mr. Sparkles, actually." The voice comes from behind me. I whirl around. Meg's disembodied head sticks in through her window.

A tiny part of me tenses to scream, but the rest of me must be acclimatizing to Meg's . . . uniqueness, because all I say is, "I thought it was Snappy."

"Well, yeah, it was Snappy. But now it's Mr. Sparkles." The rest of her body, I have figured out, is on the small bit of roof just under her window.

"You changed his name?"

"What's wrong with that? He's a turtle. It's not like he knows what his name is. Now come on out. Weather's nice. The interweb says it's supposed to snow this weekend, but screw that." It's only September 29. In Ottawa, the leaves are probably still rich oranges and reds, the monochrome of winter still weeks if not months away.

Meg ducks her head back outside. I inch over to the window, keeping my own head inside the house as I glance past the roof to the ground. A hard cement sidewalk winds its way across the lawn, much too far below Meg's striped-socked feet.

If I fell the right way, feetfirst, I'd probably only break a limb. But if I was caught off guard—and, let's face it, if I'm falling, I was probably caught off guard—I could fall headfirst and crack my head open on the sidewalk, tendrils of brain scattered about like the seeds from the cantaloupes Meg wanted to spatter across the walk.

Meg peeks back around the window frame. "Hurry up and—" She breaks off and stares at me. "Are you scared?"

Scared? No, I just get completely uncontrollable panic attacks. Which I'm not admitting to Meg the Fearless. Well, fearless except when it comes to LotS. "No, of course not." My hands tremble involuntarily, stupid things. I hide them behind my back. *One spaghetti . . . two submarine . . . three scrambled eggs . . . four scrambled brains . . .*

Meg clambers back through the window and pushes past me. "Hang on. I'll be right back." She disappears into the hall, and when she bursts back into the room a minute or two later, she's carrying two long cloth jump ropes, the double-dutch kind, which she ties together. "Thread this through your belt loops," she commands, handing one end to me.

"Through my—what? Why?"

"Here, just—" She grabs my waist and starts to shove the end of the rope through one of the loops of my jeans.

"I've got it. I've got it!" I say, swatting her hand away. "No need to molest me." When I've threaded it through the last of the loops, she grabs it again and twists the ends together into some weird knot. I give it a tug, expecting it to unravel at the slightest hint of tension, but instead it tightens. "How'd you learn to do that?"

"What? Oh, the knot? From a book. I used to—" She breaks off and her face sags, as if her mind has disappeared to some dark corner that requires all her concentration and she has none left to control the muscles in her face. Then they tighten into a smile. "I've got lots of weird books on all sorts of topics. Ventriloquism, sign language, astronomy—or is it astrology? I forget which is which."

"Ventriloquism? Really?"

"Well, I didn't get far with that one. Lizard balls, that crap is hard! I made it to about page five before giving up."

"You learned to sign, though? That's cool."

"Well, like two words. Sea turtle and dog."

"I guess I should feel real confident about this knot then," I say, tugging it again. She has tied the other end of the rope to the bottom post of her heavy wood bed.

"It's fine. See?" She gives the rope a good yank. The rope goes taut. The knot holds firm. The bed barely even trembles.

"Come on," she says, only a little bossily. She clambers out the window, then reaches back in and grabs my sweaty hand. She waits for a minute while I breathe—*one iguana . . . two name-changing turtle*—then steadies me as I crouch and inch slowly over the smooth white sill and onto the coarse black surface. She doesn't let go until I am seated firmly on the roof, legs stretched out ahead of me.

The tree above our heads is bare, but it still whispers as the last warm winds of autumn weave through it. I have to admit: as long as I don't look at the ground, it's actually pretty nice up here.

Meg hands me a plum. For some reason, she has a whole bowl of them sitting up here on the roof. I bite into it and have to hurriedly cup my other hand under it to keep the sugary juices from dripping onto my jeans.

"This is really good," I mumble, mouth full of plum.

"Just don't eat too many. They'll give you the runs."

I laugh—one spastic puff of air—and almost choke. "Shut up."

"It's true. I know from experience."

"TMI, Meg," I think about saying, but don't because I can't decide if it would come across as übercool or übernerdy.

"Where are your siblings today? Nolan didn't take my coat."

"Half siblings. It's their weekend with their dad." She bites savagely into a plum, juice spurting everywhere. A slow trickle of it drips onto her pant leg, painting a small, dark circle.

"Right." I have no idea what to do. Ask more questions? Stop prying and shut up? Offer her a Kleenex? I don't even have a Kleenex.

Thankfully, Meg is not the kind of person who needs questions in order to provide answers. "Stephen-the-Leaver." She bites the pit out of her plum and spits it toward the ground. It bounces once off the roof, then plummets below. "He lived with us for seven years. I called him Dad and everything. Those books I mentioned— ventriloquism, sign language, oh, and this one about how to make your own lightsaber—they were all from him. Instead of making me read the boring books they assigned at school, he'd take me to the bookstore and let me pick out any book on any topic I wanted. I can read for hours if it's something I actually care about, which I hadn't realized before. Of course, then he got tired of us and left."

"I'm sure he didn't get tired of you."

"He applied for custody of the halflings, but not of me. 'Cause I'm not his real daughter." Her grip tightens on the plum, and more juice drips onto her pants, though she doesn't seem to notice.

"Oh," I say.

Meg ignores my profound contribution and rambles on. "It's ironic because people used to always think I *was* his real daughter, since we look so alike, and he never ever corrected them. But I guess he was always correcting them in his head." She wipes her hands on her pants. "The one upside is that Mom feels sorry for me. On weekends when he has the halflings, I can get Mom to agree to pretty much anything. Watch." She sticks her head back through the window. "Mom! Hey, Mom!" she yells. The window's wide enough for me to join her, so I do—though not in the yelling.

After a moment, there's an echoing thumping on the stairs, and then the door opens and Meg's mother pokes her head inside. "Meg, dear, you don't have to yell," she says, showing no surprise at our bodiless twin heads.

"Sorry, Mom, I just—can Kat stay over?"

My heart races, and I sit up, pulling out of the window. Stay over? I didn't bring my toothbrush, or my earplugs, or my face mask. Where would I sleep? What if I can't sleep? What if Meg snores? What if I snore? *One toothbrush . . . two conditioner . . . three sleeping bag . . .*

"Of course," Meg's mom says, her voice loud enough to reach out here on the roof. "If Kat's parents say it's okay. Anything else?"

"Brownies!" Meg declares.

Her mom must nod her agreement, because when Meg reclaims her head, she's grinning. "See?" she says.

Eleven vampires . . . twelve darkness . . . thirteen insomnia . . .

Meg jumps to her feet, right there on the roof. She stretches fearlessly, then crouches down and heads back toward the window.

"Come on," she says. "I want to play more LotS. *Lots* of LotS. We can both play. Mom'll let you use her computer and I'll use my laptop."

We're supposed to work on our project proposal. That's the whole reason I came over. But at just the thought of LotS, my breathing slows a little. *Sixteen archery . . . seventeen computer . . .* In LotS, I feel at home. In LotS, I'm in control.

"Can I go on your server?" Meg continues. "I want to see your underwater thing."

My breathing slows even more. *Nineteen chat log . . .* "Probably. If the others say it's okay."

Hanging out in my server home is almost as good as being in my real home. Better, sometimes. Maybe Mom will bring over a bag of my stuff—earplugs, toothbrush, PJs—if I ask nicely. And we can work on the proposal tomorrow.

"Hurry up, slowpoke." Meg holds out her hand, and I grasp it with one hand and the jump rope with the other as I ease back inside.

LEGENDS OF THE STONE

KittyKat has logged on.

[]Sythlight: Hi

KittyKat: hey

KittyKat: no one else is on?

[]Sythlight: Nice to see you, too. :P

KittyKat: sorry, I just wanted to ask if I can bring my
friend on

[]Sythlight: Fine by me.

KittyKat: you don't think I should ask everyone?

[]Sythlight: I'm sure it's fine. I mean, if you're really
worried about it, you could talk to Lucien. But I
haven't seen him on here in a while.

KittyKat: that's true. and if he's not going to be online,
he really can't complain.

[]Sythlight: If anyone bothers you about it, just tell
them I said it was ok.

KittyKat: because you're the boss?

[]Sythlight: King of the world, actually.

KittyKat: oh, I didn't know that. though I am the
Supreme Emperor of the Universe, so that's to be
expected. I don't concern myself with such pitiful,
lowly matters.

[]Sythlight: So you're the one I should talk to about
that pay raise.

KittyKat: I wouldn't recommend it. I have a policy of
demoting anyone who asks for a raise.

[]Sythlight: Smart. I understand how you became the
SEU.

KittyKat: and I behead anyone who is too lazy to spell out my entire title.

[]Sythlight: Oops. Forgive me oh Supreme Emperor of the Universe. I beseech thee.

KittyKat: well, fine, just this once. but don't make the mistake again.

[]Sythlight: Never. So is your friend coming on now?

KittyKat: oh yeah right . . . give me a min

[]Sythlight has entered the badlands.

[]Sythlight was slain by a mutant shadowwolf.

[]Sythlight has entered the badlands.

[]Sythlight was slain by a mutant shadowwolf.

[]Sythlight has entered the badlands.

[]Sythlight was slain by a mutant shadowwolf.

MEGAdawn has logged on.

KittyKat: back

KittyKat: this is Meg

MEGAdawn: HIIIIIIII

[]Sythlight: ABSOLUTELY NOTHING HAPPENED WHILE YOU WERE GONE DON'T LOOK AT THE CHAT LOG

KittyKat: ha ha ha

MEGAdawn: oh good ur as good at this game as me!

[]Sythlight has entered the badlands.

KittyKat: want help getting your stuff back?

[]Sythlight: Sure. There's a whole pack of them.

KittyKat: be right there. just giving Meg some gear

[]Sythlight was slain by a mutant shadowwolf.

MEGAdawn: lolol

[]Sythlight: I should probably actually gear up a little before heading in there.

KittyKat: be right there. where'd you die?

[]Sythlight: By the tower.

KittyKat has entered the badlands.

MEGAdawn has entered the badlands.

[]Sythlight has entered the badlands.

MEGAdawn: I hit one!

MEGAdawn was slain by a mutant shadowwolf.

MEGAdawn: welp I hit it once I'm calling that a win

[]Sythlight was slain by a mutant shadowwolf.

MEGAdawn: we're good at this

[]Sythlight: Remember how I said I was going to gear up before going back in? Definitely should have done that.

KittyKat: okay, they're all down. I'll grab your stuff.

[]Sythlight: Thanks! Meet you at your castle.

[]Sythlight has entered the waterlands.

MEGAdawn: is that where I spawned?

KittyKat has entered the waterlands.

MEGAdawn: hiii

[]Sythlight: Hi

KittyKat: here's your stuff

MEGAdawn: we should do one of those rift things

KittyKat: yes, I'm sure that'll go well

[]Sythlight: Oh, come on. They just caught me by surprise the first time. After that, if I'd been geared up, I'd have destroyed that pack.

MEGAdawn: and I'm an expert at this game. from all my lumberlegs watching.

[]Sythlight: I watch him sometimes. He's funny.

MEGAdawn: the funniest

MEGAdawn: i'm going to marry him one day

[]Sythlight: Does he know that?

MEGAdawn: in his heart i'm sure he does

[]Sythlight: lol

MEGAdawn: let's do it do it do it

[]Sythlight: I'm game.

KittyKat: fine

KittyKat: but only that easy one in the drylands

MEGAdawn: YASSSSSS

MEGAdawn: TO THE RIFT!!!!!!!!!!!!

[]Sythlight: Lead the way.

KittyKat has entered the drylands.

MEGAdawn has entered the drylands.

[]Sythlight has entered the drylands.

6

IF MY AVATAR AND LEGS'S GOT TOGETHER, THEY'D ACTUALLY MAKE A PRETTY cute couple. My green hair and his tree-stump legs against a nature background—the perfect fit. Though purple skin isn't very nature-y. It is definitely badass, though, and Legs is badass, too. Sort of. More funny and kind, I guess.

"How many?" Kat's question breaks into my thoughts.

I'm not admitting to her that I wasn't listening. Again. I could just tell her about my ADHD, but what if it scares her away like it seems to do with everyone else? And it's her own fault I'm so scattered. She insisted we work on our science proposal today, even though we stayed up way too late last night playing LotS.

"Um, ten," I say.

She chews her lip and studies her page of neat, straight writing. "Do you know that many people?"

"What, ten people? Of course!"

"Okay." She writes it down. "So this week we'll both do some research on sugar so we can ensure our hypotheses make sense. I think this is a good start."

A good start. Sweet. "Hey, don't you think my avatar and Legs's would make a cute couple?"

She purses her lips, and for a moment I think she's going to ream me out for changing the topic, even though she basically just said we're done. But then she says, "Well, his is quite a bit taller than yours. But your dwarf's green hair would go well with his legs."

I grin. "An excellent point." The image of Legs's face slips out of my mind and is replaced by another. "Hey, what did you think of Grayson?"

She looks back up from her paper. "Who?"

"Boxer Boy. I pointed him out in the caf, remember? Looks kind of like Legs."

She shrugs. "I don't think I actually saw him."

"You didn't? I'll have to point him out again on Monday." I wonder what type of character he'd play in LotS. An archer, obviously. "He's a dragonlord archer," I decide.

"Oh, cool," Kat says, looking much more interested than she did a moment ago.

. . .

All week I watch for Grayson in the cafeteria so I can point him out again to Kat, but he must eat elsewhere sometimes, because I don't spot him until Friday. "There!" I say, pointing to a table in the back corner.

"Don't point," Kat snaps, then turns her head ever so slightly in that direction. "The guy with the floppy hair and black shirt?" She's whispering, as if there's any chance he could hear her all the way across the busy room.

"That's the one! Doesn't he look kind of like Legs?"

She shrugs, then jerks her head down. "He's spotted us."

"He has?" I stand and turn, and sure enough, he's looking right at us. I wave, then immediately regret waving, then don't regret it at all because he actually waves right back and grins this grin so magical it should be named Perfection.

I sit back down to find Kat blinking wide-eyed at me, cheeks tinged with red.

"Isn't he adorable?" I ask.

She shakes her head. "Let's just work on our proposal," she whispers. She pulls our drafted and redrafted plan from her backpack.

"I told you, I don't do homework at lunchtime," I say, but I'm too happy to really protest. "Maybe Grayson can be one of the people we test. That's a good idea. Write that down."

Kat just rolls her eyes.

EVEN THOUGH OUR PROPOSAL IS PRETTY FAR ALONG, MY HEART POUNDS AS Mr. Carter leans over my desk to peer at it.

One judgment . . . two approval . . .

"Nice hypotheses," Mr. Carter says.

"We want to do a bit more research on sugar this weekend," Meg pipes up, which surprises me because I didn't think she was listening when I told her that the research we'd done—and she had actually done a bit after I texted her to remind her—didn't quite answer all my questions. "To make sure they make sense."

Mr. Carter nods, eyes still on our paper. He reaches out and taps a line with his pencil. "You're going to need to test more than ten people, though."

More than ten.

Seven crowds . . . eight socialization . . .

"How about thirty?" Meg throws out.

"Yes, thirty would be much better."

Meg grabs the sheet, turns it toward herself, and I'm forced to watch her make the revision as if in slow motion.

We will test ~~ten~~ thirty people.

Thirteen strangers . . . fourteen panic . . .

"Good work so far," Mr. Carter says, then walks toward the next group, his legs disappearing from my field of view as I stare down at the page.

Sixteen introvert . . . seventeen conversation . . .

Thirty people.

When Meg and I decided on our science project, all I thought was: *Legends of the Stone. Video game. Awesome.*

I did *not* think about the fact that we would have to test real people. And I did *not* think about the fact that we would have to recruit those people.

I'm thinking about it now.

Twenty extroverts . . . twenty-one doomed . . .

"He said, 'Good work,'" Meg says, beaming like she's never had a teacher say that before, though I know she's acing history and drama. She's sitting backward in her chair, leaning over my desk, doodling on the corner of our proposal.

I can't admit to her that I'm panicking. Can't tell her that even though I've been here for more than a month, she's the only person I know. We don't need to actually finish the testing until February, with a check-in in January. That's loads of time. Months and months. Which means I can push it out of my mind for now, and we can deal with that issue later. The people issue.

I hate people.

"Even me?" Meg asks, which could mean she's a mind reader, but probably just means I accidentally said that out loud.

"You're not people. You're Meg."

And something about the way she grins at that makes me feel the tiniest bit better.

LEGENDS OF THE STONE

[]Sythlight: Good job, team.

MEGAdawn: I only died five times!

KittyKat: you're definitely improving

MEGAdawn: yeah now that we've handed in our
proposal and you're actually letting us play again
instead of working all the time

KittyKat: oh shush. we played tons while we were
working on it.

[]Sythlight: I should probably go soon. Need to go for
a run before it gets dark.

MEGAdawn: u run in the snow?

[]Sythlight: No snow yet. It's only October.

KittyKat has entered the waterlands.

MEGAdawn: we have a ton already

MEGAdawn: it snowed all weekend

MEGAdawn: u down somewhere south?

[]Sythlight: Nope, near Toronto.

[]Sythlight has entered the greenlands.

MEGAdawn: WOOOOO TEAM CANADA

MEGAdawn: we're in Edmonton

[]Sythlight: A lot of us on here are in Canada. I think
Pterion's in Halifax. That's how I connected with
Lucien on the forums in the first place. Discovered
we were both in Ontario and he invited me on here.

MEGAdawn: ur not a true Canadian if you don't have snow yet, though

MEGAdawn has entered the waterlands.

KittyKat: stop perpetuating Canadian stereotypes

MEGAdawn: there's no one else even on

Private Message from MEGAdawn to KittyKat:

MEGAdawn: u and Sythlight should totally get married

KittyKat: you're ridiculous. I don't even know if Syth is a girl or boy

MEGAdawn: boy

KittyKat: you don't know that for sure

MEGAdawn: hey Syth, u a guy or a girl?

Private Message from KittyKat to MEGAdawn:

KittyKat: you are sooooo embarrassing

[]Sythlight: Guy. Why?

Private Message from MEGAdawn to KittyKat:

MEGAdawn: told you so

KittyKat: gah, he's gonna think we're stalking him

KittyKat: and maybe he doesn't even like girls

KittyKat: BUT DON'T YOU DARE ASK THAT

KittyKat: and also I really don't care

MEGAdawn: I have a theory that boys play girl and boy characters, but girls only play girls

KittyKat: that's not confusing at all

[]Sythlight: How many people have you asked?

MEGAdawn: 1

MEGAdawn: so far 100% right. :P

Private Message from KittyKat to MEGAdawn:

KittyKat: if you want me to marry him, then you
should probably stop flirting with him

MEGAdawn: OMG am I? so sorry!

KittyKat: dude, I'm not actually going to marry
him. flirt away

MEGAdawn: no I'll stop

MEGAdawn: random fact—I'm lactose intolerant so I
fart after I eat ice cream

Private Message from KittyKat to MEGAdawn:

KittyKat: OMG!

MEGAdawn: no problem

MEG

NORMALLY, I LOVE SNOW—LOVE THE WAY IT TURNS GRAY STREETS WHITE AND
piles up on lawns like mounds of fluffy pillows and makes everyone look like they have white hair. A city of grandparents.

As I bash my knee into the washing machine, though, I curse
the stuff. Loudly.

The rest of our house is draped in carpet—except for the living room, but Mom yelled at me when she found me skateboarding on the hardwood floor. Which means that I'm stuck trying

to learn this kick turn in our laundry room. The room may have cement floors, but it is way too tiny to do this trick right, let alone to do it wrong.

I let the skateboard skitter away toward the drain as I jab pause on the YouTube tutorial. My knee has taken enough bashing for now, and so has the washing machine. I pat it apologetically as I hop up to sit atop it. Then I text Kat.

I m bored.

She won't respond. It's Tuesday evening, which means she's supposed to be out helping her granddad do I forget what. Maybe smoke a pipe and sort through old newspapers, snipping out articles about capitalism and world wars and the weather. I wonder if he has a weather clipping from every day *since* the war. Is he old enough to have been alive during one of those big ones? I could probably try to calculate it, but why bother?

My phone rings and I snatch it up, thinking it might be Kat, but it's stupid Stephen-the-Leaver. I refuse to give him a moment's thought. I hit the ignore button, hop off the washer, and head in search of my real parent who actually cares. She's in her computer room, furiously typing numbers into some Excel spreadsheet. She's been spending a lot of time doing that since her marketing company started doing so well.

"I'm going for a walk," I report, then duck back out of there before she can subject me to some boring rant about how much she hates accounting. "You should hire a bookkeeper," I always tell her, and she always says she can do it herself.

"Meg!" she calls after me, and my heart sinks.

"What?" Reluctantly, I stick my head back inside.

"Take your sister with you," is all she says, not taking her eyes away from the screen.

I see her then. Kenzie sits on the floor at Mom's feet, rolling Mom's pant leg up and down. She gives me an impish grin.

"Come on, little wingling," I say, swatting her lightly on the back to corral her out of the tiny room. Upstairs, I bundle Kenzie up in her fluorescent-pink snowsuit and alligator hat, then grab my own winter coat, and we head out.

Kenzie purrs some song about a pirate mermaid as we march along—probably one that she made up, but possibly not. It wouldn't be the weirdest thing she's learned at day care. The wind is nippier than I expected. It seeps through my jeans, making my not-so-recently shaven leg hair stand on end. Fashion be damned; I should have worn snow pants like Kenzie.

"Hey, Meg!" The call comes from across the street. Boxer Boy—Grayson—is waving at us. At me.

There's a busy street just a few blocks away that hums with constant traffic, but cars are rare on this side avenue, so Grayson barely glances each way before crossing the street to meet us. I stand up straighter, instantly relieved that I didn't wear snow pants, the ugly things. They'd make my butt look about five sizes larger. Though maybe that wouldn't be such a bad thing. Big butts and all that.

"You babysitting?" he asks as he draws up beside us. His green scarf is bunched around his neck, like a strangling boa constrictor.

"Kind of. This is my sister. Kenzie, say hi."

She pops her thumb into her mouth, glove and all. Mom has been trying to get her to stop sucking her thumb for about a year, but even mittens won't deter her.

"I like your snowsuit," he says, grinning at her. She looks down at her body, brow furrowed, as if she's just realized what she's wearing.

"She likes pink," I tell him. I think that's why she likes Kat so much, since at least half of Kat's wardrobe is pink. Kenzie tries to clamber into Kat's lap pretty much every time she comes over. Kat never seems to mind, though, and she's better at LotS than me even with Kenzie's hand under her own on the mouse. "Where are you going?"

"Heading home from archery. I practice Tuesdays and Fridays, usually."

I glance down the street at the nearby park he must be coming from. It's really more a square of lawn than a park—snow-covered now, of course—with one large rock and a single line of planted trees. "What do you do? Practice on squirrels or something?"

He laughs, and a little wrinkle forms in his forehead, just above his eyebrow—adorably cute. "It's target archery, not hunting archery. There's a range at the club. About five blocks that way." He waves his hand haphazardly in the direction he had been coming from.

"Oh. That makes a lot more sense."

"Hey, you going to Schiller's party on Friday?" Grayson asks. I know Ryan Schiller, but I didn't know that he was having a party. Now that Lindsey and I don't talk anymore—we haven't texted since that weekend she went away—I never know about the good parties.

"Of course," I say. "You?"

It might just be the snow reflecting in his pupils, but I swear his eyes lighten a little at my words. He nods. "Do you want to— Hey, should your sister be doing that?"

I whirl around, cursing Kenzie in my head before I even see her. She's two houses away, on someone's porch, pouring their small tub of ice melt into a heaping mound right in front of the door.

"Kenzie!" I shriek at her. "Put that down!" She doesn't, of course, and blue crystals keep pouring like a landslide from the tub in her hands.

"At least they won't have to worry about slipping on ice when they step out the door," Grayson calls after me, laughing, as I run toward her. I bound up the front steps, snatch the bucket from Kenzie's hands, and point at the blue pile.

"Clean that up," I demand, and she scowls at me. As I scoop up gloved handfuls of the stuff, I look back to the sidewalk. Grayson has already moved a few houses down the street, but he's still looking at us.

"See you Friday!" he shouts, waving.

My hands are full of blue crystals, and I can't wave back.

MEG POPS HER HEAD INTO THE KITCHEN, HER SNOW-DUSTED BLACK CURLS hugging tightly together, free from their frequent ponytail. Snow in October is something I'm not sure I'll ever be able to get used to, no matter how long I end up living here.

"Did Mom let you in?" I ask. "I didn't hear the doorbell."

"No, your door was unlocked, so I just came in."

"It was?" I smother the panic in my voice.

"Yes. And an evil murderer named Meg broke in. Be very afraid."

"Shut up," I yell over my shoulder as I duck into the hallway to lock the door. When I return to the kitchen, Meg's sitting in a kitchen chair, backward—she has actually gone to the effort of turning one of the chairs around just to sit in it that way. Her chin rests on the top of the chair back.

"So, let's talk about what we're going to wear to Friday's party." Since she doesn't lift her chin, the rest of her head bobs up and down as she talks.

"I thought you came over to borrow my math textbook." She texted me that she forgot hers at school, and apparently she's going to get a detention if she fails to do her math homework one more time this month. "And wait, what party?" There's no way I agreed to go to a party. I would never agree to go to a party.

Meg slips off the chair and heads toward the fridge. "And people say I have a bad memory. I messaged you about it last night. Grayson's going. Remember?"

"Oh, yeah. I just—I thought you were going with *him*." *One baboons . . . two drunken revelry . . .* "I can't go."

"What? No! You have to come with me," Meg whines, opening the fridge to pour herself a glass of milk. If we were at her house she'd grab a Coke, but we don't usually have pop in the house unless someone else brings it.

"There's no way," I tell her flatly. "I don't do parties." *Three panicky stampede . . . four trapped in crowded corners . . .*

"Don't do parties *yet*."

The only time I've ever been to a party, it was an accident. My so-called friend invited me over with "just a few people." Turns out "just a few" meant at least thirty. Not as many as those huge parties you see in movies, but enough that when she disappeared to make out with her boyfriend and I found myself alone on a couch in a dark corner surrounded by strangers, I forgot how to breathe. I sat there forever, the chatter and faces and laughter swirling around me as I struggled to remember where my lungs were, until finally I pulled myself together enough to go outside and call my mom to pick me up.

I'm not going through that again, but how do I get out of it without telling Meg about my panic attacks? Because there's no way I'm telling Meg the Fearless that just sitting on a couch with strangers can make me hyperventilate. "Can't you just go by yourself?"

"Not when I'm trying to impress a guy! What if he's watching for me? I'll look like a loner if I show up by myself." Meg pouts as she slides back into her seat. "Don't be nervous. It'll be fun."

I nibble on a hangnail. The party she's talking about is probably the full-blown movie type. If she thinks it's silly for me to be nervous about that, she's going to think it's completely ridiculous that a party with thirty people lounging around on couches induces full-blown panic mode. I definitely can't tell her that. I can't even tell her that I'm freaking out at the thought of testing thirty people for our science project. Ever since we handed in our proposal, I've been waking up in the middle of the night thinking about it. *Eight overstimulated . . . nine disappearing friend . . .*

"Who is this guy again?"

"Grayson. The guy I pointed out in the cafeteria. Like, multiple times. You know, Boxer Boy. You'd like him, Kat. He's an archer."

"We don't need a new archer," I protest. "We need a tank."

"No, not in LotS. In real life."

"What, like with a real bow and arrows and stuff?" I stop gnawing at the tiny, loose flap of skin and nail. "I didn't know people actually did that."

She giggles girlishly. "Right? That's exactly what I thought. So cool."

"And you think he likes you?" It comes out sounding skeptical, which is not what I mean. Thankfully, Meg doesn't notice.

"I think he was going to ask me to go with him. Before Kenzie screwed it up." She scowls and pushes my math text away.

"Well, problem solved then." My tension-filled shoulders

relax. "Call him up and the two of you can go together. You don't need me."

Seventeen romance . . . eighteen archery range . . .

Meg plants both her hands on the table, elbows in the air, and stares me down. "I'll call him up and invite him *if*," she challenges, "you pick up your phone and invite any guy in the world on any date of your choice."

I break eye contact first, glancing down at my phone, then back at her, as my shoulders reunite with their familiar tension. I can't do that. Obviously I can't do that. "All right, fine, you win. But I'm still not going."

"Not going where?" Granddad asks as he shuffles into the kitchen. He was downstairs with Mom and Dad, watching some documentary on whales. I don't know how he got up the stairs without me hearing him. I don't know how he ever manages to get up those stairs without breaking his hip again.

Meg hops up from her chair. "Hi! You're Granddad. We haven't met yet." She strides toward him.

"And you're Meg," Granddad says. "And no, we haven't."

Meg sticks her arm out and I think she's going to shake his hand, but instead she offers him her fist. Granddad doesn't even hesitate, just presses his own bony knuckle up to hers in a fist bump.

"I've been dying to meet the man with the epic eyebrows," Meg says, and my face flushes instantly hot. But Granddad just grins and makes the white, bushy caterpillars on his forehead bob up and down. Meg laughs appreciatively. "You sure seem to go out a lot. You're never here."

I'm always bumping into Granddad around the house and trying to figure out what the heck to say to him, so it seems to me like he never leaves. But I guess he's been out when Meg's visited before.

"Well, I'm not going to let this thing"—he waves his hand toward his hip—"stop me from living my life."

That's a sentiment I don't understand. If I had an excuse to never leave the house, I'd take it.

"You're even cooler than I expected," Meg says. Granddad laughs at that, and my stomach twists. This is the first time Meg's ever met Granddad, and she's already talking more comfortably with him than I ever have.

Meg heads back to the table, and Granddad hobbles after her. "So, where were the two of you going?" he asks.

"Nowhere, apparently," Meg says as she plops back down on her backward chair—sideways this time. "Kat's being a real party pooper. Literally. There's this party on Friday night, and she refuses to go for no reason."

"A party?" His eyes travel far away for a moment, before drifting back to us. "You should go, Katharina. Your grandma and I used to go to quite a few before she stopped leaving the house. I met her at a party."

Even though we're so different, I've always felt like Granddad somehow gets me. But if he thinks I should go to this party, maybe he doesn't get me at all.

Meg raises her eyebrows at me, as if Granddad meeting my grandma at a party is so romantic that I can't possibly argue with it. But it does nothing to quell my panic. I might find it more compelling if I had ever met my grandma, but she died before I was born. Granddad has always just been Granddad. *My* granddad.

"Was she a good dancer?" Meg asks, and Granddad's face lights up. How does Meg always know what to say? Even to people she's just met?

"Oh, was she ever," he says. "She could dance a mean twist."

"Man, I wish I could dance the twist," Meg says, climbing to her feet as if she's going to try right now.

"If it wasn't for this hip, I'd teach you."

Their banter is so smooth. They're both so adventurous.

I've always known how much Granddad loved me. Always. Except, now that we live together, now that he's seen how terribly scared I am all the time, I wonder if that's changed. Not that I think he doesn't love me anymore, but if he doesn't understand, then maybe he's unimpressed. Disappointed.

Meg and Granddad chatter away about different dance moves, old and new, as I try to imagine going to another party. I can't picture it. My brain shoves the image away and I see only darkness. Feel the tightness in my lungs from holding my breath.

I let it out. *One elephant . . . two fear . . .*

Granddad should just go with Meg. He'd probably love that. *She'd* probably love that. They could go together, and I could sit alone in my room watching LumberLegs like I've done so many times before.

Except I don't want that. I don't want to be left behind and forgotten about. Don't want to never leave the house because I'm too afraid. Don't want to fail our science project because I can't talk to people. Meg laughs at something Granddad says, and I scowl, but neither of them notices. I'm already being left behind.

Would it really be so bad to go to this party? I wouldn't have to talk to people there, just be around them. It's a baby step, really. If I can just be around hordes of people, then maybe I'll be able to test hordes of people for our project when the time comes. Maybe I'll be able to stop being a disappointment.

Meg and Granddad won't *need* to understand me if I can just keep up with them. And I'm a capable, competent person; I should be able to keep up with them.

Seven baby steps . . . eight bravery . . .

"Fine, I'll go," I spit out, interrupting them.

Meg stops the pop-and-lock dance move she's showing off to Granddad and spins toward me, beaming. "Really?"

No, not really, I want to say. No way in hell. No way in the badlands. No way in an epic rift of doom. But with both of them grinning proudly at me—proud of me for being brave, for being adventurous, for being more like them—there's no way to back out.

Meg and I are going to a party.

MEG

I CRANK THE VOLUME ON MY SPEAKERS AND LEAP ONTO MY BED. THE MUSIC acts like a duck call; Kenzie comes flapping into the room and hops up beside me. I twirl her around and we leap, spin, and head pound around the room together.

I've already showered and scrunched styler into my hair and hung upside down off my bed while diffusing it and dressed and put on my makeup for tonight's party, which means I should probably sit quietly with my ankles crossed until it's go time. But screw that.

Droplets of sweat gather in my armpits. Thankfully, the sleeves of the hugely oversized green shirt I'm wearing over black leggings are too big and flowy to get noticeable pit stains. I texted Kat pictures of all my different outfit options yesterday, and this is the one she picked. Well, actually, she picked a different one, but I vetoed that one, and this was her second pick.

Aside from outfit choices, I tried not to bring up the party too much this week, because Kat's already-pale face gets even paler every time I mention it, but yesterday, Grayson waved at me again from across the caf, and then, admittedly, I couldn't really talk about anything else all day. Kat will be fine, though—more than fine; she'll have an epic time. We'll dance together, and then I'll introduce her to Grayson, and then we'll all dance together, and she'll loosen up so much that we might even scope out a cute guy for her to say hello to.

My phone roars its Chewbacca cry. Speak of the devil—or the Wookiee or whatever.

I can't make it. Sorry.

Ha-ha, funny. I tap out my response.

lol good try, see u soon

I know she's a bit nervous, but I also know she won't stand me up like Lindsey used to. Kat's dependable that way. And she has nothing to be nervous about, because she'll be with me. BFFs together forever. I stick my pinkie up in the air. "I promise I won't leave your side for any reason whatsoever. Pinkie swear."

Kenzie yanks at my leggings. "Who're you talking to?"

"Invisible Kat," I say.

"Oh," she says, as if this makes perfect sense, then continues her own special version of headbanging—ducking her head down between her knees, curls hanging almost to the floor, before whipping up so quickly she almost throws herself backward.

My palms are sweating, but I'm not sure if it's from dancing, nervousness, or excitement. I can't wait for Kat to meet him, not just have him pointed out from across the room. I want her to tell me if he likes me or if I'm reading it all wrong.

I pick up Kenzie and twirl her around so fast the giggles burst out of her like a sneeze. A rainbow sneeze. I set her back down and she wobbles on her feet like a little drunken woman. Or squirrel. I wonder what squirrels would be like drunk. Now that would be an interesting science project thingy.

"When's Princess Kat coming?" Kenzie asks.

"Soon." I check my phone. No texts. She should be here by now, should have been here a while ago, actually. "She's not coming to play with you, though. We're going out." If she ever gets here. I message her again.

dude where are u?!!?!?

Kenzie sticks out her lip and puts her hand on her hip in a queen-of-brat pose that she definitely did not learn from me. I pat her on the head with one hand and dial Kat's number with the other. It rings. And rings and rings. Then her boring, automated voice mail. "You have reached 780-5 . . ." I hang up, then try again. Still nothing.

I try another message.

Kat?!?!?

Nothing. I call again, and then again. Nothing and more nothing.

I flip through my text log and stare at her original message:

I can't make it. Sorry.

Mom ducks her head through my doorway. "Meg, what time is Kat coming?" Her voice is more high-pitched than usual. A stray curl sticks out at the back of her neck. Did it come loose from her bun, or did she miss it when she put her hair up in the first place?

"I—I don't think she is," I say. "I mean, she was supposed to be coming, but now she's not. I guess."

"You're not going out, then? That's a relief. You can watch Kenzie and Nolan. I've got to pop over to your aunt's. Teddy's having another seizure."

"No, Mom, I—"

She's gone, though, before I can even figure out how I want to protest. "Kenzie, Nolan—Meg's in charge," she calls, already somewhere far away—probably at the bottom of the stairs. "I'm going to help with your cousin. I'll be back in a couple of hours."

And then I'm stuck at home. In my bedroom. Alone. Looking after two miniature monsters. Not dancing. Not drinking. Not making out with Boxer Boy. The outfit we spent hours deciding on, the wave from across the cafeteria that made my heart race all day—all for nothing.

And all for nothing why? I don't get it. Why isn't she coming? Why would she abandon me like that? Without any explanation. Just like Lindsey. And Brad's friends. Why does everyone end up being the same?

Why do I somehow always end up alone?

I drop my phone on the floor, kick it across the room, then flop down on my bed and start on what is now officially my most exciting activity of the evening—staring at the ceiling.

KAT

WE SIT OUTSIDE MEG'S HOUSE FOR A LONG TIME, MOM AND ME. SHE KEEPS the car running the whole time; she has to, it's twenty below. She doesn't say anything, just waits for me, patiently, to get out of the car. Like she has been since we arrived, which was long enough ago that my knuckles are stiff and uncomfortable from gripping my knees so tightly.

That's all I have to do—get out of the car. Take a dozen steps down the sidewalk. Knock on Meg's door. All of which I've done multiple times before. Plus, I'm wearing my confidence-inducing pink shirt (not to be confused with my lucky pink shirt). So I should be able to get out of the car.

But thinking of getting out of the car makes me think of facing Meg's eager excitement, which makes me think of the party, which makes me think of my fear of standing alone and awkward and overwhelmed in a corner while crowds of people jostle me and trap me in and judge me with their piercing eyes because I can't remember how to do the most basic task of living—breathing. I hate my brain. I hate crowds. I hate people.

I wish that one "party" I went to provided a full explanation for my fear. But I was afraid of parties—afraid of people, really—long before that. I have no excuse. I'm just scared.

I drop my head between my legs, searching for breath somewhere other than my lungs. I can't find it. *One* . . . I try to count. *One* . . . I can't remember how to count.

"Kat." Mom puts her hand on my shoulder. She hands me my phone. I'm not sure why she even has it. "Tell Meg you can't make it."

Obediently, robotically, I tap out the message. Breathe. Breathe. Head back between my knees. Tires rolling. Somewhere far away a phone is ringing. Somewhere in my head a phone is ringing. I don't know how to answer it.

I awake Saturday morning to more ringing, though it turns out to be my normal weekend alarm, not the telephone in my head. In fact, my mind is unusually quiet as I get up and have breakfast. After spending some time last night with a paper bag, a hot bath, one of my anxiety pills, and hours of listening to *The Velveteen Rabbit* on repeat before I finally fell asleep, I feel almost like myself again. Sort of. A heaviness still weighs down my chest, like my lungs have turned to lead.

I need to call Meg, though. I need to explain. I need her to know I tried. I really tried. And I need her to know I'm sorry.

I stare at her name on my phone screen for what feels like an eternity before I finally fill my leaden lungs with air and jab at the call button.

It barely rings before she answers. "Okay, dude," she says, without even saying hello. "Did someone die or something? Because that's the only reason I can think of for you standing me up."

"I . . . no—"

"Then what? Seriously! How could you leave me hanging like that? I had to babysit Kenzie all night."

"Well, I—"

"Kenzie fell asleep in my bed and peed in it. *Peed* in it. Have you ever slept on a mattress that smells like pee? Even like a million spritzes of Febreze can't mask that smell. Ugh. Seriously, ugh. What the heck, Kat?"

"You're not even giving me a chance to explain," I snap, more angrily than I mean to.

"Fine. Explain."

The pause draws out into one second, then three, then five. It is not silence, exactly. I can hear her hurried, angry breaths, and my shaky, shallow ones. The tension builds like radiation around a frog in a microwave in a cruel, psychopathic joke. Each breath counts down to its doom. This is my chance to explain, to make it right. To hit stop and rescue the frog before it—well, before. But what exactly am I supposed to say? I'm sorry that I'm incapable of acting like a normal human being? I'm sorry I'm overwhelmed by crowds and terrified of small talk? I'm sorry I agreed to go to your stupid party in the first place?

"I don't know," I mumble moronically.

"Then I don't know why I'm even bothering to talk to you," she snaps, then hangs up the phone.

The line is dead.

The frog's in a million tiny pieces.

Even the air in my lungs turns to lead.

MEG

I AM REDEFINING THE TERM BFF. LYRICALLY. NO, LIMERICKALLY. NO. COME *on*, what's the word? The one that means for real, not just for pretend, not exaggerated. Gah, I feel so stupid sometimes. I kick my desk, making my laptop screen shudder. Screw it. Whatever the word is, that's how I'm doing it.

I bring up the slang site, log in, and enter the definition:

BFF: Big Fat Frog, or Blind Friendly Fish, or Bean Fueled Fart.

Because it definitely doesn't mean Best Friend Forever. Not for me. I don't know if I have some kind of built-in people spray—like bug spray, but for people—or what, but no one sticks with me forever. Not best friends, not anybody.

The friendship bracelet girls lasted three months last spring; Lindsey lasted—I count on my fingers—three weeks; I had a boyfriend for just two months; my birth dad only stuck around for four years of my life; Stephen-the-Leaver lasted seven, and those years were obviously for Kenzie and Nolan, and not for me.

I thought Kat could make it at least seven years. I thought Kat would be around for*ever*.

Nope.

Try a whopping . . . one . . . two . . . two months! Not even.

Well, screw you, too, Kat.

Screw you all. Why don't you all go shove a hive of hornets up your butts?

Oh, and literally. The word is "literally."

In the laundry room, I practice ollie after ollie, bashing my knee on the washing machine every time I glide over to check my phone. No messages.

I set my phone on the arm of the couch as Nolan curls up beside me to read his dinosaur book. I check it as he reads aloud a page about herbivores. No messages. Nolan notices my distraction and starts the page over from the beginning.

There are no messages as I wrestle with Kenzie, do homework, help Mom cook beans and rice, watch Lorenzo the turtle swim in circles, play dolls with Kenzie, and try to watch a LumberLegs video, then give up because I keep turning to grin at Kat but she's not there.

No messages when I shower, change, climb into bed.

No messages until I lean over and flick out the light. Then, from out of the new darkness, my phone dings. I flick the light back on.

There's a message—not in my texts, but online.

Dear Flash,

I looked for you at the party last night, but didn't see you. Any interest in going for coffee with me sometime? My treat, as a thank you for protecting planet earth.

—Grayson

It's Grayson, which is, hello, amazing!

But it's not Kat.

I roll over and press my face into my pillow. No text messages. Not a single one, all day long. I hug the pillow to my chest. Then I roll over again and type a message back to Grayson—because I may be made of people repellent, but I'm not stupid.

KAT

MEG DOESN'T TEXT ME ALL DAY, AND I DON'T BLAME HER. SHE SHOULDN'T have hung up on me, but I probably should have been honest with her about my attacks. But how do I tell Meg that sometimes my heart races and my palms sweat and my lungs completely forget why they exist, all because I can't handle parties? Because I can't remember what beans to buy?

One pinto . . . two black . . . three French style . . .

Although my breathing's calmed since last night, I still feel like my heart is racing—though it's not. I held my fingers to my throat and timed it to check. And I still feel like an elephant is sitting on my chest.

Meg probably wouldn't even answer if I called, but maybe Luke would for once. Luke never gets panic attacks, but he always understood mine.

I call him, listen to it ring and ring and ring until the ring's replaced by his stupid voice-mail message about being too busy partying or studying or whatever to answer. He never answers now that university has gobbled him up and swallowed him whole. Maybe he's joined some fraternity cult. Or he could be dead on his dorm room floor. We'd never know.

I don't leave a message.

I wander downstairs and throw YouTube onto the big-screen TV. I choose an old LumberLegs series, where he and his buddies decide not to close up any of the rifts that spawn, and their world becomes completely unstable—walls falling apart, equipment disappearing, underworld beasts rising up from the earth in the middle of their castles. Hilarious. I grab a blanket and wrap it snug around and around me in a cocoon before settling on the couch to watch my favorite episode, which is the one where Legs will lose his legendary sword to the rifts and have to fight off a mob of filthworms with a boot.

The tightness around my heart loosens just a little.

I'm only a few minutes into the episode when I see Granddad wander into the room out of the corner of my eye.

"Is it too loud? Sorry, I'll turn it down." I wriggle my shoulders to free my arms from my blanket cocoon. Mom's always telling me to turn things down. "Granddad is sleeping" or "Granddad is reading."

"No, it's fine," he says, just as I manage to free my arms and reach for my tablet. He lowers himself onto the other end of the couch, and even through Legs's squeals as the filthworms start rising from the earth, I can hear Granddad's bones creak from the effort. I hit pause, freezing the screen on a close-up of a filthworm—with its cartoony, eyeless face—crawling over Legs's feet.

Granddad peers at the screen, then looks at me. "You feeling any better today? Where's your friend Meg?"

I shrug. "Mostly."

I don't know how to answer the other question, but he doesn't press. Instead, he just nods. His bushy white eyebrows rise. "Does watching funny things help?"

Help what? Distract my mind? Encourage every tense muscle in my body to relax? Loosen the death grip around my heart?

"Yes," is all I say.

He nods again. "Used to help your grandma, too. She had panic attacks. Has your mother told you that?"

I shake my head. She's never mentioned it. Granddad offers the information like it might help me, but since I never knew her, it doesn't.

Except that it feels like maybe Granddad understands me after all. Maybe.

He waves his bony arm toward the screen. "Don't let me stop you. Carry on." He relaxes into the couch cushions, which I wish he wouldn't do because I worry he'll never be able to get back up again.

"You won't—" I say, then break off. I have no idea what Granddad does and doesn't like to watch, and it's not my place to decide that for him. He can just leave when he realizes he doesn't like it. If he can manage to get back up off the couch.

I press play and try not to look at Granddad as Legs lets out another high-pitched squeal. The filthworms surround him. As he swats at them, his sword disappears. Another squeal.

"Is he—is he fighting those things with a boot?" Granddad asks. And then he chuckles.

I grin.

We watch the rest of the video in silence, except for Granddad's laughter, which rings out at all the right spots. Just like Meg's.

MEG

I AM GOING TO GET ICE CREAM. TEN FLAVORS OF ICE CREAM AND CHOCOLATE and sauces and that marshmallow fluff stuff, and then I'm going to spend my Sunday afternoon eating it all instead of wailing about Kat's departure from my life. But as I search through our closet for some mittens, the doorbell rings. And there she is. Kat. On our front porch. She pushes past me into the front hall before I can decide whether to slam the door in her face.

She kicks off her heavy black boots, scattering snow across our welcome mat, then sets her bag down on the floor with a thud and slides off her ginormous coat and hands it to me, wordlessly. I take it, also wordlessly, and hang it in the closet, because I don't know what else to do. By the time I've closed the closet door, she's halfway down the stairs to the basement with her bag. I take the stairs two at a time after her to catch up. I don't want to freak her out again by jumping the whole thing.

Kat kneels on the floor and starts rummaging through her bag.

"I thought we were fighting," I finally say.

"We are." She starts pulling stuff out of her bag. Some cables. Batteries. Then a Wii remote. More batteries. Another remote.

"So what . . ." I trail off, not sure what I'm trying to ask. *What are you doing here? What's all this stuff? Isn't our friendship over?*

"I wasn't sure if you had a Wii." Her words aren't inflected as a question, but she looks up at me expectantly, waiting for an answer. She needs to pluck one of her eyebrows; it's a little fuller than the other.

"We do." I gesture toward the cupboard below the TV. "It should already be hooked up. Nolan was playing his car game yesterday."

"Oh, good, that's easy then. Here are the games I brought." She spreads six Wii games across the floor. "Pick one."

"What? Why?"

"I brought only games that I haven't played in years. So it's fair. And you can pick which one. Best of three to determine who wins."

"Wins what?"

"The argument."

She's talking nonsense, but she's here, in my house, apparently ready to play a video game. With me. I point to a game at random. "Okay, then that one."

"Freddy's Farm Frenzy," she says, picking it up and heading over to the Wii. "An excellent choice."

She pops it in, and next thing I know, we're perched on the edge of the couch, waving our arms around, trying to herd animals into a pen. Fighting to herd the most. Or not fighting. Or something.

I win the first game, but Kat wins the next. She's about to win her second, but right before the timer ticks to zero, she pauses the game and turns to me.

"Good call," I joke. "I was about to win."

She doesn't laugh, and when I turn to look at her, her face is somber. She takes a deep breath, then lets it back out before saying, "I have panic attacks."

"Panic attacks?" I parrot back.

"Yes. About stupid things. A year or so ago, I was at a grocery store, and I couldn't remember what type of canned beans Mom had asked me to pick up, so I had a complete meltdown. Started hyperventilating right there in the lentils aisle. The store manager had to use my own phone to call Mom to come get me.

"Mom found me a counselor after that. She was mostly crap, but she must have helped a little, because I haven't had one since we moved here. Or rather, *hadn't* had one. Until Friday night happened."

"Oh," I say. "So that's why you couldn't come?"

She nods. "I had one at a party before. I really can't do parties. I'm sorry."

I should be disappointed, maybe, that there won't be any parties in our future. But I'm just so relieved to have her back.

"I have ADHD," I spit out.

"Yeah, I figured."

"Shut up," I say, smacking her in the arm. There's no malice in her voice, though. Not like Lindsey used to have when she talked about my hyperactivity like it was a disease. I tug at one of my curls, even though Mom always tells me not to. "I thought our friendship was over."

"I don't want it to be over. Do you?"

I am suddenly giddy. "Definitely not." I lean into her shoulder. "We should fight more often."

She scowls at me in her normal, grumpy, wonderful way. "I'd really rather not."

8

KAT

THE SNOW NEVER LEAVES HERE. THE SKY'S BEEN CLEAR FOR A WEEK, BUT the ground is still covered in white. It doesn't melt away, then snow again, then melt again like it did back home. I study a shoveled mound of it through my frosted window as Meg assures me that we have nothing to worry about. I twist the end of my ponytail around my finger as I grip my phone between my shoulder and chin. "It's just—we're already almost halfway through November. We should start doing some testing soon, shouldn't we?" I bite my lip.

"Dude. Kat. You remember I called to talk about my date tonight, right?" Her voice fades in and out as she speaks; she's pacing back and forth around her room, with the phone set to speaker on the bed.

Grayson asked her on a date a couple of weeks ago, and it's pretty much all she's talked about since, as their plans have jumped about in typical Meg fashion from coffee to a movie to a Friday-night dinner date. To be fair, it *is* a big deal. A big deal that's happening *today*. I let go of my ponytail. "You're right. Sorry. Are you nervous?"

She laughs. "You have got to stop asking me that. It's a first date. I'm excited. Oh, that's the doorbell! That'll be Grayson. Better get to him before Mom and the halflings do. Bye. Love you." And then she's gone.

My stomach twists at the thought of her meeting him at the front door, awkwardly trying to figure out what to say. Except Meg never has a problem figuring out what to say. She'll be fine. I hope.

I stare out over my binders and textbooks spread across the table. In front of me is a pathetic first draft of the questionnaire for all our test subjects to fill out. And beside that is my list of potential candidates. Which currently looks like this:

1. MEG	16.
2. KAT	17.
3.	18.
4.	19.
5.	20.
6.	21.
7.	22.
8.	23.
9.	24.
10.	25.
11.	26.
12.	27.
13.	28.
14.	29.
15.	30.

At least there's a bonus to Meg going out with Grayson. I write his name in slot three. Of course, slots one and two assume we can even test ourselves, which we probably shouldn't because of bias and stuff. I shove the papers into a binder and slam it shut. The test results aren't due until February anyway. It's only November.

Still, we're going to need to come up with a plan. Soon.

We can't do that while Meg's on a date, though. So I neatly stack my binder and textbooks, and then go watch a Legs video instead.

MEG

I DON'T BEAT MOM, KENZIE, OR EVEN NOLAN TO THE DOOR. BY THE TIME I get there, Grayson stands in the front hallway, practically mobbed by the three of them. Well, Nolan hovers back near the kitchen, peering at him from afar, but Kenzie makes up for that by literally sitting on his snow-covered boot. He keeps glancing down at her, hair flopping forward adorably with each uncertain tilt of his head, as Mom asks him where we're going for the evening.

"Out. We're going out," I say as I grab my coat off the floor and slide on my boots. "We'll be back by ten."

I grab Grayson's arm, but he resists my pull and stares down at the Kenzie-monster still on his foot. Mom steps forward and scoops her up, and Kenzie decides it would be hilarious or fun or who knows what goes on in her brain to go limp like a rag doll, and I take advantage of their distracted moment of struggle to slip out the door, dragging Grayson behind me.

"You're going somewhere public, though, right?" Mom shouts after us once we're already halfway down the walk.

I spin around so I'm walking backward. "Yes, Mom, don't worry! We're going to go make out somewhere super public!" I shout back at her.

She shakes her head at me, and I whirl back around to look at Grayson, whose cheeks are flushed so adorably pink, I could kiss them. When I showed my cousin Charlotte a picture of him online, she gave me pretend crap for dating another white guy, but if I only dated black guys, my pool of options would just be a puddle. There are two other black guys in my whole grade, and just sharing a skin color doesn't make us magically fall in love.

"So, where *are* we going?" I ask, as I hear the door click shut behind us.

"It's a surprise."

My stomach grumbles with either excitement or hunger or both. "It's somewhere to eat, though, right? I haven't eaten supper."

He laughs. "Yes. Do you need me to tell you where? I can tell—"

"No! No. Surprises are good." I love surprises.

We've made it to the bus stop, and Grayson leans against the signpost, all cool and nonchalant. Tonight's going to be epically awesome; I can already tell.

"So that was your mom?" Grayson asks, tilting his head toward our street.

"Yeah, sorry, she's usually buried in a spreadsheet. Not sure what made her decide to surface tonight."

"What does she do?"

I glance up at the bus sign, wondering which of the three listed buses we're taking. "Marketing consultant. Runs her own business. She's been working like twelve-hour days."

"And your dad?"

I kick at the ground. "He . . . died when I was four."

Grayson straightens so he's no longer leaning against the sign-post. "Oh, I'm sorry. That sucks." Then he starts telling me about his grandpa who died a couple of years ago, and it must not occur to him that my siblings are too young to have been born before my bio dad died, because he doesn't ask about them, so I don't tell him about Stephen-the-Leaver at all.

Which is good, because Stephen-the-Leaver deserves to be left out of the story. He doesn't belong in my story. Not anymore.

A bus pulls up, and it must be the right one because Grayson marches toward it, and I follow, and the strangeness of not mentioning stupid Stephen-the-Leaver follows both of us right onto the bus and settles onto the seat beside me. I shove it away and try to focus in on Grayson's story, but the white couple seated across from us on the bus is fighting, and even though they're doing it quietly, with looks and gestures instead of shouts and names, it's super distracting.

No one else seems to notice. Grayson certainly doesn't. He's chattering away to me about—to be honest, I'm not entirely sure what. I thought he was talking about archery. That's definitely where this story started, I'm sure of it. But he just mentioned his grandma's house, and I can't think how that relates.

"That's so cool," I say.

"I know, right?" he says, then we're both quiet for a minute or two as the bus turns onto a main street.

The guy—across the aisle, not Grayson—shifts his body away from the girl. His black toque is pulled so low it covers his eyebrows, which almost makes him look angrier, as if his entire toque is one big, furrowed eyebrow. The girl thrusts the blanketed bundle in her arms at him, then drops a bottle unceremoniously into his lap.

"You feed him," she says loudly.

Mom and Stephen-the-Leaver used to fight like that. Back when he was a person I mentioned when people asked me about my parents and not just a stupid nobody. If this couple splits up, maybe the guy won't even seek custody of that baby. Then he won't have to worry about feeding it.

Except it's probably his real kid. So probably he will.

Worrying about this random couple when I'm on my very first date with Grayson is ridiculous.

I leap to my feet. "Let's get off here." I skip toward the door, where an elderly man has just disembarked. It's already dark outside, but the glimmering streetlights call to me the same way the warring couple pushes me away.

"But wait—we're not—" Grayson calls after me, but I'm already off the bus.

It's been almost a week without fresh snow, and the snowbanks lining the street outside the bus are already grimy with dirt. I stand on the snowy, gray, business-lined sidewalk, and for one long heartbeat, I'm afraid that Grayson won't follow me.

But then his adorable Boxer Boy self pops out the open bus door and onto the sidewalk beside me. His crinkled forehead is confused, not angry, which is a sudden relief even though it didn't occur to me until precisely this minute that he might get mad.

"So," he says, raising one eyebrow in a perfect arch, "you really needed a payday loan?"

I laugh as the bus pulls away with a groan and reveals all four corners of the intersection. Payday loans. Payday loans. Payday loans. Pawnshop.

"Come on, Boxer Boy," I say, setting off down the street, "let's have some fun."

"Meg," he calls after me, "your mittens!" He holds them out to me—my favorite fluffy white ones, with embroidered eyes and noses and a little flap of pink above the thumb for a tongue—and I suddenly realize how cold my hands are. I must have left them on the bus. I lose a lot of mittens.

"Oh my gosh, thank you! My hero," I say as I pluck them out of his hand and slide them on.

Kat would probably smack me if she were here. She hates the idea of guys as superheroes and girls as helpless princesses. But Grayson did once call me "Flash," so he obviously doesn't think I'm a helpless princess. I spin around, imagining a superhero cape whipping out behind me—does the Flash even wear a cape? Who knows—as I march down the street and Grayson scurries to catch up to me.

We stop at the next light. Grayson looks at me with a sort of bewildered happiness in his wide eyes and half grin, and I hook my arm through his. Which brings us awfully close.

"So, um, where *are* we going?" he asks. I might be imagining it, but I swear I can feel the warmth of his breath on my face with each word.

"You talk as if I have a plan. Where do you want to go?"

His stomach rumbles with an answer loud enough for both of us to hear, and though his face blooms with red again, we both laugh.

"Clearly we're both hungry," I say.

"Well, I did make dinner reservations. But I don't think we're going to make it." He gestures in the direction of the faraway restaurant district.

We stand awkwardly at the light for a moment, and then I grab his hand.

"I have an idea." I pull him toward the other crosswalk, perpendicular or parallel or whatever to the way we were going. The orange hand is in its final seconds of blinking down, and we have to dart across the road. We make it not quite before the light changes, but before any cars start honking.

I guide Grayson inside the 7-Eleven across the street and ask the guy behind the counter for two hot dogs. They spin round and round at the back of their glass cage, shiny with sweat. The guy grunts as he fishes them out and tucks them inside their buns, on little cardboard serving trays.

"I've got this," Grayson says, and he pays while I take the dogs over to the machine on the counter that boasts "Free Chili and Cheese" and load both of them up. The chili stutters out of the machine in gross regurgitated globs, but when I close my eyes, the smell is heavenly. I wonder if angels eat chili dogs. Might be dangerous in those white robes. Though in heaven, dry cleaning is probably free.

"You ready?" Grayson asks as he sidles up beside me, and I nod and hand him one of the heaping hot-dog mounds.

We eat outside, on a bench inside a bus shelter. The wall behind us is advertising some new tablet or phone, but the side walls are plain glass, giving us a clear view of the street. Snow has started trickling down—flickering down? Sprinkling down? Whatever it's doing, it's turning the trampled ground fresh and sparkling again.

"You know, I had this whole evening worked out," Grayson says as he swallows down the last bite of his dog. "And for the record, sitting at a bus stop eating chili dogs wasn't part of my grand romantic plan."

"Is that bad?" I don't really want to know the answer, but I can't help but ask.

Thankfully, he laughs. "Are chili cheese dogs bad?" he says as if it's an answer, not a question, then moves his hand from his lap to my knee and looks up at me as if to check that it's okay. The chili dog turns over in my stomach.

"Grayson, do you like me?" I ask, because he still hasn't actually answered my question.

His eyebrows rise and his forehead crinkles in that way that I love so much. His hand is still on my knee. Its warmth seeps through the fabric of my jeans. "I didn't think you worried about things like that."

"What, you think I go out with boys whether they like me or not?"

"No, that's not what I . . . I just mean that you seem so confident."

I don't feel confident, but I like that he sees me that way. So I lean in and kiss him. His mouth is a flicker of heat escaping through a wall of ice. His breath swirls with my breath as our lips move in unison.

When I pull away, the air that rushes in to take the place of his breath is frigid.

"For the record," he says as he touches my cheek with his slightly sticky hand, "I do like you. A lot."

So I lean in and kiss him again.

LEGENDS OF THE STONE

KittyKat: behind you

[]Sythlight: thx

MEGAdawn has logged on.

MEGAdawn: LOTSCON IS GOING TO BE IN TORONTO
   IN MARCH

[]Sythlight: Seriously? Sweet. I'll have to get tickets.

KittyKat: that's cool

[]Sythlight has entered the waterlands.

MEGAdawn: LUMBERLEGS IS GOING TO BE ON THE
   SAME GROUND IN THE SAME COUNTRY AS ME

KittyKat has entered the waterlands.

KittyKat: hey Meg, as long as you're on, we should talk about our project.

MEGAdawn: CAN'T TALK NOW TOO EXCITED

MEGAdawn: THIS IS SUCH A GREAT WEEKEND

KittyKat: we need to soon

MEGAdawn: gah look we can talk about it at school then you can come over on Friday and we'll work on it then

MEGAdawn: just

MEGAdawn: be sure to show up before 6

MEGAdawn: or after

MEGAdawn: just not at 6

MEGAdawn: stupid jerkface will be here

KittyKat: ok

MEGAdawn: ugh, now jerkface has made me grumpy

[]Sythlight: HEY MEG, DID YOU HEAR LOTSCON'S GOING TO BE IN TORONTO?

[]Sythlight has entered the greenlands.

MEGAdawn: OMG WHAT? THAT'S AMAZING!!!!!!!!!!!!!

KittyKat: you guys are ridiculous. I'm logging off now.

KittyKat: bye

[]Sythlight: bye :)

KittyKat has logged off.

MEGAdawn: you going to go?

[]Sythlight: For sure. You thinking of flying out here
for it?

MEGAdawn: I will hijack a plane if I have to.

[]Sythlight: She's just kidding, NSA.

MEGAdawn: um right. plane hijacking is a bad idea. but
we'll find a way.

MEGAdawn: there's no way we're missing out

[]Sythlight: Well, I hope you do come. Both of you.

MEGAdawn: oh don't you worry, we will. both of us.

—————————— KAT ——————————

AT LUNCH ON MONDAY, MEG MEETS ME AT MY LOCKER AS ALWAYS. "OKAY," I
say, "so I've been thinking about our project—"

"Hang on—*that's* what you want to talk about after the most
epic weekend ever? Why aren't we talking about LotSCON?
Aren't you going to ask me about my date?"

I blink at her. "You told me about your date all weekend."

She leans against the locker beside mine. "That wasn't in person, though."

"Fine. How was your date?"

She grins. "Glorious. Now come meet Grayson." She slams
my locker door, grabs the lock out of my hand, and snaps it shut.

Here's the thing: we can't avoid our science project forever. I can't avoid testing people forever.

But here's the other thing: I do want to meet Grayson. Even though it makes my stomach twist. "Okay, but then we should go work on our project."

She scowls. "No way. You know how I feel about homework at lunch. We're eating with Grayson and his posse."

My stomach twists even further. It must be facing back to front.

Meg's expression softens. "Look, we can eat in the stairwell instead of in the caf. Then you won't have to be so on edge."

I'm already on edge. We started a group project today in Ancient Civilizations, and Mr. Bates put me with these two guys, Eric and Sunil, who I've never spoken to in my life, and who only ever seem to talk about hockey. They want to write about the impact of the Neolithic Revolution, and I don't even know if they can spell "Neolithic." Or "Revolution," for that matter.

One paleontologist . . . two spelling . . . three strangers . . .

"It's just—our project—we really should—"

"Dude, what's going to happen if we wait until tomorrow? It's not like the entire universe is going to implode or get mad at us or something."

"It might."

"Yeah, well, some days the universe is just wrong. Besides, you're coming over on Friday. We'll get a ton done then. Now come *on*." She loops her arm through mine, then pivots us around toward the back stairwell.

I sigh, giving in. "Will Grayson know to meet us out here?"

She stops abruptly. "Good point. I'll text him." She grabs her phone from her pocket and taps a quick message with her arm still looped through mine. Then she slips the phone away and drags us off down the hall, where we drop our backpacks in the corner of the stairwell and sit cross-legged on the beige concrete floor.

Meg starts babbling immediately about LotSCON and all the events they've announced. I'm not sure why she's so excited, since it's across the country and there's no way we'll be going. At least, I definitely won't. I don't do planes. But I guess it is kind of cool to have something so big happening in Canada. We get passed over so often.

I've just pulled out my lunch when the guy Meg's pointed out to me in the cafeteria a few times peeks over the banister, then grins and waves at Meg. "It's this one," Grayson shouts over his broad, bony shoulder as he comes down the rest of the stairs. His boxers peek out of the top of his pants, just like Meg said— patterned with little skulls and crossbones.

Meg leaps to her feet and bounces over to him and kisses him. On the lips. Right there in the stairwell. This guy she barely even knew a week ago. They beam at each other.

A big, teddy-bear-like guy appears behind them at the bottom of the stairs, and it suddenly feels awkward to be sitting when they're all standing, so I clamber to my feet and stumble over.

One first kiss . . . two pirates . . .

"Grayson, this is Kat. Kat, Grayson." Meg wiggles her hips and shoulders in an excited little half dance.

Shaking hands would be weird, so I shove my hands in my pockets and nod at him.

"Hey." He smiles pleasantly at Meg, then at me, and then gestures at the guy behind them. "This is my buddy Roman. The other guys already went to the caf."

"Hi," teddy-bear-Roman says, then nods at us. Then we're all nodding at one another like some sort of bobblehead convention.

Five bobblehead . . . six eternity . . .

Grayson pulls a deck of cards out of his backpack. "You guys want to play euchre?"

"Yes," I say immediately. A little too eagerly, maybe, but playing cards means we don't have to talk. Playing cards means that if eating lunch with Grayson and his bobblehead friend turns into a regular occurrence—which I suspect it will—I might actually be able to survive it.

"Great." Grayson sits down in the corner of the stairwell and, as we join him, starts to shuffle and deal out the cards, all without saying another word.

I like him already.

MEG

SOMETIMES KAT AND I DO OUR HOMEWORK TOGETHER AFTER SCHOOL, BUT we spent all our after-school time this week finishing up the questionnaire for our science project and didn't get to any of the other stuff. Which, I know, I know, is my own fault, since I refused to work on it during our lunch periods—a rule that I stand especially firm on now that Grayson and his buddies have been eating lunch with us. Alas, it does mean that now I'm stuck doing my math homework all on my own.

I wouldn't even bother, except that my snitch of a math teacher, Mrs. Brown, called Mom and told her that I'm failing math and that it's because I'm not doing my homework, and Mom told me I'm grounded if I don't start doing it.

So I settle in at the kitchen table, all by my lonesome, and give my textbook a death glare. When it doesn't disappear in a puff of smoke, I groan and drag the bloody thing across the table toward me so it's right in front of my face. Then I flip to the page I have listed as homework in my planner. Graphs. Tiny little graphs. An entire page of them. I groan again.

"Calculate the slope," the page demands.

A blur of black—a bird—swoops by the kitchen window. Probably forgot to set his alarm to head south for the winter. Kenzie's pitchy squawking floats up the stairs. She's singing along with the obnoxious melody of her show. If you can call it singing along when she clearly doesn't know the words. Or the melody.

"I'm not stupid," I mumble to myself. "I can do this." Except what does "slope" even mean? I flip through my notes and find the definition a couple of pages back, wedged between a meaningless graph and a doodle of a cat. I can draw pretty adorable cats.

"Slope = rise over run," my notes report. Great. Now what the hell is "rise" and what the hell is "run"?

I scan my notes again. Nothing. I'd call Kat, but she texted me that she was going to play a game of chess with Granddad, and I don't want to interrupt his favorite game.

Kenzie is dancing now. I can tell from the way her voice has gone breathless. And how she keeps yelling, "Head bang!" in between lyrics about three little kittens.

I can't even find the page now where it said that thing about slope.

Screw this.

I shove back my chair, skip down the stairs, and join Kenzie in a dance-off of epic proportions.

LEGENDS OF THE STONE

KittyKat has logged on.

MEGAdawn has logged on.

MEGAdawn: we're doing a rift run. ne1 else in?

Moriah: sure

<>Pterion: sry about to log off

HereAfter: I'm in

[]Sythlight: Me too. Which one?

KittyKat: there's a new one near my castle. on shore.

HereAfter: The water castle, right? I saw that rift. It's
   big. Maybe we should VoiceChat.
MEGAdawn has entered the waterlands.
MEGAdawn: sure
[]Sythlight: Kitty doesn't have a mic.
KittyKat: no mic, remember
<>Pterion has logged off.
MEGAdawn: want me to bring you one?
[]Sythlight: We can make do with typing.
HereAfter: Moriah and I are already voicechatting, but
   typing is fine.
Private Message from KittyKat to MEGAdawn:
KittyKat: I actually do have a mic
MEGAdawn: oh
MEGAdawn: wait so are you mad at syth or
   something?
[]Sythlight has entered the waterlands.
[]Sythlight: Ready whenever.
Moriah: we're on our way
KittyKat: just need to organize my stuff
Private Message from KittyKat to MEGAdawn:
KittyKat: no not mad
MEGAdawn: ur scared?
KittyKat: not scared. I just don't talk to strangers.
MEGAdawn: right

*MEGAdawn: you don't have to marry him you
know. it's just VoiceChat*

KittyKat: I thought you said I should marry him

MEGAdawn: ha I knew you liked him

KittyKat: THAT'S NOT WHAT I WAS SAYING

[]Sythlight was slain by a wingling.

[]Sythlight: So there are winglings in the rift. Bring a
good helmet.

KittyKat: ha ha

MEGAdawn: rofl you went in without us?

HereAfter: lol

Private Message from MEGAdawn to KittyKat:

MEGAdawn: it's just syth

*KittyKat: and hereafter and moriah. it's not just
about syth*

KittyKat: maybe next time

MEGAdawn: fine

[]Sythlight: Just wanted a peek.

[]Sythlight: I'm almost back.

[]Sythlight has entered the waterlands.

KittyKat: I got your stuff

[]Sythlight: Thanks

Moriah has entered the waterlands.

HereAfter has entered the waterlands.

MEGAdawn: HI!

Moriah: hi

HereAfter: hey

MEGAdawn: all right let's do this

[]Sythlight: To the rift!

MEGAdawn: to the rift!!!

10

"BLUE STRIPED SHIRT OR THAT FUNKY BLACK ONE?" I ASK THE PHONE ON my bed.

"Black." Kat's voice is distorted, like either her mouth or my phone is full of bees. You'd think in this modern age they'd have figured out how to make speakerphone work better. I mean, shouldn't we have holograms or something by now? "Did you get my email? With the final draft of the questionnaire?" she asks.

"Probably." I used to be able to get Kat to stop talking about the project for days at a time. Now, with our next check-in coming up on Monday, I'm lucky if she lasts ten minutes. "What about the purple one? With Mickey Mouse?" I lay it out on the bed beside the black shirt. This afternoon is my fourth real date with Grayson. Fifth if you count the time I skipped math class and we went down to the corner store to get slushies. Which really should count. They were good slushies.

"Did you agonize about your clothes this much every morning this week?"

"No. Yes. Wait, what was the question?" I'm holding the blue striped shirt against my chest in front of the mirror and maybe not entirely listening.

Kat laughs through her mouthful of bees. "You've seen Grayson like every day this week. And last week. And . . . the week before, right? It's been three weeks? Isn't this date just like every other?"

"If you think a date's no big deal, why don't you go on one?" The blue striped shirt makes me look like a sailor. Can't decide if that's a good thing or bad.

"Shut up," Kat says. "Just the thought makes me want to puke. About our project, though, seriously. I know we can talk about it tonight after your date when I come over, but I need to know if there's anything I should be working on before then. The questionnaire's ready to go. And we have all the control factors determined, and the steps mapped out. Do you think that's enough to show Mr. Carter on Monday? I'm worried we should have started testing. Do you think we should've already started testing . . . people?"

She says "people" like it's a bad word—not the way Grayson or I would say a bad word, but the way she would say a bad word. In other words, like a gun's being held to her head.

"No idea. Okay, I'm thinking the black one." I drop the blue shirt back on the bed and grab the black.

"The black shirt? That's what I said."

"Oh, good. So consensus." I yank the shirt over my head. The V-neck isn't deep, but it does give me the tiniest bit of cleavage. Definitely the right shirt. I touch up my makeup while Kat lets out the odd squawk. She must be playing LotS.

The doorbell rings.

"That's him. Got to go. TTYL." I blow Kat a kiss, hang up, stuff my phone in my pocket, and dart out of the room and down the stairs. Instead of barreling around the corner into the entryway, I force myself to stop at the bottom stair to pat down my frizz, and it's a good thing that I do. The voice that drifts around the corner from the front porch is not Grayson's. It's Stephen-the-Leaver's.

". . . drop it off in case she refuses to come for Christmas again. Can you just stick it under the tree?"

Mom sighs, audibly. "Steve . . . we don't have the tree up yet. It's barely even December. And she doesn't want—"

"Let her make up her own mind about what she wants, for once. Stop brainwashing—" He cuts off, which means Mom's probably giving him her signature death stare. He blows out a puff of air, like a bull preparing to charge. "Look, just—just stick it under the tree. That's all I ask."

There's a long, stony silence. I press my back against the wall and hold my breath so they can't hear me. The front door creaks and a gust of winter wind finds its way around the corner and creeps up the bottom of my skinny jeans.

Finally, Mom speaks. "Fine, just—it had better not be another tablet or something like last year."

"I don't know why you keep bringing that—I was trying to get her something she'd like."

"You can't bribe her to like you. Just be responsible and pay child support for all three of them, instead of only the two."

"The judge said—look, can we not get into this again? You've got plenty of money. You don't need mine. I'm going to go." There's a crunching of boots on snow, then a pause. "Can you put aside your own anger for once and ask Meg to talk to me? She never returns my calls."

So stop calling, jerk.

"I'm not going to make her call you if she doesn't want to."

"Fine, but if we could just—" Stephen-the-Leaver says.

"Good-bye, Steve," Mom says. Then the door clicks shut.

Mom will walk right past me in just a moment. I hurdle the stairs and dart back into my room. I won't let him get to me. I won't let him get to me. I won't let him get to me. I whirl about and stride out of my room as if I'm leaving it for the first time. The show is unnecessary. Mom doesn't appear around the corner until I'm almost back down the stairs.

"Oh, Meg," she says, as if coming out of a daze. She slips a blue gift bag behind her back. "Would you duck downstairs and check on Kenz and Nolan? I haven't—"

"Sorry, I'm meeting Grayson at the bus stop." I push past her into the hallway and start pulling on my boots.

"I thought he was meeting you here."

"Change of plans. I gotta go or we'll miss the bus." I glance out the window as I toss my scarf around my neck. Stephen-the-Leaver's silver car is gone. "Bye!" I give Mom a half wave, then disappear out the door before she can protest. I can't wait around for Grayson. I have to move, to get out of here. As I rush down the street toward the bus stop, I text him the change of plans.

We end up meeting at the mall, where we tuck ourselves away in a back corner of the bustling food court with a heaping dish of poutine on the not-quite-clean table between us.

"Let's watch Legs," I say, as I pick up a fry dripping with gravy and cheese curds. Fabulously soggy.

"Watch what?" He snares a fry with his fork.

"LumberLegs. I told you about him. He plays LotS, remember?" If he doesn't like Legs, that's a deal breaker. Except it can't be a deal breaker because I don't want him to leave just like everyone else.

I pull out my sparkly green smartphone, plug in my headphones, hand him an earbud, and crank the volume up loud enough to hear over the din of hungry shoppers. His shoulder presses against mine, lightly, like two books side by side on a shelf. His leg, too. I grab a few more fries and stuff them in my mouth before pressing play. I've picked the video where Legs fights the horde of filthworms. Grayson had better like it.

I still feel unsettled from stupid Stephen-the-Leaver, so it's harder to laugh, but when Legs's sword disappears and he shrieks, a giggle bursts out of me, and I glance at Grayson—and discover he's looking at me instead of the screen. I scowl at him and jerk my chin toward the screen, and both our gazes drop to see Legs beating the filthworms back with a boot. I giggle again. And force myself not to look at Grayson's face. I'm sure he's grinning. No one could watch this and not at least grin.

When the tiny video finishes, I turn to him. "So? What'd you think?" It takes all my concentration to keep from bouncing up and down like a four-year-old.

He studies me for a moment before answering. His nose is less than a foot from my nose, his lips less than a foot from my lips.

"I liked watching you watch it," Grayson says at last.

"That's not a real answer," I say, though my cheeks flush hot.

"No, I mean it. I mean, he's funny, sure, but your laugh— I could be watching kittens being murdered and if I heard you giggle, I wouldn't be able to help it—I'd have to laugh too."

"Oh, shut up. Who talks like that?"

Grayson's cheekbones color with red. He has nice cheekbones. "Sorry," he says, "did that make me sound like a psychopath? I don't enjoy watching kittens get murdered, I promise."

"No, I thought it was really sweet." I find his hand and thread my fingers through his.

He leans in and kisses me, just once, gently. His mouth is warm and soft.

I draw back and study his face. His shaggy brown hair falls across his forehead and disappears into his eyebrows. His lips are chapped. I wouldn't have guessed that from the way they felt.

"You're never going to leave me, right?" I ask him.

He lets out a little half laugh, half cough, like he's not sure whether I'm joking. I'm not sure whether I'm joking.

"Well," he says, "we've been dating for, what, almost a month? I am one hundred percent certain that we can double that."

"Only double?" I put my hands on his knees, turn him toward me, then press my mouth against his, guide his lips with my own, breathe my air into his lungs, and his into mine.

"Okay," he says between breaths. "Triple it at least."

I slide my tongue into his mouth. It tastes like gravy. Like potatoes and cheese and gravy and warmth.

"Or forever," he says at last, when I pull away.

That was effective.

KAT

"HOLY—" MEG FINISHES THE SWEAR UNDER HER BREATH AS SHE TUMBLES INTO a large pit of lava, then lets out a whole stream of them as the screen pronounces her death. Again. She was all dreamy when I first arrived this evening, and I let her replay her entire afternoon's date for me even though I was—still am—desperate to talk about our project. But then as soon as I started talking about all the things we need to get done by Christmas, she muttered, "Bah, Christmas," then hopped to her feet and suggested a LotS break. Now she's been playing the same speed run over and over for the last twenty minutes, getting more and more frustrated with each death.

I sit on the bed, supposedly watching over her shoulder, but mostly just playing with a button on my sweater and thinking about our science project. And how we're going to fail. We're definitely going to fail.

One science failure . . . two high school failure . . . three life failure . . .

Meg moves her cursor toward the retry button, and before she can hit it, I snap, "Will you stop playing for a minute and talk about our project?"

She releases the mouse and swivels her chair to face me. I expect anger, but her face is flat and empty.

"You okay?" I ask.

She marches over to the bed and flops down beside me, staring up at the ceiling. "Fine. Just stupid Stephen-the-Leaver getting into my brain." With her arms limp at her sides, she's unusually still, and it weirds me out.

I'm not sure what to say. Not sure why she's suddenly thinking about him instead of about her date. "He must have been a crap dad," I try.

"No. That's the worst part. He was actually a good guy." She huffs as if affronted by his appalling level of goodness. "He'd take me on trips sometimes. This one time he took me down to Calgary for the weekend. Just the two of us. We spent the entire Saturday at the zoo. The polar bears had this plastic barrel that they liked to toss around and float on, like chubby sunbathers. They were hilarious. He let me drag him back to their enclosure like four or five times that day."

"I'm sorry." I'm still not sure what to say.

She sits up. "It's fine." She scrunches her nose, then grins, like making a silly face has fixed all the world's problems. "Not worth any brainpower. Now, what were you freaking out about?"

"I'm not—" I break off. I am. I am freaking out. It's already December and we haven't tested a single person. "We're supposed to show Mr. Carter our update tomorrow. And we've got nothing."

One failure . . . two . . . two . . .

"We're fine. We've got that questionnaire, and—" She stops, looks at me, then hops off the bed and points at the blankets. "Do your cocoon."

Two . . . two . . .

I obediently lie down on the edge of the bed, grab Meg's blanket, then roll, wrapping it tightly around me. When I reach the other side of the bed, Meg grabs the remainder of the blanket and pulls it over me, tucking it in.

"Feel better?" she asks.

I feel ridiculous, is what I feel. And safe.

Two caterpillar . . . three warmth . . . four security . . .

Meg sits on the now-blanketless bed beside me. "Look, we'll be fine. We just need to show Mr. Carter we have a plan, right? We've got to test how many people? Twenty?"

"Thirty." *Seven testing . . . eight planning . . .*

"Right," she continues. "Okay, so here's the plan: over the Christmas break, I'll do ten and you do ten. Look, I'll even do fifteen and you can do five, if you want, since people aren't your thing. And then we're already, what, three-quarters—"

"Two-thirds—"

"—right, that's what I said. Two-thirds of the way through. Then we've still got a month or two to finish the rest." She leans an elbow on my cocoon.

"And do all the data analysis," I add.

"That's easy."

"And make the presentation board."

"Dude, I'm sure you could do that in like, what? One night?"

She's right. The presentation board is the easy part. Last year I did the whole thing on a Saturday. "You really think you can do fifteen people over Christmas break?"

She giggles. "Well, I don't think Grayson would be very happy about that."

I roll my eyes.

She grins, then forces on a serious face. "Yes, I definitely can. I mean, Grayson's posse is like seven people right there. Easy-peasy."

"Okay," I say. My breath comes normally. "Okay."

MEG

KAT MUST STILL BE FREAKING OUT ON MONDAY MORNING, BECAUSE WHEN Mr. Carter comes around to do our project check-in, she lets me do all the talking. And I nail it. I talk about the timelines we've written up and the questionnaire we've made and the control factors we've identified, and I knock that thing so far out of the park it bounces off a UFO passing by Mars on an expedition to conquer the earth, scaring the aliens away.

"Sounds great," Mr. Carter says. "Just be careful not to fall behind on those deadlines."

Sounds great. Because it is. Everything is. Kat looks relieved, I've decided not to care about Stephen-the-Leaver anymore—not that I cared in the first place—and I've finally got this school thing figured out.

And I've got Grayson. After school I ride the bus with him all the way to his archery club, like the perfect girlfriend I am, then stand with him in the swirling snow as he kisses me gently, passionately good-bye, like the perfect boyfriend he is.

I run all the way home, imagining the snow's gone and I'm soaring on my skateboard instead.

It's Monday, which means Mom won't be home with the

halflings for an hour or two, and I've got the house to myself. I can amp up the music, or watch LumberLegs videos while dancing around like a maniac.

I do a little pirouette, hopping about as I whip into the kitchen. I'm so amped up, I don't even notice her until I pull the pitcher of no-name red punch—the drink of champions—out of the fridge and whirl around to grab a glass.

"Mom! What are you doing home?"

Mom sits at the kitchen table, arms crossed, eyebrows furrowed. "Your math teacher called today. Again."

"Holy gumdrops. She's basically stalking me at this point. I think we should probably call the cops."

Mom doesn't laugh. "She said you still haven't been doing your homework. And that you've got a big test coming up next week."

Ugh, I hate math. It's basically the worst. "I know, I know. I'm sorry. But I'm doing awesome in science, so it balances out."

Mom stands up, almost toppling her chair. "Meg, this is serious. You're in high school now. You've got to start figuring out how to—"

"I will. Scout's honor." I make a peace sign and hold it over my heart. That's a thing, right?

"Yes, you will," Mom says. "Because there will be no more going out, no more television, no more video games until you start consistently getting your homework done."

I drop my peace sign. "I'm grounded?"

She sighs and holds her hand against her forehead like she's checking for a fever. She's still wearing her work clothes. "Don't think of it as grounding," she says. "Think of it as eliminating distractions so you can get important things done."

Right, as if it was as easy as eliminating distractions. Stephen-the-Leaver should have given her a tutorial before he left. He was the one who got me diagnosed in the first place. Before that, Mom's go-to response was to lecture me on respecting my elders, then send me to my room. Stephen-the-Leaver, on the other hand, would just remind me not to talk over people, and he was always researching ways to help me focus and get homework done. The medication helps, but it's never enough.

"That's not how ADHD works, Mom," I want to say. But I don't know how it *does* work. Stephen-the-Leaver should have given *me* a tutorial before he left.

I can't exactly call and ask him now. So instead, I swear at Mom, then storm off to my room. The last time I did that, Stephen-the-Leaver stormed right after me and made me apologize—to Mom, to him, to myself. But Mom is too tired or too jaded or too sure I'm a lost cause, and she doesn't bother to follow me.

MEG IS GROUNDED. APPARENTLY SHE HASN'T TURNED IN A SINGLE HOMEWORK assignment for her math class in weeks.

"Why didn't you tell me?" I ask her on Tuesday at school. "I would've helped you."

"Math is stupid."

"It's not—" I start to say, then stop myself. I love math. I love that it's predictable. And orderly. Five plus five is always ten. Always.

It's not the same for Meg, though, I know that. I think she'd be happier if five plus five sometimes equaled twelve. Or purple.

Meg being grounded means she's not allowed to use her phone. Or her computer. Or leave her house at all except for school. Which means no texting, no talking on the phone, no LotS. For two weeks.

Which means my evenings are quiet. Ordered. Peaceful. Studious.

Lonely.

I'd forgotten what it feels like to be lonely.

LEGENDS OF THE STONE

KittyKat has logged on.

<>Pterion: You in for a rift raid, Kitty?

KittyKat: naw, think I'll work on my castle today

Private Message from Sythlight to KittyKat:

[]Sythlight: You okay?

KittyKat: what do you mean?

[]Sythlight: I've never seen you turn down a rift raid.

KittyKat: yeah, well, I'm just not in the mood today

[]Sythlight: Is Meg coming on?

KittyKat: no

LucienLuck has logged on.

KittyKat: LUKE!

LucienLuck: Hey, Katsup. Just finished an exam and
   need a break. Wanna play?
KittyKat: of course.
Private Message from KittyKat to LucienLuck:
KittyKat: just let me plug in my headphones and
   I'll call.
LucienLuck: k
Private Message from Sythlight to KittyKat:
[]Sythlight: So . . . guess I'll talk to you later
   then?
KittyKat: yep. see ya :)

KAT

LUKE HAS RESURFACED OUT OF THE CHURNING, ENGULFING WATERS OF HIS
university life at the perfect time. He's got just one exam left
and his girlfriend—who I'm not supposed to tell Mom and Dad
about, for some reason—has already gone home for the holidays,
so he has all sorts of time to play with me.

And I have all sorts of time to play with him. Halfway
through her grounding, Meg gets grounded for even longer—at
least until Christmas—for some "stupid reason" that she refuses
to tell me. So with Meg unable to hang out or chat or even
text, and with teachers giving in to the holidays-are-nigh cheer
and assigning much less homework than usual, my evenings

continue to stretch out empty before me.

The server's pretty quiet, too, aside from Luke and me. Pterion joins us for one raid, and HereAfter and Moriah for another, but Sythlight isn't around much, which is strange. He's usually on when Meg and I are, which I thought meant he was always on. But he's not, apparently. At least not this week. Maybe he's busy, or on vacation. Or dead. Now that Luke's proven himself to be alive, maybe Sythlight's taken his place among the unknown deceased.

He's not dead, though. On Saturday evening, a week before Christmas break, he logs on just as Luke and I are about to start a rift raid. Luke's invitation to him to join us appears in the chat log. And then, when he agrees, Luke's invitation to join us in VoiceChat follows. Luke knows I don't like talking to strangers, but apparently university has stuffed his brain so full of stupid facts he's forgotten the important things.

You have a mic now? Sythlight types.

My heart thuds heavily. But Meg's words swirl around my head to the same rhythm. *You don't have to marry him. It's just VoiceChat.*

Here's the thing: I don't like talking to strangers.

But here's the other thing: Syth isn't a stranger, not really.

It's just VoiceChat. And if I say no, Luke might out me as a liar, since he's clearly not thinking straight.

Yeah, I type into the chat. My stomach turns over. But I can't take it back.

I already have my headset on, since Luke and I were already planning to use VoiceChat, and I barely have a chance to breathe before the call rings in my ears.

One it's just VoiceChat . . . two it's just VoiceChat . . .

I click "Accept call."

"Hi," Sythlight says. His voice is cheery and smooth, like caramel drizzled over freshly popped popcorn.

"Hi," I croak. *Three it's just VoiceChat . . . four it's just Voice-Chat . . .*

"Where's Meg tonight?" Sythlight asks.

"Who's Meg? You have a friend?" Luke butts in before I can answer.

"Shut up," I say, thankful to slide into our usual banter. The routine of it creates a veil of calm that keeps the nerves at bay. "You only had friends back in Ottawa because they wanted to hang out with me."

The line is silent as Luke tries—and fails—to come up with a clever response. University has made him weak. Sythlight ends the quiet instead of Luke. "Do you—do you guys know each other in real life?"

Luke laughs. "Kat's my bratty little sister."

"Oh!" Sythlight says.

"I'm not little, jerk," I spit at Luke. "Or bratty."

"That's good to know," Syth says. "I thought—well, never mind." It's impossible to tell for sure, but it sounds like he's smiling. The caramel in his voice is warm and melty.

The veil of calm disintegrates, and my stomach floods with butterflies. Butterflies whose wings are laced with acid.

"Well, Supreme Emperor of the Universe," Syth says, "why don't you take point? I'll follow you."

Okay, maybe wings laced with acid is going a little far. They're just plain butterflies. A hundred butterflies.

"Supreme Emperor of the Universe?" Luke laughs. "What have I missed?"

"A lot," I say. "Now hurry up and get your butt over here. Syth and I are both ready to go." I draw up beside Sythlight at the rift. His dragonlord does a little dance. My elf warrior dances back. Just like normal, but with voices in our ears instead of words in the chat log. It's okay. Meg was right; it's just VoiceChat.

"Okay, okay, I'll be there in a sec," Luke says. "Should I bring anything special?"

Planning over VoiceChat is definitely easier than planning over regular chat. I advise Luke on what to bring, we talk strategy as he runs over, and we enter the shadowy rift in record time.

"How's the science project going?" Luke asks once we've established our positions and descended far enough into the rift that we have time to talk about more than just strategy. "Have you figured out who your guinea pigs are going to be?"

My hand spasms at the unpleasant reminder, and I miss my shot. The mutant shadowwolf gallops toward us. I steady my bow, aim, and release a second shot. The arrow pierces the wolf right between his beady eyes, and he falls down dead.

"You mean besides Mom and Dad? No." If only our test subjects actually were guinea pigs instead of people. That I could manage.

"What's the project?" Syth asks. As I explain, he executes his tank role flawlessly, rushing in and taking several sword slashes to the face—our human shield—then withdrawing to the shadows at the perfect moment. In other words, he can't possibly be listening to me. I keep my explanation short.

"Sounds like fun," Syth says as he dodges a venomous wereboar, ducking out of the way just in time for me to fire an arrow into its back hoof.

"Yeah, except we have to test actual humans. The horror," I say, aiming for sarcasm, but not quite reaching it. An idea comes to me as Luke slices the maimed beast open with his ax. "Hey, Luke, do you think you could recruit some of your friends to do speed runs?" I'll have to check with Mr. Carter to make sure it's okay, but I think it will be. I mean, we've created detailed instructions, which would allow for self-testing, and it would be good to get a variety of ages and locations anyway.

Another venomous wereboar creeps out from amid the rocks. Green poison-slime drips from its nostrils as it stalks toward Luke, backing him into a murky corner. Luke's battle-ax ability is still on cooldown.

"Um, yeah, probably?"

My fingers pulse with adrenaline at his response and I hit the beast with an arrow, right below the neck, where its armored skin is weakest. It crumples to the ground. If Luke tested four friends plus himself, I could be halfway done with my share before Christmas break even started. Meg said she could do fifteen, leaving me only five, but if I can find a way do my fair share, then I will.

I start to explain the steps—the multiple tests, the importance of randomization, the timing—to Luke as we loot the corpses and head farther into the darkness, but he cuts me off. "Just send me an email."

Well, of course. The tests have to be done right or there's no point, and there's something about the way he's holding his battle-ax in one hand and a glittering, freshly looted sword in the other that makes me think he's not taking notes.

"Shall we head into the depths?" Syth asks, obviously bored with my science project rambling. Obviously having no interest in me and my boring life.

I tighten my grip on my mouse. "Mm-hmm," I say, and Luke and I follow him into the dark forest.

MEG

WHEN MRS. BROWN SETS MY MATH TEST ON MY DESK UPSIDE DOWN ON THE Monday before the holidays, I know it's not going to be good. I flip it over immediately. Across the top is a big, red *47/100*.

I stick my hand up in the air.

"Yes, Meg," Mrs. Brown says. The jingle bells on her red sweater chime softly as she hands a test back to Chris beside me. She's worn a different Christmas top every day this month. She must have an entire closet devoted just to snowmen and reindeer.

"Have you ever thought of marking in a different color than red?" I ask. "Red is so demoralizing. The color of blood and all that. Maybe you could mark in purple or green. I have like a million green pens at home. I could bring one in for you if you like."

She clutches the rest of the tests to her chest and sighs. "Meg, just—be sure to study next time, would you?"

I flip my test back over to hide the angry red, and she continues up and down the aisles, bells jingling cheerily. I lean over and whisper to Chris, "She should study how to dress fashionably," and he laughs.

Actually, I love her sweater.

And actually, I did study. Or at least, I tried. I mean, I've been doing my homework. I have to or Mom will never let me leave the house again. The problem is that my math textbook might as well be written in Egyptian, so I had to start just writing down random numbers, because what else was I supposed to do? But of course, since Mom thinks I'm stupid, she started looking at my notebook and eventually figured it out, and I ended up grounded for even longer.

I shove the math test into my backpack. When I get home, it's going straight into the shredder.

• • •

"Okay, so I asked Mr. Carter," Kat says when I stop at her locker between classes. "He said it's okay to have Luke do some of the testing for location diversity purposes, as long as we're doing the majority ourselves."

"Have Luke what?" I don't know what she's talking about half the time.

"I told you. I asked Luke when I was VoiceChatting with him and Syth—"

"Wait. Wait! You were VoiceChatting with Syth? I thought you were just—"

"The bell's going to ring," she says, cutting me off. "I've got to get to class."

"But—"

"Talk to you at lunch," she says, then disappears into the mass of students flowing by. She is basically the worst. And the best. And the worst.

At lunch, I catch up to her in the hall and punch her in the arm. "Dude," I say, "I can't believe you made me wait an entire class to find out what happened with you and Syth. That's mental cruelty."

"What do you mean?" She frowns at me like she has no idea what I'm talking about. "What *did* happen with me and Syth-light?"

"That's what you're supposed to tell me!"

We're in the hall by then, at Kat's locker. She opens it and starts sorting through her books, casually, as if she didn't just tell me that she went on the forbidden VoiceChat with a guy she doesn't like to talk about, but who, even though she refuses to admit it, she is clearly head over heels in love with. She doesn't say anything.

"You are infuriating!" I say as dramatically as I can, then march off to our lunch spot, leaving her to sort her boring textbooks in peace.

KAT

I TAKE A MINUTE TO ORGANIZE MY STUFF BEFORE I FOLLOW AFTER MEG.

The thing is, I know exactly what she's talking about. But I refuse to make a big deal of it, for multiple reasons:

1. It actually isn't a big deal. Like she said, it's just VoiceChat. It was just a rift raid. We've done dozens upon dozens of rift raids.
2. Syth lives near Toronto, which means he's not here.
3. When things become a big deal, my chest constricts, and I can't remember how to breathe.
4. Syth didn't listen to my science project explanation.

WHEN KAT ARRIVES AT THE STAIRWELL, SHE IGNORES MY GLARE AND TUCKS herself in beside me, cross-legged on the floor.

"It was fine," she says quietly. "He's a good tank. It was nothing special."

My mind whirls with a thousand different questions—What does he sound like? Did he make any jokes? Did you turn on video? What were you wearing? Can you please recite every single thing he said from start to finish?—but something about the solemn, almost sad way she says it makes me bite my tongue. Seriously, I don't ask a single probing question. "I'm growing as a person, everybody!" I want to announce to the group. If only I could grow a little in body, too. Stupid short gene.

"But it was fine?" I say. "You went on VoiceChat and you were fine?"

Her mouth quirks into a half smile. "Yeah. Yeah, I guess so."

"Cool," I say.

Roman interrupts us. "You guys in this round?" He gathers the cards strewn about the circle, stacks them, and begins to shuffle.

Kat shakes her head and answers for both of us. "Meg and I have some science stuff to talk about."

"We do?"

She scrunches her nose at me like a bunny. "Ha-ha, hilarious." Then she rummages through her knapsack and slides out a red folder. "Here's the email I drafted for Luke," she says, handing it to me. "And the step-by-step instructions we wrote. You'll need them for the tests you do."

I flip the folder open, study the pages of tiny black text, flip it closed again. Kat's head is buried in her knapsack. She reemerges with a slim white box, which she holds out in my direction.

"Sugar cubes," she says, then narrows her eyes. "Don't eat them."

"What do you think I am? A horse?" I give a loud whinny, and Grayson laughs. He's playing cards, but he must be listening to us, too.

Kat's mouth stretches into a fake, impatient smile. She points to the red folder in my hand. "I'll email that to you, too. Do you think your mom would let you go on the computer just to print it out? If you lose it, I mean?"

"I won't lose it," I snap. I'm tired of people treating me like a child.

"Sorry," Kat says, bumping her shoulder into mine. "You're right. I'll stop being all overbearing. I just want to do well, you know?"

"Yeah," is all I say. Because contrary to popular belief, I want to do well too. I grab my own knapsack and start to slip the red folder into it, then stop. If I put the folder in here, next to my science book, then end up shuffling my books around and putting the science book back in my locker, I might pull the red folder out with it, not even noticing. It's the kind of thing I do—the kind of thing my ADHD does.

I whip open the red folder, pull out the perfectly smooth white piece of paper with our instructions, and start to fold it—one . . . two . . . four times. Then I slide it along my leg, down into my shiny black hooker boot. Grayson cocks his head at me, puzzled, as the guys start badgering him to take his turn. Kat just nods. She gets it. This is the only way I can think of to make sure I actually take it home. Well, short of eating it and pooping it back out again, which probably wouldn't be particularly effective.

I pick up the little white box beside me on the floor, tear it open, pull out a grainy white cube, and pop it into my mouth, pulverizing it with the first bite.

Kat rolls her eyes at me, then sticks out her hand, palm up. With exaggerated solemnity, I place a glittery cube in the center of it.

"Neigh," she says, deadpan. Then she pops it into her mouth and chomps down with a satisfying crunch.

12

---— KAT ---—

LUKE IS DUE TO ARRIVE IN EDMONTON AT 13:57 ON FLIGHT AC 2157 ON THE last day of school before the holidays. In geography, I watch the clock and say a silent prayer that the plane's landing gear doesn't stick and that the runway isn't icy and that visibility is clear enough. I hate planes. When we moved here, Dad flew out first for work and to help Granddad, and I drove in the moving truck with Mom. I wish Luke could have driven instead of flown. *One blazing inferno . . . two emergency exits . . .*

When the clock ticks to 1:58, then 1:59, then eventually around to 2:30 and my phone still hasn't buzzed with horrified messages saying, "Oh no, Luke's plane has crashed and he's dead," my heartbeat slows to a normal speed, and a grin creeps onto my face.

For the rest of the school day and my entire bus ride home, I sing in my head, to the tune of "O Christmas Tree": *O Luke is home. O Luke is home. It's Christmas break and Luke is home.*

When I get home, I barrel through the front door, get directed downstairs by Mom, and find him in the basement bedroom, where I bury him in a bear hug. Neither of us are big huggers, but I don't care.

"Hiya, champ," he says as I pull away.

"Hiya, sport," I say right back. "I bet I'm taller than you now."

"You are not. There's no way." He drops the shirt he was folding and turns around, back to me. I whirl around and we stand back-to-back, smacking each other on the head as we try to measure. We end up having to call Mom down to judge; it's that close. In the end, though, at least according to Mom's nonexpert judgment, he is still half an inch taller than me, which, though I wail at the injustice of it, is actually just fine. I would happily stop growing; if I get much taller, I'll start standing out.

For supper, Mom serves up a feast almost as elaborate as we can expect for Christmas dinner in a few days. Except with ham instead of turkey and with applesauce instead of cranberries. And no stuffing, of course, since it would be weird to stuff a ham.

Luke keeps tossing glances at Granddad as they both shovel down their mashed potatoes. Granddad looks stronger to me now—not strong, just stronger. More like a ravenous zombie than a fleshless skeleton. And he doesn't wobble so much when he walks. But Luke didn't see what he looked like three months ago, hasn't seen him for probably a year, since Granddad last visited us in Ontario. I've gotten so used to zombie Granddad, I can't remember what he looked like then, but judging by Luke's raised eyebrow, I bet it was not like this.

Aside from that, though, and aside from the fact that we're all in Alberta instead of Ontario, everything is the same as it was before Luke went away to school. Dad asks Luke what book he's reading—a murder mystery, of course. I beat both Dad and Luke to complimenting Mom about the food, stealing all the points for best manners. Luke glares at me. Dad is oblivious. Luke tells a bad joke. Mom tells a worse joke. Granddad tells a good joke, which is different from before because Granddad wasn't at our family dinners in Ontario, but I'm so used to Granddad being around now that it feels the same.

Luke asks Dad about his work and actually listens to Dad's answer. I was worried that university life and independence were making Luke selfish and unreliable, but he's back to the same old Luke.

"Hey, Luke," I say, changing the topic, "how many of your friends did you end up testing?"

Luke chews and chews, swallows, takes a huge gulp of water, then finally looks at me. "What?"

"My project. Did you do all five?"

"Your project?" He stabs another piece of ham with his fork.

"Yes, you dunce, my science project."

"Kat!" Mom says.

Luke's eyebrows rise in understanding, then fall in something else. Something not good. He swears.

"Luke!" Mom says. She hates swearing.

"What?" I say. "What happened?"

"I completely forgot," he says. "Sorry, champ."

"But you said—"

"Yeah, I know, but I had that exam and stuff. It was a busy week."

I stare at him, unblinking, waiting for the "Ha-ha, I fooled you. I actually tested fifty-seven people!" But it doesn't come. University's changed him after all.

"Sorry," he says again. Then he shoves the mouthful of ham into his mouth and starts chewing again, as if he hasn't just told me that the world is ending. I can't believe him. I wish Meg wasn't still grounded so I could call her and complain about what an idiot he's become.

One cumulous clouds . . . two lightning strike . . .

"What's this testing?" Granddad asks. "I'll be a lab rat if you need one."

Granddad, zombie lab rat, doing a speed run in LotS—I can't help but smile just a little at the thought. I scrape my heart off the ground and gather its remains into a bloody pile, press it back into my chest. Meg said she would do fifteen; that leaves only five for me. I can do five, I can.

"Thanks, Granddad," I say. Also, I kick Luke in the leg under the table. Just once. But hard.

MEG

ON CHRISTMAS MORNING, A SHARP PAIN IN MY SHINS STARTLES ME AWAKE. When my eyes flicker open, Nolan's face is inches from my own. His dark-brown eyes stare right into mine. "It's Christmas," he whispers, like a creepy but excited little doll. Then I register the singing.

I roll over and sit up. Kenzie is jumping up and down on the bed, sometimes landing on the mattress, sometimes on my shins. Her Little Mermaid nightgown flaps up and down as she sings, "Christmas Christmas Santa frog. Christmas Christmas Christmas dog." I grab her and pull her onto my lap, and Nolan and I both tickle her bare feet as she squeals.

Then we all tiptoe—not so quietly—past Mom's room and downstairs to survey the loot. Nolan's and Kenzie's eyes light up as they spot the tree and all the presents beneath it, but my gaze catches on something else—a glint of green. My phone is on the coffee table, sparklingly beautiful. Mom's finally returned it to me. I snatch it up. It's only six thirty a.m., but as Nolan and Kenzie crawl around, practically drooling as they examine the heap under the tree, I type out a Merry Christmas message to Kat and then to Grayson.

I drop down onto the floor beside Nolan, and he nuzzles against my arm like a cat. Kenzie violently shakes a Santa-covered box. I think I love the halflings most on Christmas. "Should we open our stockings?" I ask, and they both nod frantically like little woodpeckers.

Later, after Mom comes downstairs and we all have breakfast—leftover Christmas ham from last night and poppy-seed cake, as always—we sprawl out on the living room floor with our mugs of hot chocolate and tear into the colorful heap. I open a jar of skateboard wax and some funky neon wheels that look like candy Life Savers from "Santa."

Then Mom tosses me a blue bag with green tissue jutting out the top. It bounces into my lap with a crinkling of paper. For a moment, I catch the faintest whiff of sawdust before the scent is overwhelmed by ham and pineapple and candy canes.

"From Stephen," Mom mouths uncomfortably at me. My stomach churns, but I ignore it. I will take whatever Stephen has given me. I will take it, I will enjoy it, and I will not say thank you. I rip the tissue out, dive in with my hand, pull out a fluffy white lump. It stares up at me with adorable glass eyes.

Kenzie bounces over, pressing her face into its fake fur. "Aw, polar bear," she purrs.

Stephen-the-Leaver and I spent so much time watching the polar bears, that day at the zoo. The baby polar bear was the cutest. Over and over, she would gleefully clamber onto the barrel, then slip off with an epic splash. I could almost hear her laughing along with us, along with me and Stephen, except then he wasn't Stephen, he was "Dad."

"I don't want it," I say, shoving the thing off my lap.

"Mine," Kenzie says, claiming it with a smothering hug to her chest.

"Fine, whatever, just take it away." I climb up off the floor and onto the couch beside Mom. In a few days, the halflings will scamper out the door, off to celebrate a second Christmas with Dad—their dad, not mine. I rest my head on Mom's shoulder. "Can I go to Grayson's tomorrow? Helen said—"

"Helen?"

"Sorry, Grayson's mom. That's what I meant, sorry. Grayson said that *his mom* said that I could come over anytime over the holidays." I hurry onward before she lectures me about how she's fine with me dating a white boy as long as I don't pick up any disrespectful habits, like calling adults by their first name. "So can I?"

Mom kisses me on the forehead, right along the hairline. "All right," she says, giving my shoulder a squeeze. At least my grounding is over.

—————————— KAT ——————————

CHRISTMAS AFTERNOON IS THE EYE OF THE STORM, HALFTIME IN A basketball game.

Christmas morning is a flurry of wrapping paper, spinach

frittata and fruit salad, arguments over who gets to open their presents first—or in the case of me and Dad, who gets to open their presents last. This evening will be another flurry, this time of turkey and Christmas pudding and a family game of Clue.

The afternoon—the in-between—is peaceful nothingness. No traditions or festivities. Just a moment to breathe. Dad reads his new book. Mom scurries about in the kitchen. Luke taps away on his phone, probably chatting with his secret girlfriend. Granddad slides a rook forward three spaces. It bumps a pawn, and the gentle clatter as it topples over sounds like the rattling of bones in Granddad's fingers. His face and shoulders have fleshed out in the past few months, but his fingers are still just skin wrapped around bone.

He rights the pawn and nods at me, a silent "your turn."

My phone chirrups as my knight charges into the fray, and because it's Christmas, I allow myself to pick it up and read the text.

My grounding is over!!!!!!! Its a Xmas miracle! :D

"What are you grinning about? Some boy writing to you?"

"What? Granddad. No, of course not." Boys don't write to me. Which is good, because I think I'd die of a heart attack if one did.

"Well you're grinnin' like a raccoon on garbage day."

I laugh, a breathy laugh that is no sound, just air. "It's just Meg. She's not grounded anymore."

Granddad sets down his pawn with a thud. "Well, let's go then." His chair's shoved backward as he lurches to his feet.

"Go where?"

"To Meg's. You've had that package sitting there for weeks." He points with his thumb. "It's about time we delivered it."

Meg's Christmas present sits on the table by the door—a blue, misshapen, snowman-covered lump. I probably should have put it in a box before wrapping it, but that always feels like cheating. It arrived a few weeks ago, but with Meg grounded, I couldn't go to her house, and I didn't want to take it to school and have her open it with Grayson and Roman and any random passerby looking on, even though that's what she did with mine.

Granddad is at the door already. He walks now as if his hip is his own, instead of comprised of some foreign material cemented onto his bones like there was a crack in his foundation.

"We're going for a drive," he calls into the kitchen. "Back in time for turkey." He slips his coat on, fishes keys out of the pocket, and jangles them in my direction like a lunch bell. "Let's go, slowpoke." Then he picks up my gift and disappears out the door, leaving me to scurry after him.

MEG

STUPID POLAR BEAR. KENZIE KEEPS HUGGING IT AND PETTING IT AND pretending to feed it candy canes.

"I'm going downstairs," I declare, snatching up my new fluorescent wheels and the wrench that came with them. In the laundry room, my board is in its usual place, but wheel-less. The metal rods stick out like stubby arms and legs. I examine the new wheels in my hands. The wheel nuts are inside their imitation candy Life Saver doughnuts. Mom must have done her research and had the nuts from my old wheels transferred over at the shop.

The wheels go on easily with a few twists of the wrench, and within minutes the board is in the middle of the laundry room floor, balancing on its shiny new rollers. I hop aboard, shift my weight, pop an ollie. Or at least try to.

My knee bashes into the washing machine as my phone rings. I curse, loudly, rubbing the bruise-to-be.

"You are always in the way!" I kick the machine. "Ow!" Stupid, hulking thing. I pull my phone out of my pocket.

Stephen-the-Leaver is calling.

I could answer it. Could listen to him wish me a Merry Christmas. Thank him for the gift. And then what? Then he'd pick up Kenzie and Nolan for Christmas in a couple of days and they'd get to spend a second Christmas with their dad, and I'd have a stupid stuffed polar bear to stare at alone in my room, remembering when he was my dad, too.

"Stop calling me!" I shout at the ringing phone. "I don't want to talk to you." I jab the ignore button. Then, when that doesn't feel like enough, I stab about in the menus until I find the right option. And I block him. "Now you can never talk to me," I tell the phone. If he wanted to talk to me, his not-my-real-daughter, he should have told that to the judge.

I kick the washing machine again. Even though it's only a halfhearted kick, it still hurts.

I abandon my skateboard to the washing monster and trudge out into the rec room, where I sprawl on the floor, limbs stretched out into a star, eyes fixed on the ceiling.

Stupid Stephen-the-Leaver ruining Christmas.

I roll over onto my stomach and rest my chin on my hands. From here, I can see under the couches. The carpet needs vacuuming. A hundred-year-old Cheerio has made its home under the couch beside a Barbie hairbrush. At least that means we probably don't have mice.

I sweep the rest of the carpet—with my eyes, not a broom, though there's enough grunge under the couch that a broom might be surprisingly effective. The shabby brown rug stretches to the back of the room, under the shelving units piled with toilet paper and packages of noodle soup, where it curls up against the wall. Curls up, away from the floor.

I hop to my feet, grab at a fortunately-not-that-heavy shelving unit, and pull. The shelf lurches away from the wall, dragging the carpet with it.

The carpet isn't glued down! Or nailed, or whatever it is that construction men normally do with carpets.

When Mom clomps downstairs in her slippers a while later, I am shoving the last shelf back into place.

"Meg, the door is—What'd you do down here?" She surveys my handiwork. The couches still face the TV, but I shoved them back to clear more floor space. I've returned the shelves to their proper places against the walls, though the toilet paper and Mr. Noodles are still in mounds on the stairs, where I displaced them temporarily. And the totally unnecessary rug is rolled into a long brown log, pushed up against the side wall.

Sweat prickles along my hairline, and I swipe it away with my pajama sleeve. "I want to skateboard," I tell her. The gray cement floor boasts patches of discoloring and rug residue, but it's no rougher than the currently-snow-covered-and-unusable pavement outside. Better, probably.

Mom doesn't descend any farther into the basement, just hovers on the stairs, blinking. Her black hair's pulled back into a puffy bun, but the penguin-patterned robe hanging loose off her shoulders cancels out any severity in her expression. On Christmas Day, we wear pajamas. It's basically an unbreakable rule.

"Meg—" she starts to say.

"It's not like we even use this space much," I say, cutting her off. I am not having my past hour of hard work erased. No one ever seems to think my ideas are good, but this one *is*. "And I'll stop bashing dents in your washing machine. I've probably taken years off its life already."

"Meg—"

"And that carpet was disgusting anyway. There's probably fungus living in it. Or parasites. Or fungus-eating parasites."

"Meg! I just came down to tell you that Kat's at the door."

"And exercise is healthy, and—wait, what?"

"Your friend Kat. She's at the door."

"Oh. Our front door?"

"Yes, our front door. She's waiting for you." She turns and glides back upstairs, penguin robe flowing behind her. At the last step, she calls over her shoulder, "Just clean the toilet paper off the stairs, please."

I dart up the stairs three at a time. I haven't seen Kat since our last day of school, which was basically an eternity ago. I burst out the basement door, dart down the hallway, and suffocate her in a hug.

"Oof," she grunts. "You're squishing your present."

I pull away. "Merry Christmas!"

"You too. Nice pajamas."

She looks surprisingly put together for Christmas Day. Hair smoothed back into a flawless ponytail, dark jeans, cheeks flushed pink—though that could be from the cold and not from the tiny bit of blush she sometimes wears. She could be hiding a pajama top under her fluffy coat, but considering the look of the rest of her, probably not.

"You've seen these before," I say, holding out an arm to show off the lime-green frogs hopping around a light-blue background.

"Not at three in the afternoon, though."

"Dude, it's Christmas. It's basically a sin not to wear pajamas. You should go home immediately and change."

"Okay, I'll just take this and go then." She tucks her mangled package under her arm.

"Fine, maybe not im-me-di-ate-ly," I say, stretching out the final word.

She grins and thrusts the bundle into my arms. The snowman-patterned paper crackles in protest as the parcel squashes against my chest for the second time. Like a pillow. Or a stuffed animal. Or Stephen's polar bear.

"What is it?" I say, a little too loudly. A little too much like a frothing-at-the-mouth rabid person. Maybe I shouldn't be wearing pajamas. It's just one more thing that might convince someone to cart me away to a madhouse. Or the hospital or whatever.

She raises a single eyebrow. "I'm not sure that you understand how this whole gift-giving thing works. . . ."

"All right, you've twisted my arm. I'll open it." I pierce the paper with a jab, then grasp the torn edge and pull away one long strip after another. They fall to the floor like absurdly misshapen snowflakes.

"Oh my gosh. Oh. My. Gosh!" It's so much better than a stupid polar bear. It's better even than a not-stupid polar bear. It's basically the greatest thing ever.

I let the rest of the paper fall to the floor and hug my own personal LumberLegs to my chest. My very own red-cloaked, elven warrior with tree trunks for legs. The material is soft and oh-so-cuddly.

"Where'd you find him?" Legs has never been big into merchandising. It's not like you can just find Legs stuff in a store.

He's got a few shirts—all of which I own—in his online store, and that's it.

"Online. I found this girl who makes them."

"He's perfect. I love him. You'll be the maid of honor at our wedding, right?"

She laughs. "Careful, you'll make Grayson jealous." She leans down, gathers the discarded wrapping paper into a neat little ball, and hands it to me. "I'd better go, though. Granddad's in the car, waiting. I just stopped by to give you that." She moves toward the door.

"You saved Christmas," I tell her.

She pauses with her hand on the doorknob and looks me in the eye. "Did it need saving?"

"I'll tell you later. Go home and put on some pajamas. Like seriously. Now."

She laughs again, then disappears out into the cold. I toss the wrapping paper back on the floor and give Legs another hug.

13

LEGENDS OF THE STONE

[]Sythlight has entered the waterlands.

[]Sythlight: You guys up for a dungeon run?

KittyKat: actually, I'm really tired. think I might sleep.

MEGAdawn: It's only 10pm!

KittyKat: I know. I'm just so tired. and I need lots of sleep if I'm going to survive the new year's thing.

MEGAdawn: Fine. <3 <3 <3 good night party pooper!

[]Sythlight: Good night.

KittyKat has logged off.

MEGAdawn: you still want to play something?

[]Sythlight: Actually, I might head off too.

MEGAdawn: of course you will

[]Sythlight: What?

MEGAdawn: never mind

MEGAdawn: good night

[]Sythlight: Hey, thanks for always texting me when you guys are playing.

MEGAdawn: np

[]Sythlight: OK. Ciao.

MEGAdawn: bye

[]Sythlight has logged off.

KAT

Mom. Dad. Luke.   *Mom. Luke. Dad.*
Luke. Mom. Dad.   *Luke. Dad. Mom.*
Dad. Luke. Mom.   *Dad. Mom. Luke.*

There are six different ways to organize the set, but no matter which way I choose, there are still only three items in it. We're already halfway through Christmas vacation, and I've only done three tests. I have no idea how to go about the others.

Granddad is fine with a tablet, but not so great with a mouse, so despite his offering, he's out. Which means I've run out of family-member lab rats. Meg's extended-family Christmas party is in a few days, and she swears she can get fifteen tests done just from her cousins alone. I have cousins too, but they're older. And in different provinces. And countries. I always got along with Tarah, my youngest cousin—youngest, but still seven years older than me—but she's in Kenya for a year delivering babies or building schools or something. I don't think she can even get email, let alone do a speed run in LotS. Maybe I should try her anyway.

"Kat."

Then again, even if she did find some internet café, the connection might be too slow.

"Kat! Earth to Kat!"

I blink, bringing the world outside my head back into focus. A snowman mug, ringed with the powdery remnants of my hot chocolate. An LED screen boasting a flickering countdown.

New Year's Eve at Meg's house.

Everyone—Meg, Grayson, Grayson's buddies, even Luke, who had nothing better to do and decided to come along—is gathered by the front door, all peeling off their socks in some foot-fetish orgy. The living room couches around me, packed with people just moments ago, are deserted. The noise hasn't stopped, though. Everyone's still laughing and talking like they're on a radio show and can't have dead air.

Meg bounds barefoot across the room toward me and starts tugging at my socks like I'm some obstinate child refusing to change for bed. "Come on, come on," she says. "It's almost time."

"I can do it." I hook my thumb under the topmost stripe and slide my sock away to expose my wintry-pale, naked flesh. "We're all going to get pneumonia," I mumble, just loud enough so that she can hear me but the weirdos by the door can't. I fold my socks and set them in a tidy pile on the rug.

"Then we can be hospital buddies," she says. Before I can protest that we might pass the pneumonia on to Granddad, she grins, grabs my arm, and hauls me to my feet. "Come on."

We draw up to the front door just as Grayson starts the countdown, reading from the TV screen like it's a teleprompter. "Ten . . . nine . . ."

Everyone joins in. Luke's sonorous tenor harmonizes with Grayson's gruff bass. Luke has always had a knack for blending into groups of strangers.

"Six . . . five . . ."

Meg's hand hovers on the front door handle. It's not open yet, but already my toes curl, retreating from the winter wind. This—this ridiculous midnight celebration Meg has convinced us to do—is bananas. I've gotten swept up into some alien culture that shoves aside all reason in favor of a herd mentality of recklessness. Foolish idiocy.

"Two . . . one . . ."

With a shout of "Happy New Year!" Meg whips the door open and the alien cows lumber past me with surprising speed, bursting out onto the porch, then onto the snow-piled lawn. There's no time to flee. Meg latches herself onto my arm and kisses me on the cheek—actually kisses me on the cheek, the silly fool—and then we both tumble out the door and into the snow. Barefoot.

MEG

I WILL GO ON RECORD AND SAY IT: THIS IS THE BEST NEW YEAR'S SNOW RUN of my life. Big white flakes flutter down and settle on our heads like sprinkles on cupcakes. A passing car hoots and honks, chiming in with our cheers of "Happy New Year!" And the snow has a crispy pie-crust top that lets us walk on it and race a lap around the house in record time—all except Roman, who ends up waist deep in a drift. We have to backtrack and hoist him out by his armpits, which sets everyone laughing.

Kat grabs my arm and huddles up to me, hopping from one bare foot to the other. "Okay, we did it, jerkmuffin. Can we go inside now?" Her teeth chatter, but the corner of her mouth twitches upward.

"You liked it!"

"Shut up!" She scowls, but her eyes twinkle. "I'm going inside!"

"Okay, I'm com—" A force collides with my shoulder and pushes me backward onto a cushion of snow. Grayson's face is inches from my own.

"Kat, help, I'm under attack!" I call out to her retreating back.

She turns, shakes her head at me. The porch light illuminates the grin that she's finally given up hiding. "Sorry, but you're on your own."

I look up at Grayson. The snow obscures his dark hair, giving him a mane of white, and for a moment we're both seventy, having just raced a New Year's snow run together for—what, the fiftieth time?

I've never done a snow run with the same people more than once. Last year I probably could have rallied some duplicates; I was at a house party and some girls there had done it with me before. But I didn't even do one, because I was too busy dancing or something.

Next year, though, I'm doing this again with Grayson. And with Kat. Because I've finally figured it out, this relationships thing. And we are going to be a big, happy family forever.

"Forever!" I shout up at the snow or the stars or maybe both.

"What?" Grayson asks.

"Nothing."

Grayson shakes his head at me, then leans forward and presses his perfect mouth to mine. His familiar heat grazes my lips, skips to my heart, and floods right down to my toes. My feet suddenly burn as if they've been stamped with a cattle brand—but one of ice instead of fire.

"Get off. Hurry, hurry, hurry." I smack Grayson's arm until he hops up, snow showering off him like a life-threatening dandruff affliction. "So cold!" I yelp, leaping up after him. I grab his arm, spin him around, and hop up onto his back, liberating my feet from their prison of snow. "Mush, mush! Hurry! Inside!"

He laughs, his chest rumbling under my own with each "ha," and piggybacks me inside to warmth.

───────────── **KAT** ─────────────

I RAN THROUGH SNOW. SNOW. IN MY BARE FEET. AN ABSURD, STUPID THING to do, but I can't stop grinning.

I ran through snow in my bare feet, and I didn't die.

I can do this, too.

I can ask Roman to do our science fair test.

He stands beside me in the kitchen, swirling powdery grains of chocolate into warm milk. The otherwise-empty room echoes with the clinking of metal on ceramic as I stir my own mug of cocoa. Roman doesn't love LotS like I do, but I know he's played it before. And it wouldn't be poaching one of Meg's subjects; she's doing all of hers at her family party in a couple of days. Asking him should be easy.

I rest my spoon against the side of the mug and rehearse the question in my head. *Would you be willing to—*

"Mini marshmallows?" he asks, holding up a bag.

I blink at him. "Oh, um, no thanks," I say. Which is stupid, because of course I want mini marshmallows. Who doesn't want mini marshmallows in their hot chocolate?

"Okay," he says, then starts to hum along with the cheery song that trickles in from the living room radio as he pours a stream of marshmallows into his own mug.

I can just change my mind. Ask for the marshmallows. Though really, I should skip that and ask about our science project before I lose my nerve. But is it rude to interrupt someone when they're humming?

I grab my spoon and give my hot chocolate another vigorous stir.

We both look up as Roman's girlfriend, Leila, waltzes into the room. Their relationship is all new and shiny; they smile every time they see each other, like some Pavlovian dog's response. Leila's grin makes her high cheekbones and thick dark eyebrows even more striking; Roman's makes no difference—he's a teddy bear whether he's grinning or not.

"You making one for me?" she asks.

He lifts his mug as if toasting her. "This is for you."

"Aw, you're so sweet." She kisses him on the cheek, then takes his hand and leads him out of the kitchen.

I stand there, alone, for a moment or two. Stir my hot chocolate. Listen to the melody of clinks. The cacophony of voices floating in from the other room. Leila's giggle. The dissonant chorus of multiple stories being told at once. Meg's cheery "Shut your mouth!" Roman's hyena laugh. Everyone's boisterous laughs.

I peek my head around the corner. People are settling in the living room, a scattered mishmash of still-bare feet, snow-damp clothes, and adrenaline-laced voices. Leila sits on Roman's lap and squeals as he tickles her. Luke is squashed on the couch between Grayson and one of his friends, waving his hands about as he tells some apparently hilarious story. I search for Meg and spot her by the radio in the back corner, wiggling her hips as I swear three different songs come on at once. She's partly hidden by the tree, which blinks with red and yellow and blue. Every light in the room is on. It's after midnight, and still the whole place bursts with it—light and noise and chaos.

I've had enough. I want to be surrounded by darkness. Smothered by it. Not in a suicidal kind of way, just in a floating-on-a-noiseless-matterless-void kind of way.

One eternity . . . two nonexistence . . .

I pluck my hot chocolate from the counter, step out into the hall, and turn left instead of right.

MEG

I DANCE INTO THE KITCHEN JUST AS KAT DISAPPEARS OUT THE OTHER DOOR. I hurry to catch up to her. We could follow each other from one room to the other—kitchen, hallway, living room, kitchen, hallway, living room—never meeting, if we went at the same speed and in the same direction.

Kat doesn't turn right toward the living room, though.

Instead, she swerves off course, up the stairs. Her blond ponytail waves good-bye before she disappears into the darkness. I want to skip after her, draw her back to me like a kite on a string. But she has rambled on enough times about needing "alone time," and I suppose she deserves it. She did let me drag her to my party and out into the snow like yetis, with only minimal kicking and screaming.

So I let her go.

I miss her already.

A bag of mini marshmallows sits open on the counter, and I grab a handful. Mmm, sugar.

"Hey, Meg, do you have any lip balm?" Leila stands in the kitchen doorway. The snow has wilted the waves out of her dark-brown hair, though it's still smooth and shiny. I wonder if everyone has perfect hair in Turkey. (I think that's where she said she was born. I'll ask Kat later.) My own curls just get frizzy when they've been wet, so my head is probably a beehive of frizz.

"Um, yeah, I think so," I say. I've definitely got some upstairs in my room, but if I go up there, I'll be risking an "alone time" lecture, and I think I've got some in my backpack, anyway, which is probably still out in the hallway where I dropped it like a million years ago on the last day of school before the holiday. "Here, hold these," I say, grabbing Leila's hand and dropping my remaining marshmallows into it. Then I step past her into the hall where, sure enough, my backpack sits under the bench, half buried by my hooker boots.

I elevate—no, excavate—it, and unzip the small front pouch.

I find only pens and pencils and the mascara I thought I lost. No lip balm. I unzip the main pocket. A big, ugly, red *47* jumps out at me. My math test. I had almost forgotten about the stupid thing. If Mom sees it, I'll probably be grounded again. I grab it, crumple it with a satisfying crunch, and shove it down into the bottom of my bag with all the other unwanted debris—including my lip balm. I knew I had some in here. I grab the pink tube, shove the bag back under the bench, and march victoriously back into the kitchen.

"Here," I say to Leila, dropping the stick onto the counter beside her.

"Sweet, thanks," she says. "Want these back?" She holds out the palmful of mini marshmallows.

"Nah," I say, waving her off.

"Okay, I'll just—" She discards them in a little pile on the counter, picks up the lip balm. "Thanks," she says again, then flounces back into the living room.

I hop up onto the counter, sitting beside the little white mound. I pop one in my mouth. White marshmallows are blah. I should've told Mom to get those multicolored ones. Another failure. Bombing a math test or choosing the wrong mini marsh-mallows—I'm not sure which is worse.

Grayson sticks his head through the doorway. "Hey, you coming back in?"

I shrug. "In a minute." The snow in Grayson's hair has melted, leaving tiny droplets of water that sparkle under the kitchen light. If I was a tiny little person living in his hair, I could swim in those droplets.

A burst of laughter erupts in the living room. It does sound like fun in there.

"Okay," Grayson says, turning back toward the hallway. "Well, I should—"

I reach out and grab his arm. "You should stay in here with me for a minute." I'm not letting stupid math get me down. I turn him and pull him closer to me. He resists for only a second.

Sitting on this counter, I'm almost as tall as him. I lean forward and kiss him, pressing my lips into his, tracing the inside of his smile with my tongue.

"Phew," Grayson says, once we come up for breath. "You are—" He breaks off, wordless. And grinning.

At least this I'm good at.

I grin too, then kiss him again.

KAT

LAUGHTER FOLLOWS ME UPSTAIRS, ECHOING THROUGH THE HALLWAY. I SHUT Meg's door to muffle the sound. Not quite quiet, but close enough. The reflection of moonlight on the snow outside Meg's window transforms inky darkness into a gray light, illuminating

Meg's room just enough to navigate.

I sink down onto the bed, lean over the side, and trace the divot in the wood post where Meg tied the jump rope on that one fall day, an eternity ago, when we sat on the roof.

I sat on a roof. I can definitely ask Roman to do a speed run in LotS. Not today, maybe, but once we're back at school. I can do it. I *will* do it.

My stomach seethes with the urge to vomit. *One socialite . . . two . . .*

I hop to my feet and stride over to Meg's laptop, flipping it open. I need to distract myself. There's nothing I can do about Roman or our science project right now.

I check my email first, out of habit.

My in-box boasts a new message from a "Dan Martin." The subject heading is "Science Project," which could just be a bizarre coincidence, but it catches me so off guard that by the time my usual worries about viruses and malware even pop into my head, I've already clicked on it.

Kitty,

Happy New Year! It's already the new year as I write this, but you, being a couple of hours behind, are still in last year. Good news: the future is epic. We all have hover cars.

I wanted to send you this for Christmas, but your email said Redpath sugar cubes and they didn't have that brand at our supermarket and I didn't want to somehow screw up your entire experiment, so I had to order them online and wait for them to come in. I asked your brother for the info, and he forwarded me your email. I hope that's okay. I tried to follow your instructions to a T. If anything's not quite right, let me know and I'll fix it. Since you are . . . what was it? . . . the Lord High Empress of the Universe (please don't chop off my head if I got the title wrong), your wish is my command.

Hopefully we can do a rift run again soon.

All the best,

Sythlight (aka Dan)

I slide the mouse over to the attachment, then click.

A chart—the chart I made and emailed to Luke—filled out with results. Seven of them.

And scanned, completed questionnaires. Seven of them.

Seven.

With my three, we are a third of the way there.

"Happy New Year, Syth," I whisper into the empty room.

14

LEGENDS OF THE STONE

KittyKat: your family thing is at 3 tmrw, right?

MEGAdawn: something like that

KittyKat: do you have the questionnaires packed?

MEGAdawn: of course mom :P

KittyKat: and the sugar cubes?

MEGAdawn: shoot I ate them all

KittyKat: frick, really? hang on.

MEGAdawn has entered the greenlands.

MEGAdawn has entered the waterlands.

KittyKat: OK I've got two extra boxes. I can bring them
   by first thing tomorrow. when are you leaving?

MEGAdawn: dude chill out. I was joking. I only ate a
   couple.

KittyKat: how many are left?

MEGAdawn has entered the barrenlands.

KittyKat: ???

MEGAdawn: tons. I ate like 5.

KittyKat: do you have enough for all 15 tests?
   remember you need 3 for each person.

MEGAdawn: there's loads of them. relax. I got this.

KittyKat: OK. just remember I'm home tomorrow. call
   me if you need help.

MEGAdawn: stop worrying. youre gonna give yourself a
   brain anemia

KittyKat: aneurysm?

MEGAdawn: that 2

KAT

THE BREAD DOUGH DIDN'T RISE. IT STARES AT ME FROM THE BOTTOM OF
the silver bowl, a pathetic, globby mound. A molehill instead of a
mountain. Which means I forgot the yeast.

I pull the white garbage bin out from under the sink, invert the silver bowl, and smack the bottom until gravity draws the mass into the garbage bag with a thump. Right beside the who-knows-what-I-messed-up failure from yesterday.

Yesterday, when all I heard from Meg was: Awesome day. Ill come over tmrw at 2.

No answer to Tests going smoothly? Or to How many did you end up doing? Or to Don't forget to randomize. Though to be fair, that last wasn't a question, so I suppose it didn't technically need an answer.

I shove the trash bin away, slam the cupboard closed, and glance at the clock. 2:15. This is typical Meg lateness, but it still makes my fingers itch. If the bread had risen, I could have used the time to split it in two, transform the mountain into logs, and stretch them out across the bread pans to rise for the second time. But again—that only works with yeast.

The doorbell rings. Finally.

When I open the door, Meg is staring off toward the road, so all I can see is her lime-green backpack instead of her face. The test results are probably in there.

"Hi," I say.

She whirls around. "Oh, hi! Did you know that your neighbors don't have curtains? What if they wanted to walk around their house naked? Have you ever seen them just walking around with their junk hanging out?"

"No, of course not."

She shrugs, wanders inside. "Probably a good thing."

"How was your party yesterday?" I ask, politeness winning out over my desire to demand that she show me the test results immediately.

"It. Was. Amaze-balls. My cousin Charlotte is so hilarious. She can do this perfect imitation of Bugs Bunny. Seriously, I practically peed myself." Meg kicks her boot off and it topples over, snow forming piles of slush on the mat. "And my cousins that I never see came up from Lethbridge. I didn't know they'd be there. Someone threw on some soca music and their dance moves are beyond epic. Brian—he's the oldest—is seriously your double. Like not in looks—that'd be weird—but in interests and stuff. If you and Syth ever get divorced, you should definitely call Brian."

"Syth and I aren't—"

"Do you have apple juice?" She waltzes past me toward the kitchen, backpack still slung over her shoulder. "I've got a superloud craving for it, which probably means I'm PMSing or something."

I scurry after her and pull a glass from the cupboard while she pokes around in the fridge. She emerges with the jug of strawberry-kiwi juice Mom just bought yesterday, twists off the lid, and tips it forward over the glass in my hand.

"That's not apple," I warn her.

"It's a fruit. Same difference." She caps the jug, then twirls around to stick it back in the fridge, which she's holding open with her foot. "Do you think that's a thing?"

"What? Strawberry and apples being the same?" I want to

snatch the backpack right off her shoulder.

"No, having cravings while PMSing. Like with pregnancy."

The backpack has slid down to the crook of her elbow. It sways back and forth as she raises the glass and sips.

"I don't know," I say. "You're not, though . . . right?"

She laughs, spewing her mouthful of pink liquid across the floor. "Pregnant? Dude, you have to have sex first. Did they not have sex ed in Ontario?"

I grab a roll of paper towels from under the sink. "Well, you might have done it and just not told me." *It* is a thing teens our age are doing, right? I assume based on health class and movies that they are, but I've never thought to ask. I have a bajillion other things on my mind. Like science.

"As if I could keep something like that to myself. No way, José!"

I start scrubbing at the floor, harder than I need to. This is not the first time Meg's laugh has had a juice-spewing side effect, and even when she kneels down to help, my annoyance doesn't abate. It weighs down my shoulders like a backpack that's supposed to be full of test results but instead is full of rocks. Why are we kneeling on the floor talking about something stupid like sex when our entire science project hangs in the balance?

"How many did you do?" I spit out.

"What, guys? Only LumberLegs, and only in my dreams. You know that."

"No, not—I mean test results! How many tests did you do?"

She stares at me, face blank, eyes blinking stupidly. "Tests for what?"

It's a peculiar sensation, the blood draining out of my face, down my body and legs, and out through my toes to pool with the splatters of pink liquid on the floor.

MEG

KAT'S FACE IS WHITE, LIKE PURE WHITE, LIKE WEARING-A-BLEACHED-SHEET-as-a-ghost-costume white.

"I'm kidding," I tell her. "Holy cheese balls, you're so gullible." I expect relief, or at least color, to flood back into her face, but it remains motionless and colorless. Seriously, she's whiter than a mutant rabbit.

Her silence is unnerving. I reach for my backpack. Maybe I should have sorted the papers before coming. Too late now. "Look, stop worrying," I say. "I did a ton. Do you really think I could forget with you reminding me like every ten seconds? You're worse than my mom." I mean it as a joke, but she just scowls at me. At least the scowl brings a bit of color back. "Okay," I say. "Don't joke about our science project unless I want a stare of death. Got it."

She gives her head a shake, as if dispelling those creatures the weird, awesome girl in Harry Potter thinks make brains go fuzzy. "Sorry. Good. You have them with you?"

"You betcha." I unzip my backpack and plunge my hand into the jumbled mass of paper. Last night, when Mom decided out of the blue that it was time to go home, I had to dart about like I was playing tag, gathering up questionnaires from under coffee mugs and off the bed upstairs and stuffing them into my bag. But I ran through the house three times, and I'm confident I found them all. I deserve a pat on the back for that, or maybe even a shiny gold medal. "Okay, here's . . . my aunt Hilda's. No, never mind. She had to leave early and never did her speed runs, so we can just throw that one away."

I crumple the paper and toss it across the room. My house just has a kitchen, with a marker-scribbled plastic table. Kat's kitchen opens into a proper dining room, with a long, fancy, mahogany table that they use every day, not just for special occasions. The paper ball skips across the ground toward the table, coming to rest under one of its carved wooden chairs.

"I'll get that later," I say, then dig my hand into my bag to pull out another. I smooth out the paper on the kitchen floor, then slide it across the tile toward Kat. "There you go."

She snatches it up and stares at it in silence. I watch her face, waiting for more of its color to flood back, but it doesn't. She bites her lip. "This is empty."

"What? No, it's not." I stretch forward and grab it out of her hand, but she's holding it so tightly that a corner of the page tears off and remains behind, snared between her thumb and pointer finger. Her nail polish is pink, no surprise there. I scan the page. "This isn't empty."

"Well, it isn't full either."

I look back down. The first two questions are dutifully filled out in red pen. After that, nothing.

"Okay, you're right, bad example. But I have like a gajillion papers. I haven't had time to sort them yet."

Kat doesn't say anything, just sits there on the floor in her favorite pink polo shirt, one foot tucked under her, paper towel still balled up in her hand, staring blankly at me like a mannequin. A spooky about-to-come-to-life mannequin from a horror movie.

"You're kind of creepy sometimes," I mumble, as I grab my backpack again.

"What?" she asks, but I ignore it. One thing I have learned about Kat is that when she's cranky like this, my jokes to lighten the mood are rarely—if ever—successful.

A pencil-scrawled name jumps out at me. "Aha," I say. "My cousin Leah's." This one I know we got right. Leah had never played LotS before, and every death resulted in gut-splitting, infectious giggles. I shove the paper into Kat's hands.

She looks it over. "Where are the test results?"

"Bottom corner."

"There's only two."

"No, there's three."

"Definitely only two." She scrunches her face like she's trying not to cry. Like it's a letter advising that her aunt died instead of just a boring science questionnaire. I snatch the paper from her and glance at the corner where, sure enough, only two times have been recorded in my signature green pen.

"Lizard balls!" Yesterday was a frenzied blur of LotS runs between charades rounds, questionnaires lost in wrapping paper, and trying to time sugar cubes around chocolate cake. There were definitely a few, like Aunt Hilda's, that never got finished, but this isn't one of them. "We did all three tests for sure," I say. "I'll text Leah. She'll remember what her third time was."

"Just—can I look through them, please?" Kat gestures toward my backpack, and I toss it over. She pulls out paper after paper, smoothing each one on her leg, studying it, then placing it onto a pile on either her left or her right, using a sorting system that I can't make sense of until she puts two blank ones in a row on the pile to her right.

"I took more than fifteen questionnaires with me," I explain. "In case we needed them." She doesn't reply, just smacks another questionnaire down on the pile to her right. I lean over to look at it. I can't see anything wrong with it, aside from the streak of chocolate down the middle. "I told everyone not to eat cake until after doing their speed runs," I tell her. "If they didn't listen, that's not our fault."

She's apparently so lost in the riveting task of sorting that she doesn't hear me, but before I can grab the chocolate-smeared one and move it to the other pile, she holds up another questionnaire. "What's this number?" she asks, jabbing at the corner.

I lean in to study my green scrawl. "Five, I think. Or maybe eight."

Her eyes bulge as if they might pop out of her head. "We need an exact number."

"Okay, it's a five." I look at it again without really seeing. "Yep, definitely a five."

She hesitates, then slowly lowers it onto the left pile, grimacing like it physically hurts her to admit that it's okay. Which means tossing the next two on top of the chocolate-smeared one on the right should give her relief, but she keeps scowling as if smiling might kill her.

When she gets to the end, she sticks her arm all the way into the bottom of my backpack, as if she expects it to extend past the floor, like a Mary Poppins bag. "Is this it?"

I stop myself from rolling my eyes. "Guess so."

She picks up the left pile—the much smaller pile—of smoothed-out papers off the floor, licks her finger, and counts them. "There's only five," she moans.

I point toward the other pile. "Plenty of those are perfectly fine. You're just being too picky."

"Meg, this is a science project, not a finger painting. The results need to be accurate." She sets the papers back down on the floor. "We're doomed," she breathes, leaning backward against the cupboard with a thud. She closes her eyes and presses her lips into a thin line.

"Dude, stop being so overdramatic or melodramatic or whatever. We're not doomed. We've still got—what?—two months?"

Her eyes fly open. "Two *weeks*! The next check-in's in two and a half weeks, and we're supposed to have finished twenty tests by then!"

Well, that's news to me, but I still think she's overreacting. "Stop worrying. I bet I could finish another fifteen tests in like a week."

"You were supposed to do that already! And you completely screwed it up. You are the people person and you were supposed to get lots of tests done, and you *didn't*. I did twice as many as you!" She glances at the big pile on her right as if it's stacked with her oh-so-perfect ones instead of with my apparently-not-good-enough hard work.

"You didn't actually do more, though! You did a whopping three. Your whipped boy toy did the rest. I did five—more than that if you weren't so picky—and Grayson had nothing to do with it." I give the failure pile a shove, and the top questionnaires fly off, revealing that stupid chocolate-smeared one that she refused to move. "Maybe I didn't finish that many to your perfect standards, but at least I wasn't too scared to try in the first place!"

I stand, grab my now-empty backpack, and storm out of the room. I wore my chunky slip-on boots today instead of my zip-up hooker boots, and they slide on like my feet are sticks of butter.

Kat appears in the hallway as I yank open the front door. "Where are you going?"

"Somewhere people don't think I'm a failure," I snap, then stalk out the door and slam it behind me with a not-quite-satisfying bang.

15

SOMEWHERE PEOPLE DON'T THINK I'M A FAILURE. THAT'S THE PROBLEM.

I failed my math test. I failed to keep Stephen-the-Leaver from leaving.

And now I've failed to live up to Kat's ridiculous standards. Even in *her* eyes, I'm a failure. A screwup.

The bus is taking forever to arrive, so I run the however many blocks to catch the 7 instead. It stops five blocks past Grayson's, so by the time I run up to Grayson's front step, I'm gasping like a slimy trout at a fisherman's rubber-booted feet.

"Grayson!" I half shout, half wheeze as I pound on his door. "Grayson, open up!"

The door swings open as if he was waiting for me, though he couldn't have been, since I was too busy jogging myself to death to text him. Maybe we're developing a psychic connection. Maybe every time I kiss him, it makes it stronger.

"We have a doorbell, you know," he says, hooking his thumbs into his pockets instead of throwing his arms around me.

"That's some greeting," I say, pushing past him. "Aren't you happy to see me?" I push my bottom lip out in my saltiest pout—no, that can't be right. Sultanest? Is that a word?

His face softens. "Of course. Sorry. I just—I'm about to head to the range." He steps back to close the front door, wobbling like a peg-leg pirate. He only has one boot on. As usual, he's laced it halfway up, tying it in a loose, single knot at ankle height.

"Guess I got here just in time, then." I lean down and yank at the pathetic knot, unraveling it.

"Meg!" He pulls his foot away and frowns at me again. "I have a competition in two weeks, remember? I have to practice." He leans over and snatches up his other boot, wiggling the tongue back and forth to loosen it. He doesn't even look at me.

I'm losing him. Maybe I've already lost him. Maybe "archery" is slang for "some blond-haired, white-skinned preppy chick who's smarter than you." On the way over here, I'd thought of asking him to do the LotS speed runs like Kat and I had planned before I got the idea to do all of mine at my family thing, but when he's grumpy like this, I'm not about to ask. He doesn't love LotS like I do.

I step closer to him. I'm not failing at this too. Am not. Will not.

I place my hand lightly on his boot-holding one and pull out my sultriest voice. (That's the word—sultry.) "But your parents aren't home."

He sucks in a breath. I draw even closer, slip my hand into his back pocket. Am not, will not, cannot fail.

I stand on my tiptoes and kiss him on the bridge of his nose. Then on the mouth. He lets the boot drop.

Success.

Upstairs in his bedroom, he shoves a book and some clothes off his bed and we stretch out along it, hands and lips falling swiftly into ravenous patterns. I think about his fingers gliding up my back and the bed's occasional creak and his kisses electric along my neck and hardly at all about my chocolate-stained surveys strewn across Kat's kitchen floor.

I grab the hem of my shirt and yank upward, over my head. Grayson has to dart backward to avoid an elbow to the face, but when I emerge from the fabric, his eyes are not angry, but devouring.

"You are so sexy," he whispers.

I'm not going to tell Kat about this, about taking my shirt off for Grayson for the first time. She doesn't deserve to know.

Grayson's fingers reach out toward my chest, and I look down in a burst of panic. What bra am I wearing? Purple and green stripes with white lace. Thank goodness. If I was wearing some grungy sports bra, this could've been embarrassing. And very not sexy. When I get home, I'm throwing out every nonsexy bra I own.

Grayson presses his body against mine, and his fingers feather up and down my shirtless back. It doesn't feel much different from having his fingers sneak up under my shirt, but I lose myself in his touch anyway. Because I am *not* a failure.

KAT

I'M NOT SCARED.

Yes, I worry. And yes, I get nervous. And yes, I have panic attacks.

But I'm not *scared*.

And Syth is definitely not my "whipped boy toy."

Still, I don't play LotS for the rest of the weekend. I don't even play LotS when I sit at the library computers on Monday during lunch period. I just pull out my notebook and pen like I have research to do, then stare at the screen and type random things into Google without clicking on any of the links. *Lightning storm. Pickle sandwich. Anxiety disorder.*

Here's the thing: true does not equal right. I could walk up to Granddad and say, "Just so you know, you are old and frail and probably going to die soon." And even if it was true, it'd still be wrong. It'd still make me a jerk.

Which is why I'm not eating lunch with Meg or any of her jerk-by-extension friends.

The freckle-faced librarian coughs, a fake, pointed "ahem," and when I look up, she's glaring at me, though I don't know why. I'm not playing LotS, and I scarfed my food down in the hallway before coming in. I even put my juice bottle in the recycling bin.

Then the *clickclickclickclickclick* noise reaches my ear. I set my pen down, and the librarian releases me from her stare of death and returns to her book.

My search results blink out at me from the screen. Wikipedia. WebMD. Answers.com. This is stupid. I close the search and pull up LotS. Sythlight is at school right now and won't be online anyway. And even if he was, I have no reason to avoid him.

I log on to our server, and of course, it's empty. I'm the only one on.

As if he's a monster who feeds on the worries in my brain, the first thing Mr. Carter does in Monday afternoon's science class is remind us that our next check-in is in two weeks, and that we need to have met our first testing goal by then.

Our goal was twenty tests. Out of thirty. We only have fifteen. Out of thirty. I don't think I know five more people, and I definitely don't know fifteen more.

My throat tightens.

One Sesame Street . . . two anaphylactic shock . . .

Thirteen days is not enough time to start a new project. We have no choice but to push forward. Maybe Meg's come up with a brilliant plan that she hasn't told me yet. I glance at her. She's facing forward instead of in her typical sprawling posture of legs in the aisle, one arm on my desk. Her usually relaxed shoulders are rigidly straight. She didn't look at me when she sat down, hasn't looked at me this entire class.

Meg's hand shoots into the air. "*Someone*," she says, so pointedly that it's obvious she means a very specific *someone*, "is clicking their pen a lot. . . ."

I don't listen to the rest, just drop my pen on my desk with a thunk as the entire class turns to stare—thirty sets of eyes burning into me. *Seven center of attention . . . eight this is all her fault . . .*

So Meg isn't going to be any help, isn't going to talk to me at all, apparently. However I do this, I'm going to have to do it alone.

16

MEG

I WALTZ UP TO GRAYSON'S LOCKER AT THE END OF THE DAY AND TUG AT the red-and-gold-striped scarf his older sister gave him for Christmas.

"Ready for awesomeness?" I ask as I drape the end of it around his neck.

"Awesomeness?" he echoes, like a parrot.

"Yeah, let's go somewhere. All-day breakfast at Smitty's or something. Or we could rent skates and go on the ice rink at West Ed Mall. I've always wanted to do that."

"I can't," he says, shrugging his backpack on. "I need to practice."

"All you do is practice lately. Come on, it's ice-skating! I can be Tessa Virtue and you can be . . . did she have a partner or was she just singles?"

"Meg!" he says, then pauses as if I should know what's coming next. When I don't say anything, he sighs. "I have that competition, remember? I need as much range time as I can get."

Right, competition. Is it this week? Next week? Regionals? Finals? I can't quite remember, but I know it's a big deal.

Grayson has already started striding down the hall, and I rush to catch up to him, the anvil on my back slowing me down just a little. I don't know why I'm taking so many books home. I don't think I have any homework to do. Well, maybe math. It's probably in my planner.

"Okay, I'll come with you," I say as I draw up next to him and slip my bare hand into his mittened one. "I'll be your own personal cheerleader. Prepare you for having an audience. There'll be lots of people at the competition, right?"

He turns to look at me, brown eyes sparkling with hope for just a moment before his caterpillar eyebrows drop and crush the twinkle. "Nah, you'll just get bored."

"I won't," I protest, feeling suddenly like a three-year-old. "I'll be your own Jenna Matheson. You know, that girl who wears her cheerleading uniform around school like she's in *Glee*?"

He laughs, deep and perfect. "Well, all right then. Let's go."

. . .

I've always pictured Grayson's archery club as full of boisterous Robin Hoods, but the place is empty and painfully quiet.
Aside from the targets on the far wall, it just looks like a boring
old community hall, with beige walls and beige floor and beige
ceiling. While Grayson fetches his bow from the probably-beige
locker room, I study the posters on the bulletin board. There are
ads tacked onto ads tacked onto ads, like those layers of rock my
teacher was rambling on about in geography. They should come
here to date dinosaur remains. Peel back the layers until an adver-
tisement announces, "Dinosaur in need of new home. Rarely
bites." Then rip off one of those slips, call the number, and ask
how long ago it was posted.

I tear off one of the slips at random—it's satisfying, like popping Bubble Wrap—just as Grayson walks up, bow dangling
casually from his left hand as if to say, "Yeah, I'm über strong.
Deal with it." He leans over to look at the board. "You're looking
for a . . . 'tidy, middle-aged male roommate'?"

"You never know." I shrug and tuck the number into my
pocket.

There are no chairs in the range area—I know people shoot
standing up, but what if someone wants to watch?—so I grab one
from the table at the entrance and drag it across the hall. I lean,
standing, against the back of it while Grayson prepares his first
shot. His arm muscles bulge as he pulls his hand back to his ear,
pauses, then releases.

Kat can hit a speeding wingling between the eyes from miles away, but I'm sure real-life archery is way harder, so I throw up my hands and cheer. My foot hits the chair and sends it skittering forward.

Grayson whips around and glares at me.

"What?" I drop my hands to my sides. "I thought I was here to be your cheerleader."

"Yeah . . . just . . . maybe save the cheers for the bull's-eyes."

"As you wish," I say, waving my hand with a flourish and bending at the waist in a dramatic bow. I pull back my runaway chair with a scrape as Grayson turns to stare down his stationary enemy.

It would be wicked if the targets moved, darting about like winglings in LotS. Maybe four at once. They could flash with alternating lights, and if you hit the lit-up one, you'd get bonus points.

"Did you see that?" Grayson is beaming at me. I glance at the bull's-eye. Two long stalks poke out from the outer rings, one from the padding behind the target, and, at last, one smack-dab in the red center.

"Wooooo!" I throw my hands up. "Good job, bae!"

Grayson's smile melts off his face. "I knew you'd get bored," he mumbles.

"I'm not! You look badass," I tell him, but he's already turned his back on me again.

I wonder if something like that rotating light show of an

archery contest actually exists. That would be epic. I pull out my phone to look it up. As always, the browser opens on Lumber-Legs's YouTube channel. There's a new video I haven't seen yet, so I mark it to watch later.

I glance up just in time to see an arrow slam into the middle red, just at its edge.

"Wooooo!" I cheer again, and this time, Grayson grins at me, running his hand through his wavy hair before reaching for another arrow.

LumberLegs has an email address on his info tab. I'm sure that wasn't there before. I click on it, wait for my email to open, swipe my finger across the tiny keyboard.

Dear LumberLegs,

I am your biggest fan. You probably think it's that girl who calls herself Mrs. LumberLegs, but it's not, it's me.

Just thought you might enjoy a hello from your biggest fan.

HELLO!

Ta-ta for now

With love from your biggest fan,

Meg

P.S. By biggest I mean #1, not fattest. I'm not fat. But also not anorexic or a stick or anything. Just regular size, with curves and stuff. Like someone who exercises lots but still eats cookies. Because cookies are an important food group. obvs.

I tap send, then open my messages to text Kat.
Guess what! Legs has—
I stop and delete the text. Right. Kat and I aren't talking, and I don't know how to stop not talking. Last time, Kat showed up with video games. Maybe she'll do that again this time.

Another arrow plunges into the red with a thunk. I whoop, and Grayson grins at me for like the umpteenth time. At least I've got this girlfriend thing down. I put my phone to sleep and wedge it back into my pocket.

KAT

"I GOT YOUR EMAIL," SUNIL SAYS TO ME AS SOON AS OUR ANCIENT CIV teacher releases us to finish our group essay, which is due next class. "Your section looks great. I loved the joke about the plow."

Heat rises up my neck and into my cheeks. Maybe getting assigned to this group wasn't such a bad thing. "You don't think it was too corny?"

He chuckles and shakes his head. "No, it was funny. Did you get a chance to look over mine?"

I nod. "It was good," I say, relieved that I don't have to lie. Actually, it was beautiful. I couldn't even find a typo to complain about. Eric's, on the other hand—good substance, but awful execution. So many misuses of *its* and *it's* that I gave up on cringing. I'm not sure how to broach the subject, though. Eric keeps nodding his head so optimistically along with us, eyes wide as a basset hound's. How do I tell him his writing's crap?

"Okay," Sunil says, "so I'll just do a good edit of Eric's section tonight, then combine them all together."

"Oh, I did that." I grab the paper—complete with my fully revised version of Eric's section—out of my binder and set it down in front of Sunil.

He flips quickly through the first few pages—his section and mine—then slows to read Eric's, nodding as he goes. "Good. Good. This is great." When he gets to the end, he holds it out to Eric. "Want to see?"

My chest constricts. Eric's section is barely recognizable as his, though all his research is still there. I just . . . gave it a makeover. A really intensive makeover.

But Eric just flips through the thing once, too quickly to actually read anything, then hands it back to Sunil. "Looks good."

"Let's hand it in now, then," Sunil says, then gets to his feet and strides over to the teacher's desk and back again, empty-handed, before I can even stop him. I was going to give it one more edit.

If I don't, though, that gives me one more hour to spend on our science project. One more hour to figure out how not to flunk out of grade ten science. How not to flunk out of life.

"Do you guys—" At my words, Sunil and Eric break off their gesticulating about some game—hockey, probably—and turn to look at me, expectantly. Not exactly killer stares, but still, my mouth becomes a desert, arid and hot and empty.

One sandy dunes . . . two blazing sun . . .

"I mean—" The words come out as a rasp. I swallow, breathe, try again. "Do you guys play LotS at all?"

"Sometimes," Eric says.

Sunil shrugs. "I've seen my brother play. Do you?"

"Yeah. And I just—I'm doing—for science, you know the science fair project? We're—I'm doing LotS. I mean, speed runs. We're testing speeds. In LotS. After eating sugar, I mean. To see if you're faster, you know, after eating sugar. Anyway, test subjects. We still need some test subjects." I force the words out before they disappear wherever my saliva went, but I can't get them right.

Somehow, Sunil seems to understand me anyway. "That's cool. Way better than my power source testing. Can we do them at school? My house is out in the boonies."

The librarian hasn't complained about me playing LotS for fun, so surely she'd be okay with us playing it for science. "Yeah. I mean, I think so."

"Sweet," Sunil says. "Lunch today, then? Where should we meet you?"

And just like that, somehow, I have two more subjects.

I just need three more. In ten days.

And then ten more, plus all the analysis and write-ups and poster-board design in the following month. Maybe let's not think about that.

MEG

Dear Lumberlegs,

Did you know that archers are supposed to engrave their initials on their arrows? They should add that into LotS. I wonder if there's a machine here at the club that does it. My bf just used a Sharpie.

I saw your video last week where you tried to gather all the ingredients to make a hellspawn cake, and I swear I almost peed myself laughing when you died to that shadowbeast. Thanks for the laugh! I needed it!

Love your biggest fan,
Meg

Dear LumberLegs,

Did you know that the world's first UFO landing pad was built just outside Edmonton (that's Alberta, Canada, if you don't know)? I just learned that and was going to tell my friend, because she'd think it was amazing, but then I remembered she's not talking to me, so I'm telling you instead. Pretty cool, eh?

That is all.

Love,

Meg

Legs,

I almost forgot to tell you that I bought tickets for LotSCON! I'm so excited to see you there! Of course, my mom noticed I used her credit card and tried to make me return them, but they're nonrefundable, so all she could do was make me clean the toilets for a month. And pay her back, of course, but I was planning to do that anyways. She thinks it's ridiculous I bought them, since LotSCON is across the country, but I think she's forgotten planes exist. I'm going to wait until she's in a better mood before I remind her.

I can't wait to tell my friend I bought us tickets. I can't tell her now because we're fighting. But that'll sort itself out soon. I hope.

Anyways, looking forward to seeing you!

SO EXCITED!

Meg

KAT

I duck out into the hallway in front of him, cutting him off with my ninja-like swiftness.

"Kat, hey! You're not dead!"

"Dead? No, I—did Meg say I was dead?"

"What? No. I'm joking. You just haven't been around at lunch for a while. I was starting to wonder if you switched schools or something."

Well, at least I know Meg hasn't been bad-mouthing me to everyone at lunchtime. Or if she has, Roman hasn't been listening.

I shake my head. "No, just busy with my science project."

Meg's imaginary protest shrieks in my head. "*Your* science project! When did it stop being *our* science project?"

There are so many ways I could answer that, but I'm too busy talking with actual Roman to argue with imaginary Meg. "I need more subjects," I say. "Meg hasn't tested you yet, has she?"

"No. I mean, I don't think so. Unless she stole my saliva or urine or something."

I laugh—one quiet, airy burst. Asking Roman is a lot easier than asking Sunil and Eric. Maybe because I'm practiced at it now. Or maybe just because I actually know Roman. My heart isn't even pounding. I press my fingers to my wrist to make sure it's still beating at all. It is. "It's not a DNA test or anything. We just need you to do some LotS speed runs."

"Oh, phew," he says with mock relief. "That's easy. When do you need me?"

"Tomorrow at lunch. Does that work?"

He shrugs. "I don't see why not."

"Great. Meet me at the library at the start of lunch tomorrow, then. Don't eat anything before you come."

He nods, and I turn to leave, then spin back toward him. "Can you bring your girlfriend, too? And her friend Tanisha?"

He's already several steps away, but he gives me a thumbs-up in reply. Then, just before I slip around the corner into ninja mode, he calls out, almost as an afterthought, "Hey, Kat, I'm glad you're not dead."

MEG

Dear Legs,

I didn't know until I watched your video from last night that box turtles are often captured from the wild in super-big numbers and then die in captivity. I have a turtle. How do I know if he's a wild box turtle? And if he is, should I set him free in the woods or something? I'm worried that if I did, he'd be lonely.

With love from your biggest fan,

Meg

LumberLegs,

Love your vids! Watching your livestream on the weekend by myself was so ugh-fest, though. I kept expecting my friend to show up like she did last time we fought, but she didn't. Maybe she's even angrier than I thought. I could ask her, but I don't really want to know the answer. I haven't even tried logging on to our LotS server in case I find out she's banned me or something. How about next time you just invite me onto your server to play with you? Deal? Deal.

—Meg

Legs,

I am sick of cleaning toilets. But it'll be worth it because Kat and I will make up soon and then we'll go to LotSCON together. Won't we?

What if we don't?

Meg

Dear Lumber Legs,

If someone ever invites you to his archery practice, I recommend saying no. Otherwise, you'll end up going to every single one with nothing to do except write emails to your idol. Also, stick to LotS archery, it's more exciting!

Putrefying with boredom,

Meg

KAT

THE QUESTIONNAIRES LIE ACROSS MY LIVING ROOM FLOOR IN A GLORIOUS blanket of perfection. All twenty of them, all ready for Monday's class. Five from Meg. Three from my family. Seven from Sythlight. And five that I did—that *I* did!—on Sunil, Eric, Roman, Leila, and Tanisha.

It wasn't hitch-less. There wasn't time to fit Roman, Leila, and Tanisha into one lunch period and still have the proper amount of time for the sugar to wear off for the third test—or kick in, I guess. I've got to do more research to determine which one. But Roman came back the next lunch period, without protest. And Leila and Tanisha came too, to see if Roman could beat their scores. (He did.)

Easy.

I still have ten more questionnaires to finish in the next month, but it doesn't matter.

You know that moment when superheroes—the ones who gain their powers, not the ones who are born with them—realize what they are, and what they can do? Like when Spider-Man wakes up from the spider bite to discover he can shoot laserlike webs from his hands and scurry up a wall, impervious to gravity pulling him down?

This is that moment.

I can do anything.

LEGENDS OF THE STONE

KittyKat: go go go!

[]Sythlight: I lost him. Where'd he go?

KittyKat: that's like the fifth one. do you lose your keys
as often as you lose wereboars?

[]Sythlight: Hey, you lost the first one.

KittyKat: no way

[]Sythlight was slain by a venomous wereboar.

KittyKat: bahahhaak

[]Sythlight: Found him!

KittyKat: ha ha I can't believe you died to a wereboar

[]Sythlight: A venomous wereboar

[]Sythlight: Can you get to my stuff?

KittyKat: yeah I think so

KittyKat: give me a min phone keeps ringing

[]Sythlight: K

[]Sythlight: Made it back to my stuff. You back yet?

[]Sythlight: Kat?

KittyKat: got to go ttyl sorry

[]Sythlight: Is everything okay?

KittyKat has logged off.

17

COMPETITIONS, AT LEAST, ARE MORE EXCITING THAN STANDING AROUND AT THE archery club watching Grayson shoot his arrows, then collect them, then shoot them again, like playing fetch with himself. I ran to grab them for him once, but he still had one last arrow left and he just missed shooting me in the arm with it and somehow it was my fault, not his, so I didn't try that again.

Late Saturday afternoon, we ride across the city to the other club with Grayson's parents, and I hold Grayson's hand the whole way, even though it's all clammy with sweat—serious girlfriend points there.

The club bustles with competitors, from a tiny blond girl with her hair in pigtails and a pink grip on her miniature bow, to a burly ape of a white guy with a red bandanna atop his head who probably shoots arrows off the back of his Harley. I don't see any black competitors, but as always, that's no surprise. Though actually, the whole place is disproportionately white. It's like I've left Edmonton and landed in . . . I don't know, some place that's way more white. I want to ask Grayson why he thinks it is that I can count the number of nonwhite competitors on one hand, but he looks too nervous for that kind of discussion.

Grayson's division is the third group—probably not up for an hour or two, he reports—so we buy nachos and sit on the chairs at the back, chomping our cheese-coated chips as we watch the bow-wielding warrior tots.

The pigtailed girl claps and giggles every time she shoots, like this is the greatest fun she's had since she mastered the potty, and she shoots better than the grim-faced kid with an arm brace, whose parents hover around him, clucking advice and reprimands.

My phone vibrates in my pocket—it's too loud in here to hear it—and I lick the gooey orange off my fingers before wriggling it out.

It's a text from Kat. A text. From Kat!

SOS! Please come. Now. Please.

And it's not even an angry text! I shove the nachos at Grayson and tap out my reply.

Your house?

I pull on my coat as I wait for her response. Grayson grabs my arm as I stand. "Where are you going?"

I pat him on the head. "Sorry. It's an emergency. I have to go."

His brow softens. "What kind of emergency? Are Kenzie and Nolan okay?"

"Yes. I mean, I assume so. It's not them—it's Kat."

"Kat?" The furrow returns. "I thought you guys weren't talking. What's the problem? Can't it at least wait until after my group?"

I just shake my head. Kat wouldn't text me an SOS unless she meant it, especially not after two weeks of silence that's been growing louder and louder every day.

My phone lights up with the one-word response:

Yes

I lean down and kiss Grayson on the forehead. "I wouldn't go if it wasn't an SOS. Get your mom to film your round for me, okay? I'll watch later and cheer lots, I promise." Then I whirl out of the bustling hall and into the winter night.

It takes three different buses to navigate across the city to Kat's house, but I manage it in only forty-five minutes. Her house is dark, except for one light shining from the tiny basement window, but when I ring the doorbell, she swings the door open like she's been sitting right there.

"You came," she breathes. Even in the shadowy darkness of her front hallway, her eyes look red-rimmed.

"Of course I came, sillyface. It was an SOS."

Then she throws her arms around me and collapses against

me in a very un-Kat-like show of affection, or maybe desperation.

"What's the SOS?" I ask once she pulls away.

She pushes a few loose strands of hair back toward her pony-tail, as if trying to glue them into place.

"It's Granddad," she says, hand still atop her head. "He's had a stroke."

KAT

IT'S MEG'S TURN TO SMOTHER ME IN A HUG. "OH GOD!" SHE BREATHES, WORDS tangling in my hair. "Is he okay?"

In other words, is he dead or not dead? I shrug as she pulls away. An hour ago, when the nurse called, he was not dead. Or at least, not dead yet. Since then, I've sat in my dark living room, looking over questionnaire after questionnaire, spreading them across the floor, counting them, searching them for some strength that, I have determined, I definitely do not have. Since then, anything could have happened.

"ICU," I say, shrugging again.

"Which hospital?" she asks as she starts rummaging in the front hall closet.

"Royal Alex." I think. After the nurse said Granddad had collapsed of a stroke at the grocery store, everything else she said was muted by the roaring of a waterfall in my ears. Maybe she said the Misericordia. Or the Grey Nuns. I should've written it down, recorded her words in black pen strokes on lined paper as if preparing for a school final. Except in this case, it's a life final.

My stomach lurches as Meg winds a pink-and-purple-striped scarf around my neck.

"Well, that's easy, then. The 125 will take us right there." She stands on her tiptoes and shoves a plain green toque onto my head.

I shake my now-green head. "We should wait for my parents."

"Oh, are they on their way?" Her face brightens as she lifts my coat off the floor at her feet. I don't know when she put it there. Perhaps it walked there on its own.

I clench my phone tightly and shake my head for like the umpteenth time. "Not answering. Date night. They're at a movie," I force out, my voice breaking. When Granddad said he was going out to run a few errands, I didn't think twice about it. He goes out a lot, and he's been so much stronger lately.

Meg nods. "Which one? What time did it start?"

I shrug for about the fiftieth time. I don't know. I don't even know what theater. Normally, I would ask. In the past, I would have asked. I'm getting sloppy. I'm never letting them go anywhere again without telling me all the details first. I'm never letting Granddad go anywhere again, ever. If he even comes home in the first place.

One . . . one . . . I try to count, but I can't even remember what I'm counting about.

"Did you leave them a message?" Meg holds up a phone—my phone, which she has somehow pried out of my fingers without me noticing, in some sleight-of-hand magic trick.

I shake my head, unable to find words again.

"I got this," Meg says. She unlocks my phone with a swipe, types in my passcode, and taps the speed dial button that, if it was a real button and not a touch screen, would be completely worn through after the past hour. Puts the phone to her ear. Waits. "Hi, Mrs. Daley? This is Meg. Kat got a message from the Royal Alex that Granddad is in the ICU there from I think a stroke, so when you're done with your movie, you should head straight there. We'll catch the bus and meet you at the hospital. We'll call again if we get any more news. Ciao."

She hangs up, shoves the phone into my pocket, pulls my coat out from where she's been holding it between her knees, and continues to dress me just like she does Kenzie—one arm, wind around, other arm, zip up right to the neck, pat on head.

"Okay," she says, "you're ready. Let's go."

I shake my head again, perfecting the part of the speechless Neolithic cavewoman I've apparently devolved into. "I can't," I say, and Meg furrows her brow, clearly confused. Perhaps if I grunted and pointed, she'd understand me better.

"Can't what?" she asks.

Just can't. I reach up and tug at my coat's cold, purple zipper pull, flipping it up and down and up and down.

One . . . one . . . one . . .

I can picture him now—face battered and bloodied from the green bean cans he bounced off of as he pitched in slow motion to the grocery aisle floor. Left side of his mouth sagging with the weight of the words his brain no longer knows how to speak. Eyes wide and expectant as he waits for me to murmur some meaningful, poetic thing that will comfort his soul as it slips out of this world into the darkness only absence brings.

"Kat?" The word's full of impatience—Meg's always impatient—but it's full of worry, too.

Meg's concern is enough to start the words flowing.

"I just can't," I say. "What if he doesn't look like himself? What if I say something idiotic and insensitive? What if he dies? What if he dies in a fit of coughing and blood and beeping monitors and there's nothing I can do? What if he dies while I'm right there?"

Meg reaches out and takes my hand like we're five years old, fingers interlocking with my own. She puts her other hand firmly on my wrist and looks me in the eyes. "Kat. What if he dies and you're *not* there?"

Then she marches out the door, pulling me behind her.

When I was little, maybe six or seven, Granddad took me to a carnival. I can't remember if he was visiting us or if we were visiting him, but I only got about ten feet inside the gates before I started crying. I don't know why. The flashing lights, the hiccuping music, the shrieking children—could have been anything. Granddad scooped me up, kissed me on the top of my head, and murmured, "It's okay, Katharina. It's okay." Then we went out for ice cream instead.

I want to go for ice cream now. I want Granddad to walk into this waiting room, dapper and tall, and tell me, "Katharina, don't worry about these fluorescent lights, or bustling noises, or contagious patients. Let's blow this joint and nab us some two-scoop chocolate cones."

Though would Granddad choose chocolate? What's his favorite ice cream flavor? What does he usually have? I can't remember. I'm losing him already.

Meg turns from speaking to the front-desk nurse and looks at me expectantly, as if waiting for the answer to life, the universe, and everything.

"What?" I ask.

"Your granddad. What's his name?"

I tell her, and she continues chatting with the nurse, and then we are following a nurse—the same one or a different one, I couldn't say—down flickering beige hallways, and I'm trying not to look in any of the rooms at the puking and the monitors and the bruises and the dark, sunken eyes.

Then we're standing in front of heavy black double doors. And the nurse turns to us and says, "I'm sorry, family only. You'll have to wait out here."

I start to sit obediently in one of the gray plastic chairs lined against the wall, but then Meg grabs my hand and pulls me back up.

"Not you, silly. You're family. She means me." She taps me lightly on the back, nudging me in the direction of the big, black entryway to hell.

I reach out and grab Meg's hand, and she looks fiercely up at the nurse. "Look," she says, "she's—can't I—"

"No," the nurse says. "Family only. No exceptions." She's tall and broad, like you'd expect a prison warden to be. She frowns at us, compassionless. I bet it's not even a real rule. I bet she just doesn't want a pair of teen hooligans set loose in her ICU.

Meg slides off my coat, undoing her previous work, and lays it over a chair. "I'll be right out here," she says, as if I'm Kenzie, except that Kenzie would just go roaring right in and start dancing with every patient, even the ones in comas.

I can't get my feet to move an inch, let alone dance.

Meg unzips her coat, revealing her favorite black cardigan with the oversized purple plastic buttons. Out of nowhere, she grabs one of the buttons and pulls. There's a snap, and then she's pressing the button into my palm and folding my fingers around it.

"There," she says. "Now it's like I'm with you."

Heat from our sweaty rush from sidewalk to bus to lobby in downy winter garb seeps from the button into my palm, and my eyes prickle with tears. Before I can dissolve into full meltdown sobs, Meg grasps my shoulders and turns me around, pushing me through the hell-door that's now being held open by the prison-ward nurse.

Then I'm trotting after her through a sea of curtains with Meg's button pressed so deep into my palm I can feel my heart pulsing through it.

I would count, I should breathe and count, except I can't remember the numbers.

Curtain. Curtain. Nurse. Cart. Monitor. Curtain.

And then, Granddad is there.

There's no blood, at least not on his face, but his eyes are shrunken into his head, and there are tubes and needles taped into his hands, and he takes up so little of what is already a tiny bed. I look away, find the nurse's face instead.

"He's lucky he collapsed in a public place," she says. "Ambulance got there and got him on TPA real quick, which breaks down the clot. And it's the right side of his brain, not the left, so his speech and language should be fine." I nod at her, barely hearing her words. I can still see Granddad's skeletal frame out of the corner of my eye. "Well, go on," she says, waving at the chair beside his bed. "Go talk to him."

The gray chair is hard and cold, and I perch on the edge of it, leaning forward to rest my hands on the bar along the side of the bed.

"Hi, Granddad," I say, softly, so whoever's on the other side of the curtain behind me can't hear.

His eyes flutter open just a crack, eyelids struggling against fatigue or drugs or maybe even another stroke. I sit back, surprised. "My Katharina," he murmurs.

I still clench Meg's button in one hand, but I reach out my other hand and slip it into his, trying to ignore the IV piercing his paper-thin skin.

I squeeze, gently. With his bony, fleshless hand, he squeezes back.

And I realize, with relief, that we really don't need to say anything more than that.

18

"WE HAVE A DOORBELL, YOU KNOW," GRAYSON SAYS WHEN HE ANSWERS MY *tap tap tap tap* on his front door.

I take off my coat and hang it in the ridiculously orderly front closet. "You've used that joke before," I tell him as I throw my mitts and scarf onto the bench in the entryway.

He scowls. "It's not a joke."

I reach down and pluck a pair of pink knit mittens out of their mitten bin. "Are these mine?"

He just shrugs.

"Someone got up on the wrong side of the manure farm

today," I say. "Did your competition thing not go well or something? No, don't tell me. Your mom recorded it, right? I want to watch."

"I don't know. Maybe. What was your big emergency, anyway?"

"Dude! Kat's granddad had a stroke. We were at the hospital until like midnight."

"Oh, I'm sorry." The scowl relaxes out of his face. "That's awful. Is he okay?"

That's closer to the reception I expected. "Yeah, I think so. Kat went over there again this morning with her parents. She said there doesn't seem to be too much brain damage or whatever, and he can talk and stuff. But he hurt his hip again when he fell."

Grayson nods, all traces of bad-day grump gone from his face. "I hope he didn't hurt it too badly," he says. Then, after a pause, "So, you wanted to watch the video from last night?"

"You bet! I'm sure you were the archeriest of all the archers. Even that big Hell's Angel guy."

"Well, he wasn't in my division. Hang on, I'll have to find my mom's camera. My parents aren't home."

I make myself some hot chocolate while he searches for the camera. By the time I settle myself on the wide navy-blue couch downstairs, mug heaped with mini marshmallows in hand, he has the camera connected to the big screen and ready to go.

"Okay," he says, "this video is of the first guy in my division, Kyle. He's from Beaumont. I thought he was a dick at first, but once you get his sense of humor, he's not so bad."

The video starts and a short, scrawny Asian guy steps up to the line and rolls his neck back and forth as if he's about to duke it out with someone.

My phone beeps with a new email, and I pull it out and unlock it, glancing at my in-box as Kyle raises his bow.

"Oh my God. OhmyGodohmyGodohmyGod!"

Grayson jabs pause. "What? Is it Kat's grampa? Is he okay?"

"LumberLegs!"

"What?"

"LumberLegs! He emailed me back. OhmyGod. Oh my God. Oh my God. I never dreamed he'd actually email me back. Look!" I hold the phone out to Grayson, but before he can even look, I pull it back to study it again. I tap on the email, fill my screen with LumberLegs's words. "Listen to this!" I stand and read it aloud:

Meg—

"Did you hear that? He called me Meg. He knows my name."

Meg—

Thanks for the kind words. I'm glad you enjoy my Let's Play.

Box turtles can go completely inside their shell, fully protected. Your local pet store or zoo can probably help you figure out if your turtle is a box turtle, and how best to care for him if he is. Please don't just release him in the wild. Your climate might not be right for box turtles.

I hope you keep watching and enjoying.

Be awesome.

Chow for now,

LumberLegs

"He wrote me back!" I do a little hopping dance as I scroll back up to read it again. Kat is going to lose her mind when I tell her! I can't wait to tell her! I'm never not talking to her again.

"Yeah," Grayson says. "To tell you that you shouldn't release your turtle in the snow. Real Einstein, that one. I could've told you that."

I glance up. Grayson's scowl is back. Combined with the darkness of his eyebrows, he looks almost—but not quite—ugly. I've never noticed that about him before.

"Well, he doesn't know it's snowy here, genius. I could be anywhere. Borneo or Libya or Hawaii."

"Borneo? Really?"

I kick lightly at his shin. "Stop being such a downer. This is a big deal!"

"To *you*. I know. He's all you ever talk about."

"He's not—"

"He *is*. All you could talk about after every practice was

whatever email you wrote to him and whether he'd read it. You'd think you were dating him, not me."

I drop my hands—and my phone—to my sides. I thought he *liked* hearing about LumberLegs. And it's not like I wasn't paying attention, but his practices were so boring. Even someone without ADHD would need a distraction, wouldn't they? Maybe they wouldn't. Maybe this is another way my ADHD scares people away. Another way *I* scare people away.

I slide my phone into my pocket. "I'm not dating him," I say uselessly.

"Look, all I know is this random gamer who has no idea who you are and who doesn't care about you at all is way more exciting to you than your effing *boyfriend's* archery competition!" He huffs out a breath and sags back against the couch.

I want to snap back that he'll have other archery competitions, whereas LumberLegs emailing me back is probably a once-in-a-lifetime event, but somehow I manage to bite my tongue. "You're right," I say instead. "I'm sorry. Your competition is more important. Let's watch that first." I settle on the couch beside him, slide my hand along his thigh. I'm getting good at this—this girlfriend thing.

"Meg," he says, lifting my hand off his leg and sliding away to create a cavern of space between us, "I don't think this is working."

It's not the answer I expected—the answer I expected being more like, "What a good idea, Meg. You're so caring and understanding. You earn three hundred and two girlfriend points." But that's okay. I haven't lost, not yet. I can still fix this.

"Of course it's working," I say. "This is just a fight. Couples fight. And now we make up." I grab my shirt, pull it upward and over my head. I glance down. Ugly gray bra. I thought I threw this one away. No matter; it can come off.

I pull at the snaps at my back and let the ugly grayness fall away into my lap. I slide closer to Grayson and reach for his belt buckle.

"Meg," he says, laying his hand on mine. "I don't think we should."

I lean into him, press my lips against his ear. "We should. I know we should." I can save this. I know I can save this. I kiss his ear—once, twice—and then he turns his head and presses his mouth firmly against mine.

LEGENDS OF THE STONE

KittyKat has logged on.

[]Sythlight: Hi

KittyKat: sorry about the other night

[]Sythlight: What happened? Everything ok?

KittyKat: my granddad had a stroke

[]Sythlight: Oh no!

[]Sythlight: :(That's awful. I'm sorry.

KittyKat: he's ok

KittyKat: I mean, considering

[]Sythlight: Do you want to talk about it?

KittyKat: on here or on VoiceChat?

[]Sythlight: Either

[]Sythlight: What do you think?

KittyKat: ok. I'll call you

MEG

IT HURTS.

That's something they don't show in the movies—how condoms can tug and grab at areas that are way more sensitive than I expected, amid all the banging of knees and elbows and noses.

Afterward, we don't curl together as one on the couch, blanket pulled up to the dimples in our chins. Instead, Grayson stands, runs his fingers through his hair, and starts tugging on his clothes.

This part I do know from the movies. This is the point where the guy pulls on his clothes and leaves. Except this is Grayson's house, so there's nowhere for him to go. He buckles his belt and sits down on the couch beside me, shirt clutched in one hand.

I lean down and snatch up my own shirt, pulling it over my head, skipping the bra, which still lies abandoned on the rug. I lift my hips, tug my underwear on. I ease up beside him so my bare leg presses against his denim-covered one.

"Do you want to watch your archery thing?" I ask, and Grayson nods, not looking at me. He reaches forward, taps some buttons on the camera.

On the screen, the short kid finishes pulling back the string and lets go. Grayson puts his arm over my shoulder. The weight of it is like that enormous snake that tiny girl on *Britain's Got Talent* wore while she recited a poem about saving the animals—as the thing basically tried to strangle her to death.

I have done it. I have saved us. We are right back where we're supposed to be, watching his oh-so-important video, not fighting.

Except that I don't care about his stupid archery. I actually could not care less if he wins or loses or gets clobbered over the head by that hairy biker who—yes, I do remember—is not in his division. I just want him to kiss me, and wrap his arms around me, and breathe his warmth into my ear, and tell me that it's okay that I feel wet with what I think must be blood. It hurts enough to be blood.

The video clip ends. Grayson leans forward to start the next. His hair flops forward toward his eyes, and he flicks it back before putting his arm once again around my shoulder.

On the screen, a mousy, freckled guy prepares his bow. Are all archers as thin as Pixy Stix?

Grayson's not breaking up with me. Grayson's not breaking up with me, because we just had sex. And I think that's the only reason.

I get to my feet, swoop down and snare my pants, pulling

them on one leg after another. My legs feel like cacti. I should've shaved them this morning. But I didn't know this morning that this was going to happen.

"I'm going to go," I tell Grayson. He doesn't protest, just hands me my bra, which I stuff into my pocket.

"Meg, I'm sorry," he says, which I'm pretty sure means *Good-bye*.

KAT

SYTH'S VOICE HOVERS ABOUT MY HEAD, DARTING FROM MY HEADPHONES TO my ears like a tiny hummingbird.

I talk about Granddad, and about how the flesh seems to have melted off him basically overnight, and how awful it is to see him as brittle bone again, when he'd been getting so much stronger. I tell him about my doll and the dresses for her that Granddad gave me, and about the carnival, even though it's embarrassing to admit that lights and music can make me cry.

He tells me about his oma and how she speaks only German, and how when he was little that made him scared of her, but now he's thankful for it because he can actually speak a little German.

"Like what?" I ask.

"Like *Fahrtwind*. It means airstream."

That makes me laugh. "You didn't really learn that from your oma, did you?"

"Okay, maybe not that one," he admits.

I tell him about how Meg and I stopped talking over our silly science project, but she came anyway when I texted and now we're talking again and that's at least one good thing that came out of Granddad's stroke. And then I feel horrible for saying that, but he says he understands.

He tells me about his friends and how one wants to be an engineer and another has no idea, and I recognize their names because their questionnaires are printed out and sitting on my desk.

At some point, we stop playing LotS, and I lean back in the computer chair with my feet up on the desk.

By the time the doorbell rings, more than two hours have passed.

"That'll be Meg," I say. "We have plans."

"Okay," he says. "Talk to you later then?"

I nod, even though I know he can't see me.

The doorbell rings again. Typical impatient Meg. I've missed her.

"Syth—I mean, Dan?"

"Yeah?"

"Thanks for listening."

"Anytime."

"How's Granddad?" Meg asks when I open the front door and usher her in. I like the way she does that—calls him just "Granddad" as if he's hers, too, because he's mine.

"No further strokes," I say, "which is good. Mom and Dad are there now. They say it's a miracle how well he's doing." It both does and doesn't feel like a miracle. Seeing him so fragile in that tiny bed—not a miracle. The fact that he's still alive—well, he's supposed to live forever anyway, right?

Right?

Meg nods, as if in answer to my unspoken question, and hands me her coat.

Something is wrong.

She smiles at me, pats me on the head in her strange, caring way, but there's a deadness in her eyes that wasn't there yesterday. That I've never seen there, ever.

"Are you okay?" I ask.

"Of course," she says, though she shakes her head almost imperceptibly, as if shaking away an unwelcome fly. "How are *you* doing?"

"Okay." I study her carefully as she picks up my mom's latest textbook draft off the front table and leafs through it absentmindedly. Her voluminous curls look normal—a bit lopsided from her toque, but that's normal, too. Makeup, bright-colored nail polish, all normal. But she's slouching, I think. Something is making her look even shorter than usual. "Do you want to maybe watch Legs or something?" Maybe that'll cheer her up.

She drops the stack of paper with a thud. "Oh! Guess what! LumberLegs emailed me!"

"Did you sign up for that fan club? I got that, too."

"No, not that. I mean, that too. But I sent him a couple of emails and he actually responded."

"He did not! You're joking." Legs gets thousands of comments on every video, hundreds of daily posts on Reddit, and who knows how many emails.

She shakes her head, pulls out her phone, unlocks it, and hands it to me.

"Holy crap! He really did! He emailed you. This is amazing."

She grins, stands up straight, and starts to recite the words on the screen in my hand in her best LumberLegs impression: "'Meg—'"

"He wrote your name," I can't help but interject. "He wrote out all three letters of your name!"

"Exactly!" she says, pounding her fist on the table, as if she's just won some argument. Whatever deadness loomed in her eyes is gone. Maybe I imagined it.

I let her recite the entire thing from memory, even though I've got it right there on the screen in front of me.

"You were going to release your turtle into the wild?"

"Of course not. I'm not stupid."

"Okay, just checking." I study her face as I hand back her phone. "Are you sure you're okay?"

"Are you sure *you're* okay?" she responds.

Granddad is not dead. That's the important thing.

I nod. "So . . . marathon watching sesh of your new buddy, Legs?"

She hugs her phone to her chest like it's Legs himself. "Yes!"

Later, when we're sprawled on the couch with our chips and chocolate, and there's a brief pause as we switch from one video to the next, I turn to Meg. "By the way, thanks for last night. For being there."

"Of course," she says. "Anytime."

Which makes twice in one day that someone has said that to me.

MEG

"MEG SAYS WHAT'S ON HER MIND."

"Meg has no filter."

"Meg is so outspoken."

I've heard it a hundred thousand times—from teachers, friends, my mom, everyone.

The Meg they're talking about would walk into Kat's house and report, immediately, that she'd had sex. "I'm wearing a pad," she would say, "because there was blood and it's not my period. Also, Grayson and I broke up, I think, but it's good riddance, really, because he was boring and a jerk." That Meg would give a complete play-by-play of how and where and what *it* looked like.

And then once that weight was gone, that Meg could move on to talking about exciting things, like LotSCON and how she bought tickets and how we can go together and it will be epic and great and it won't matter that I had sex because who cares about Grayson because I don't even like him as much as Legs anyways.

That Meg would say all the things.

I know this because the words are hopping around in my head like an angry wasp buzzing about under a glass, like a horde of winglings stuck in a lava trap, screaming to get out.

So why aren't they coming out?

19

---------- MEG ----------

THERE'S NOTHING SCARY ABOUT THE DARK. I'VE NEVER HAD MONSTERS UNDER my bed, just lost jigsaw puzzle pieces and dirty laundry and probably an old, discarded pizza crust.

But tonight I can't sleep, and it's the dark's fault. I can't see my magazines or my LumberLegs posters or my phone or even the fly that's been buzzing about in the corner even though he should be dead, shouldn't he, because it's winter?

There's nothing to distract me from the realization that I am fundamentally unlovable. Grayson doesn't want me. Neither did Brad. My friends. My dad. Even my stepdad, Stephen. All of them realized, at some point, that Meg is not worth having.

I flick on the light beside my bed.

LumberLegs—the knit doll Kat gave me for Christmas—sits across the room on the shelf he was demoted to in case Grayson would be jealous if I slept with him. I thought it was a silly fear, but I guess I was right to worry.

I don't have to worry about that now.

I get up, snatch Legs off the shelf, then cozy back into bed, the top of Legs's head tucked just under my chin. I don't need Grayson. I've got LumberLegs.

I turn on my tablet and search for flights to LotSCON. Then stare through the darkness at the glowing screen.

Lizard balls.

Lizard. Balls.

Flights are expensive. How the heck do people fly all over the place? Are they made of money? Because I am not. I drop the tablet on the floor and squeeze Legs tighter.

If I slept with Legs in real life, I bet it would be different. I bet he'd know what to do to make sure I don't bleed, and he'd be gentle and kind, and afterward we'd cuddle just like this except my head would be under his chin instead of the other way around.

I don't have real-life Legs, though, only the doll, and apparently that's all I'm ever getting, so I try sliding the doll up so his head is above my own. But then my face is buried in his belly button—or at least, where his belly button would be if he was human and not a doll—which just feels weird.

So I slip him back down under my chin and hug him close until I finally fall asleep.

—————————————— KAT ——————————————

IT'S SCIENCE PROJECT CHECK-IN DAY, WHICH IS FINE, BECAUSE I HAVE ALL twenty of our questionnaires and test results completed and ready to show Mr. Carter.

"And I hope your projects are all coming along swimmingly," he says before he makes his rounds, "because I've got some exciting news. The school board has approved our funding, and this year, in addition to the regional fair, the winners from each school in Edmonton will be flown to Toronto to compete at the national fair. It's on March fifteenth, so mark your calendars. But remember, only one team can win!"

In front of me, Meg's lying across her desk with her right arm sticking out into the aisle, her head resting on her bicep. With her left hand, she lazily flips the pages of her planner. January. February. March.

She sits up abruptly, then turns around and thrusts the planner practically in my face. "He said March fifteenth, right?" she whispers.

I nod, then look down at the page. And suddenly I understand, with a tightening of my chest, her unexpected glee. From

Friday, March 16 to Sunday, March 18, Meg has giant words written over and over across the space in green pen:

LOTSCON
LUMBERLEGS
TORONTO

"Ms. Winters. Ms. Daley," Mr. Carter says before I can burst Meg's bubble and remind her that I don't fly. "Is there something you'd like to share with the class?"

Meg snatches her planner out of my hand and whirls back around in her seat. "Only that our project is going to whup their butts!"

Mr. Carter's mouth contorts in a half grimace, half smile, as if he's not sure whether to reprimand her or to laugh. "You heard it here first, folks," he says finally. "The project to beat."

Meg glances over her shoulder and flashes me her sparkly white grin.

My heart crashes into my stomach like a plane from the sky.

─────────────── **MEG** ───────────────

I KNOW LUMBERLEGS CAN'T DATE EVERY LOVESTRUCK FAN WHO'S EVER LAID eyes on him. And I know he's got a lot of fans.

But . . .

He's got to date somebody, right? And why couldn't that somebody be a lovestruck fan? And why couldn't that lovestruck fan be me? Especially when the universe is basically handing us this free flight.

Grayson practically thought Legs and I were dating already. Plus, we both like to joke and we both like turtles and we're both bad at LotS and we're going to meet at LotSCON and I already know what our wedding colors would be.

Plus, dating him would be like a swift kick to Grayson's balls.

KAT

THE MOMENT WE STEP INTO THE HALL AFTER SCIENCE, MEG TURNS ON ME like a shadowwolf who's just spotted its prey.

"Okay," she says, "what do we have to do to win this thing?"

"We're not going to win." It's going to be hard enough just to finish our project. And there are over three hundred people in our grade, so that's at least a hundred and fifty projects to beat. So I need to stop worrying, because winning is something that I don't have to worry about. Fortunately. There's no way I'm riding in the air in a hunk of heavy metal all the way to Toronto. I start down the hall toward my locker.

Meg scurries after me and loops her arm through mine. "Don't be such an Eeyore. Come on, we can totally win. What do we have to do?"

I glance at her. Her gaze is on me instead of on what's ahead of us. Mr. Carter let us out a bit early, so it's not the between-classes rush yet, but still. Apparently she trusts that her arm through mine is enough to guide her safely through these halls.

I'm sure she knows we won't win. I'm sure she knows LotSCON tickets are probably already sold out. But she's staring at me like she's hungry for it—like she's desperate to finally conquer something. She deserves to conquer something. And she will. Even if we won't win, we can at least get an A.

"Dude, get out of your head and talk to me," Meg says. "What's the plan?"

I roll my eyes at her. "Well, we've got to actually finish the testing first. We still need ten more people."

"Okay. Easy." Meg beats me to my locker and starts entering my combination.

"And you have to be passing all your courses." She deserves to conquer more than just science.

Meg's head jolts up from the lock to stare at me. "You're lying. That's not a thing."

"It is. It's a requirement. Mr. Carter said."

It might just be the way the skin around her eyes sags, but Meg's eyes seem to flash with darkness. Like in the X-Men movies when a character's eyes flash with yellow to reveal she's really Mystique in disguise, except this color suggests powerlessness, not superpowers.

I was right. She's sick of feeling like she can't win. "I'll help you," I say. I haven't told Meg, but I've been researching home-work techniques for teens with ADHD. I've figured out that she avoids homework at lunch because there's too much going on, not because she's slacking. She's definitely not slacking. She works hard and gets a ton done—when her brain's not getting in the way.

The darkness vanishes so quickly that I wonder if I imagined it. "Okay, well, I'm only failing math," Meg says. "I think there might be a test coming up or something." She grimaces, then scares away the frown with an excited little hop. "I can't wait until we're at LotSCON! It's going to be epic!"

I thought my heart had been returned to its place in my chest, but I was wrong. It's still crashed and crumpled and heavy in the bottom of my stomach. Meg *does* know that winning is a super long shot, right? That it's basically impossible? She has to know. And she knows I wouldn't go even if we won—which we won't—right? I've told her I don't fly. Haven't I?

Before I can think through whether I have, Meg breaks into my thoughts. "Okay, so now do we just invite people to my house for testing, or what? I'd suggest a big testing party, but I know parties aren't your thing."

Of course she knows that. Meg gets me. She knows all my fears, so of course she knows about my fear of planes. She's just fantasizing, like she does about Legs all the time. I push my worries away and explain to Meg how I've been using the library computers, and how we're limited to two people per lunch period in order to fit in the cooldown periods between tests, and also how I've run out of people to ask.

"Well, that's easy," Meg says. "Hey, you two!" she calls out to two girls who have just passed us. They spin around to look at us with matching what-in-the-world-do-you-want expressions.

"Us?" the one girl says. She has one of those shoulder bags instead of a backpack, and the weight of it makes her stand a little crooked. I think I recognize both of them from my English class.

"How would you like to play video games? And eat sugar? For science!" Meg wiggles her hands near her face in an "It's so magical" kind of gesture, as if science is some kind of voodoo and not, well, science.

The crooked girl giggles. "Um, what?"

The other one smiles. They're definitely in my English class.

Meg's voice returns to its normal non-exaggerated-but-still-excited tenor. "We need a few more subjects for our science project. You guys free?"

"What, like, right now? We have class."

"Tomorrow at lunch," Meg says. "In the library."

"You can't eat lunch first, though," I say, jumping in. "It'll mess up the results."

"So, you up for it?" Meg asks them confidently. She can definitely conquer this.

Shoulder-bag girl—their apparent spokesperson—shrugs. "Sounds more fun than sitting around in the caf."

MEG

FINISHING THE TESTING IS EASY-PEASY. ON TUESDAY, WE TEST OUR BRAND-new friends, Emily and Kayla, who, it turns out, know Kat from English. On Wednesday, I grab Chris from my math class and Fatima, who I've known since like birth, and Kat asks Chris if he can write down my math homework in my planner every class, which is kind of embarrassing, but also good because I'm not letting something as stupid as math keep me from meeting LumberLegs.

Then these two guys in the library wonder what all the laughter is about, so we schedule them in for Thursday. One has a birthmark just under his eye, toward his cheekbone, which is adorably distracting, but I've sworn off all guys except LumberLegs, so I just smile at him and that's it.

On the weekend we enter all our results so far into some spreadsheets, and then on Tuesday I ask Bridget and Louis in geography. It turns out Louis has band practice at lunch, but Bridget brings her friends, and Louis shows up on Thursday with his friend.

Every day after school, we meet in the quietest back corner of the library and do our math homework. Kat's idea. Her notes make a lot more sense than mine. Her notes make sense, period. And she doesn't let me leave until I'm done.

Except on Friday, when we go for ice cream even though it's

minus twenty out, because we're done testing, and we deserve a celebration.

In a booth, Kat stops licking her scoop of chocolate and studies me as I take a bite of my bubble gum ice cream. "You realize there's going to be more than a hundred and fifty other projects, right?" she says. "That winning is almost impossible?"

"Of course," I say. That's what makes it so epic. The girl with ADHD and the girl with panic attacks—like the hobbits setting across Mordor to Mount Doom, no one will see us coming.

Until they lose. Because we are definitely going to win.

We are definitely going to LotSCON.

KAT

PEOPLE DIE IN PLANE CRASHES ALL THE TIME. PLANES CRASH ALL THE TIME. If you search the internet, you can find lists of them. Famous People Who Died in Plane Crashes. Ten Most Famous Plane Crashes of All Time. Worst Plane Crashes in History.

"But most of the people who died were on small, private planes," people say. "Commercial flights have a much lower fatality rate." As if that's supposed to make me feel better.

I force myself to put down my phone and stop researching plane crashes.

I should go downstairs and do one last review of our science project. The final, complete presentation board sits by my front door, ready for tomorrow's fair. Once we finished all our analysis and reports and write-ups a couple of weeks ago and started working on the board, Meg insisted we work on it here and only here, to ensure the halflings wouldn't puke on it or turn it into a playhouse or something. I could give it one last look-over to make sure there are no typos or other silly errors we missed.

Or I could waltz downstairs and kick it in half.

My stomach lurches with guilt. Meg hasn't stopped talking about LotSCON, and the more she talks about LotSCON like it's not just a fantasy, the more I research plane crashes. And the more I research plane crashes, the more I worry that maybe I haven't told Meg about that particular anxiety after all.

But it's too late to tell her now. She'll wonder why I didn't tell her in the first place. All I can do now is hope we won't win—which we won't, of course. And when we don't win, Meg will get over her disappointment quickly in typical Meg-bounce-back fashion. I hope. She doesn't feel quite as bouncy lately.

The doorbell rings, and after a minute or two, Mom calls up to me, "Kat, package for you."

It's probably the gaming mouse Mom let me order. I don't think I'll get to play LotS tonight with all the reading I have to do for English, but I trot downstairs anyway because, well, it's a package for me, and how often does that happen?

The only thing on the kitchen table is a white cylindrical package, about a foot long and only a few inches in diameter. It's definitely not the right shape for a mouse.

I duck my head into the living room, where Mom, Dad,

and Granddad are all sitting with books in their laps. Granddad looks up and winks at me before returning to his reading. I wish he'd sit in a different chair. His favorite oversized armchair makes him look even smaller and frailer than he is. His left arm lies limply at his side. It's been over a month since his stroke, but it still hasn't fully recovered. And even though he's starting to gain the weight back, he still looks like his spine would snap in half from the simple weight of a fedora on his head. Not that he'd ever wear a fedora. And if he tried, I'd stop him.

"Mom, where's my package?"

"On the kitchen table," she says, not looking up from her book.

So, not my gaming mouse, then.

I stride back into the kitchen and pick up the cylinder, which, sure enough, has my name on it. I open my mouth to shout to Mom that I don't remember ordering a poster, but then I see the return address.

My mouth clamps shut, and without saying another word, I slip back upstairs to my room, poster tube balanced carefully in both hands.

I set it gently on the bed, pull out the red cap in the end with a *pop*, reach inside, and pull out a small, folded piece of lined paper. I unfold it to read the careful, even scrawl.

Dear Kat,
I've been working on this for a while. Thought

I'd send it to you as a "good luck at your science fair" gift. Hope it makes it to you in time.
Good luck!
Dan

Sythlight.

I've told him all about our results and the competition and how Meg has become a workaholic Energizer bunny. But I haven't told him that first prize is a flight to Toronto, where LotSCON is, which he's going to, since he only lives an hour or two away. If I did tell him, he'd probably get excited about the possibility of us coming, and I'd have to either tell him what I haven't been able to tell Meg, or lie to him—either option feels like a betrayal.

My stomach backflips as I pick up the cylinder again.

Rolled up inside the tube is a large piece of white cardstock. I unroll it, spread it out across my bedspread, and blink at the splashes of color that greet me.

It's an elf. My elf. My character in LotS. Her pink hair flows out behind her as she stands fierce and strong in her black armor, bow ready as she stares down a frothing wereboar.

I run my finger over every painted line and stroke, tracing the contours until my fingers have them memorized.

Then I call Meg.

"Holy gumdrops," she breathes. "That's so romantic."

"It is not. It's just a good luck thing. There's probably one in the mail for you, too."

She laughs. "Yeah, sure, you keep thinking that."

I don't tell her that in the darkest part of KittyKat's shadow, my finger keeps tracing and tracing over what I'm pretty sure is a tiny, camouflaged heart.

There's a crash on the line, and some distant, muffled swearing, and it takes Meg almost a full minute to answer my repeated queries of "Are you okay? Meg? Are you there?"

"I'm fine! I'm fine," she pants.

"Are you skateboarding?" I ask.

The soft whirring of skateboard wheels is my answer.

"Study break," Meg says. "I pushed the couches all the way back in here, but there's still not enough room to perfect that back jump thing, whatever it's called."

Study and skateboard. They're pretty much the only things Meg does lately, switching between the two every five minutes.

Well, that and watch LumberLegs. She always wants to watch LumberLegs.

"Know what I love about LumberLegs?" she asked last time we curled up on her bed for a video marathon. "He never leaves. Unlike every other jerk guy in the world, he's always there when we need him."

She still won't tell me how she and Grayson broke up, and she snaps at me anytime I try to bring it up. We don't eat in the back stairwell anymore; Meg's been making us work on our project in the library every lunch hour. "Legs is the only one I'll break my no-homework-at-lunch rule for," she said when I reminded her of her rule.

Meg's still skateboarding away, so as her wheels whir in the background, I Google the LotSCON website. I haven't looked at it—have preferred to just not think about it. But seeing KittyKat's badass fierceness makes me curious what Dan'll be doing while he's there. Will other artists be there? I click on the link.

My gaze slides over the LotSCON heading, past the silver-haired dragonlord leaning casually against the *N*, and settles on the small red letters in the top right corner: *SOLD OUT.*

My stomach twists. Does Meg know? She goes on this site all the time, doesn't she? She talks about LotSCON like we've already won, like we've already bought our tickets. Maybe they only just sold out and she doesn't know.

A thump echoes through the line. "Nailed it! Finally!" Meg shouts triumphantly. Happily.

I haven't seen the powerless darkness in Meg's eyes since I told her she needed to pass math. Hopefully her recent math test conquest banished it for good, but I'm not telling her about this and risking bringing the darkness back—not when there's basically no chance whatsoever that we could win. If there was a decent chance we'd win, I'd have already told her that I don't fly.

"Now, tell me again about the painting," Meg says, panting.

So I ignore the twisting in my stomach, and I do.

After I say good-bye to Meg, I finish my English reading,

put on my pajamas, and brush my teeth. Then, instead of my recent nightly ritual of checking if there have been any more plane crashes in the world, I trace my finger over the shape hidden in the drawing's shadows again and again until I finally fall asleep.

20

I'M NOT NERVOUS.

The guys beside us are both wearing baggy geek shirts and glasses and look like they're really smart, but their project is about dung beetles, and no one cares about that. Across from us is Marcia, who's mixed but such a pale brown that she could be white-passing—especially since she's started straightening her already loose curls. She spends our entire homework time in math period talking to Dylan, which could mean she's really smart and has already done her homework, but I doubt it, and her partner is this Asian girl I don't know who looks like she's about ten years old, and long story short, our project is better than every other project in this entire place.

And there are a lot of them. Our whole grade is here. Thank goodness Grayson's a grade ahead. I don't want to have to go out of my way to avoid him like I do in the hallways.

The background of our poster board is splattered with fiery red paint—for the past week, Kat's been complaining that she keeps finding red splashed in every corner of her kitchen—which looks incredible, like splashes of lava. We've pasted screenshots from a speed run around the outside, so it looks like Kat's character is doing her own stop-motion speed run around our board. Across the top in big bubble letters, it reads, "Are your children eating too much sugar?" and then under that, in slightly smaller print, "Can video games provide the answer?"

My math teacher, Mrs. Brown, the first of our three judges, walks up to us with a clipboard. Her earrings—small, sparkly gemstones—are two different colors. Is she wearing them that way on purpose, or did she grab the wrong one from her dresser this morning? "Well, girls," she says, "tell me about your project."

I force myself to stop staring at her ears. "Parents often hate video games," I say, launching into our practiced spiel—rehearsed so many times, I could probably say it in my sleep. "Violence, obesity rates, all that jazz. But video games can also have many technological, academic, and other advantages. We were able to use the mechanics of a popular computer game to test the effect of sugar on speed and reaction rates." I explain the tests and the results, Kat goes through our analysis and conclusions, and we both answer questions.

After we finish, Mrs. Brown beams at me. Well, at both of us, but mostly at me. "Great project, girls," she says. "Meg, you're really pulling things together—a B on your last math test, and an excellent project. Well done."

"Why, thank you," I say, and give a little bow, which makes her laugh.

Our second judge—a stocky white teacher with black hair and a mustache—is much less pleasant. He doesn't even laugh at my joke about having to take only one person to the hospital due to a sugar overdose, and he asks questions we didn't practice, about control test placebos or something, which, fortunately, Kat answers without even blinking. But I watch his hand while we talk—he's wearing a wedding ring, which means he's probably kissed someone with that hairy-capped mouth of his—and every time he circles something on his paper, he does it on the far right side, which, I know from the marking grid we were given, is where he would circle all the ten out of tens.

Parents are allowed to come to the science fair, and apparently most people's parents don't have to work on Friday afternoons like my mom does, so while we wait for our final judge, Kat and I play a game I invent called Guess Whose Parent.

"Ha-ha, I win," I whisper to Kat when a tall black woman in a plaid suit, who's a bit darker than Mom, walks up to Marcia and tells her, "Honey, I'm going back to work now. Good job!"

"Man, I would not have guessed that," Kat whispers back. Considering how few black kids there are in here, people probably think Marcia's mom is mine. "How do you get so many of these?"

"I'm just gifted, I guess."

Marcia's mom turns around just then and smiles at us. "Hello, Meg," she says. "Is your mom here?"

I shake my head, feeling Kat's angry villain glare drilling holes in the side of it. "No," I say. "She had client meetings today that she couldn't reschedule. She made me present our project for her last night."

"Well, tell her I said hello," Marcia's mom says, and I promise that I will.

"You're just gifted, eh?" Kat hisses at me when Marcia's mom leaves.

"Okay, so I might have cheated on that one." When she doesn't stop glaring, I add, "All right, all right—you can have one penalty smack," and hold out my hand, palm down.

She doesn't even hesitate, just slaps it once, hard enough to make a small *thwack*.

"Ladies," comes a booming voice, "no violence in the school, you know that." It's Mr. Goldsmith, a science teacher I know for the same reason every girl knows him—his jawline alone, with its perfectly sloped angles meeting at his dimpled chin, deserves its own place on a magazine cover.

"Sorry," Kat mumbles at her feet as her face flushes bright red.

I just grin. "It's okay," I tell him, putting my arm around Kat's shoulder. "We're besties. And besides, I deserved that."

It's a good thing my part is first, because Kat's face is still red through my entire presentation. I throw in a couple of extra jokes to stretch my section out a little longer—Mr. Goldsmith actually laughs properly at them, which only makes him more dreamy—and by the time we get to Kat's part, she looks less flustered. Sure enough, she breezes through it, with barely a stutter.

And then we're done. I bump my hip happily into Kat's as Mr. Goldsmith walks away. We have won this. For sure.

KAT

ALL OF THESE PROJECTS ARE CRAP.

Like, seriously, folks, is this really the best you can do?

My fellow classmates have had almost seven months—*seven months!*—to whip together a thought-provoking, prizeworthy project, and the best they've come up with is a couple of projects about watering plants, one about a dung beetle, and way too many about the dangers or nondangers of microwaves.

My hands prickle with sweat as I wander up and down the aisles, searching for a beacon of light.

My mom's at the end of one aisle, chatting away in the corner to some other parent. She's stayed mostly out of my way, except to report quietly into my ear, "Your project is one of the best here. You could win this whole thing," and then sweep away, beaming.

I don't want to win, I almost said, except that Meg was standing right there beside me, and of course, she doesn't know that. Because I didn't think she needed to. Because I didn't think we would win. I mean, I didn't win last year, at my old school. Why would we win now? We're not going to.

At the start of the fourth row, a title pops out at me: "Dog Hair: Superman's Kryptonite or the Hulk's Radiation?" Clever. My heart levitates in my chest, unimpeded by the surrounding bone and flesh and sinew. I step toward it for a better look and start to read the introduction.

> Have you ever worndered if having a dog meant your allergies were getting beater or worse? We decided to test and find out once for all wether allergies are better or worse with time.

I blink, rub my eyes, reread the sentences. They're unchanged.

My heart is not floating at all, but tangled up in veins and strips of flesh. They constrict around it, tightening with every beat.

One Devil's Snare . . . two trash compactor . . .

This project isn't bad, really, in theory. But not exactly something the school is about to ship off to high-and-mighty Toronto as an example of our brilliance.

"Hey, Kat."

I turn around to find the voice's owner. Across the aisle and three poster boards down, Sunil, from my Ancient Civ class, gives me a military salute. I mentally bookmark my place in the aisle, then march toward him.

"You had your three judges already?" he asks. His partner, a nondescript brown-haired guy I don't recognize, is deep in conversation with the girls at the poster board next to them.

"Yeah. You?"

"One more to go. Hopefully soon, 'cause I've got to—well, you know . . ."

I laugh, which jostles my still-constricted heart. And my lungs. I should really continue my search. I glance up at his poster board to keep from rudely looking over my shoulder at the rows of lackluster projects. Their board is simple—sky-blue background and black borders around the text and pictures—but sharp. "Retrofitting for the Future: Energy Solutions," the heading reads.

"Energy, eh?" I ask.

He nods. "Not as glamorous as yours, but did you know that it wouldn't make any sense to upgrade everyone's cars to electric, because so many of the power plants are fueled by coal anyway? The energy savings are minimal unless the power plants themselves are upgraded to wind or water."

"Water?" I sound like a dunce. I don't know much about energy efficiency, other than that it's important. More important than sugar. And definitely more important than video games. My heart starts to disentangle itself. *Five windmills . . . six hope . . .*

"Yeah," he says. "It's not much of a thing yet, but it could be, maybe."

"Can I—?" I gesture toward the board, and he steps out of the way, allowing me to move in closer. I read the introduction. It's clear, intelligent, grammar-error free. Judging from our Ancient Civ paper, which we aced, by the way, I'm sure the rest of the board will be the same way.

My heart is fully free and racing. They could win this. They could be the ones trapped in a metal cylinder high above the earth. Is it wrong to wish that on them?

"Excuse me. Sunil? Chris?" Mr. Carter stands in the aisle with a clipboard. I back quickly away from the table as Sunil and his partner stand at attention, but I don't go far. Oral presentation is a big chunk of the mark. No matter how environmentally consequential or grammar-error free their project, they could still bungle this. I press my hands against my thighs as if pressure could stop the flow of sweat the way it stops the flow of blood.

Sunil's partner—Chris, I guess—starts the presentation. He's not as good as Meg—not a single joke to keep it interesting—but he's clear, succinct. Sunil explains the next section, confidently and smoothly, then it's back to Chris.

They're doing well. They can win this. Everything is going to be okay.

Then, in the middle of one of Chris's sentences, Mr. Carter jumps in with a question, and Chris's face pales. His mouth hangs slightly open like a feeding guppy. Sunil leans forward, ready to jump in, but Mr. Carter is looking directly at Chris, waiting for an answer from him. The silence grows.

Nine say something . . . ten say anything . . .

I can't watch. I turn and stride away. And almost walk right into a middle-aged black man.

He's wearing khaki shorts—even though it's only March—and a navy golf shirt that says *Rick's Carpentry* over the heart. His dark hair is shaved down short, but not short enough to hide the patches of gray sprouting from his temples. Whoever's dad he is, I don't recognize him, but that's not saying much, since I haven't recognized any parents so far except my own.

"Sorry," I mumble, and sidestep out of the way. Behind me, Chris is finally fumbling out an answer to Mr. Carter's question.

"You're Meg's partner, right?" the man asks. Sometimes I forget that Meg grew up in Edmonton and knows so many more people here than I do.

"Mm-hmm." *Lalalalalala,* I sing in my head, trying to drown out Chris's voice. If I can't hear him, his answer will be genius, right? Right.

"You and Meg have a really great project. Top-notch."

Great. Even other people's parents are noticing our project. Crap. Crap crap crap.

"I haven't seen Meg this focused in a while."

"Yeah, well, you know, when you get the right motivation." When I talk, I can't hear Chris still stumbling through his answer. "There's this convention for this game we like—LotS. Have you heard of it? Of course you have. Everyone's heard of it. Anyway, LotSCON is in Toronto the day after the national fair. It's never been in Canada before, which is pretty cool. Meg wants to go."

And then that's it. I'm not telling this random stranger that I'm afraid of flying or that LotSCON's sold out when I haven't even told those things to Meg. And I've got nothing else. Even when I babble, I have no idea what to say.

But it's okay. From behind me floats Sunil's rich tenor, then Chris's almost smooth bass, confident again, and musical. Whatever lapse in brain function they had, it's over. Hopefully it's enough.

"I've got to go." I sidestep around the guy for real this time and stride off down the aisle.

I left Meg on the other side of the gym, chatting with some girls from our science class, but when I round the corner, she appears out of nowhere and grabs my arm, jolting me toward her.

"Ow, Meg, be careful."

"Why were you talking to Stephen?"

"What? I wasn't—"

"I don't know why he's even here. Mom must've told him. I'm going to throttle her. Do you think if I asked the principal, she would make him leave? Everyone's going to think he's my dad."

I follow her gaze across the rows to Sunil and Chris's project. Mr. Carter has disappeared, replaced by the man in the golf shirt.

"Wait, that's your stepdad?"

"*Ex*-stepdad."

He's past Sunil and Chris's project now, meandering down the aisle. His shirt is tucked into his shorts, but the back tail has escaped and hangs lazily behind him. It never even crossed my mind that he might be here.

"Screw him," Meg says, taking my arm and turning us both away from him. "I'm not going to let him ruin my day. Did you notice that teachers keep going by to look at our project? Like, not our judges. Other ones. We are so going to win this."

If we did win this—which we won't—maybe instead of telling her, I could just suck it up and get on the plane like a normal person. The thought makes my heart drop straight through my stomach to my feet, like an airplane spiraling out of the sky. *Seventeen Amelia Earhart . . . eighteen seat belts . . . nineteen life vests . . .*

Of course, then I'd still have to tell her LotSCON's sold out. We can't win. We can't. "I don't know," I say. "There are some other good projects. Sunil's—"

"None as good as ours!"

"You haven't even looked at any—"

"I don't need to. We've got this. I just know it."

I hope she's wrong.

It doesn't take that long to find out. We head back over to the far end of the gym, where Meg chatters away to Emily and Kayla from my English class while I try not to look at any other projects. Then Mrs. Naidoo, one of the science teachers, climbs up onto the stage and takes the microphone.

As she delivers her introduction, greeting to the parents, and thank-yous, all the students and parents and teachers wind their way through the rows to clump up near the stage, as if the floor is tilted in that direction. I stick out my elbows to preserve as much room around me as possible. People are too close. If there was a stampede, we would all die for sure.

Eighty-seven suffocation . . .

Mrs. Naidoo finishes with her pleasantries, having skipped entirely over the part where she should have warned people not to cluster together so deathly close, and moves on to the actual awards announcements.

She reads out six honorable-mention projects first. Ours is not one of them. Meg grabs my arm. "LotSCON's sold out and I don't fly!" I want to scream at her. I pinch my lips together so the words don't come tumbling out.

Third place goes to some project about lasers that must have been down the final row that I never got to. Maybe that was the genius row, lined with project after project of sheer brilliance.

"Our next project," Mrs. Naidoo continues, "took a unique look at technology and nutrition. With a clever topic and top marks for presentation, second place goes to Megan Winters and Katherine Daley!"

Oh, thank goodness.

Relief floods through my body like water through a collapsed dam. Followed immediately by a wave of worry. Meg will probably need consoling.

I turn toward her. "I know you were—" I stop when I see her face. I expected disappointment, but it's worse than that. That eerie deadness is back in her eyes, like it never left. *Ha-ha, you'll never banish me. I know where to hide.*

"Are you okay?" I whisper. She doesn't say anything, just stares straight ahead, like a lifeless corpse.

Mrs. Naidoo begins announcing the winning project, drawing my gaze in her direction. First place goes to Sunil and Chris. They must have kept it together after I left.

"The winning team," Mrs. Naidoo reminds us, "will travel to Toronto in just two weeks' time to represent our school at the national science fair. Let's all give them a big round of applause!"

"I've gotta go," Meg says, not even bothering to whisper. I turn to follow her, but she's already slipped halfway through the still-clapping crowd. Before I can take more than a couple of steps, the crowd breaks up, and it's as if the room doesn't know which way to tilt, with some people pushing past me to the doors, others bumping my shoulders as they wind back down the aisles to their projects.

Some people start packing up their poster boards, and I glance down the long aisle at ours. Are we supposed to pack them up now? Is that a rule?

It doesn't matter; I'll get it later. Meg first.

I push through the crowd, to the door, and out into the hallway. But by the time I get there, Meg is long gone.

21

MEG

I'VE NEVER WALKED ALL THE WAY HOME FROM SCHOOL BEFORE, WHICH IS weird. I mean, I've been going there almost a year; you'd think I'd have walked home at least once, no matter how far away it is.

I count the buses that rumble past, losing count around five or seven or maybe fifteen, hating every single people-filled one. I'm never speaking to anyone but Legs ever again, which means I'm never speaking to anyone *ever*, because I'll never get to meet Legs. Ever. I shiver, then realize I left my coat and my backpack and my wallet at school, so I couldn't hop on one of those stupid buses even if I wanted to.

My phone rings from my back pocket, and I jab the volume button until it goes silent. *Didn't you hear me, world? I'm too germufflebuddoned to talk to anyone right now, too germufflebuddoned to even think of the right words for how I feel!* I scream the words only in my head, not out loud, because talking feels like too much—

Wait.

Wait!

I have a brilliant idea.

If Sunny and his freckle-faced partner couldn't talk, well then . . . I grab a handful of dripping snow off someone's heaping lawn and press it to the back of my neck, then gasp. It may be melting in the warmer March weather, but it's still darn cold. Which is good. I'll get sick, then I'll breathe all over their faces, then they'll get sick and will get whatever that thing's called where they can't talk, then they won't be able to go and the second-place winners will get to go, which means Kat and I will get to go, except I guess then I'd be sick, too, so . . . never mind.

I drop the snow back on the ground, rub the cold out of my neck.

Still, maybe there's another way. I can't let one stupid project stand in the way of meeting LumberLegs—the only person in the world worth talking to.

Maybe allergies? They've got to be allergic to something. Feeding them accidental peanuts would be a lot easier than breathing all over their pimply faces anyway. To get that close, I'd probably have to try to make out with them, and I mean, freckle-face is not bad looking for a white guy, but Sunny has that big nose that juts out of his face like a sword. Except swords don't usually stick out of faces. Well, maybe if there's just been a battle, but then he'd be lying dead on the dirty ground, in which case, I really don't want to make out with him. And besides, I'm not making out with anyone but LumberLegs anyway.

I'm still thinking of allergies when I finally stomp up our front steps. "Mom," I shout, as I open the front door, "do we have any—"

He's in our front hallway. Dad. I mean, Stephen-the-Leaver. Stupid Stephen-the-Leaver in those stupid khaki shorts that he's apparently still wearing even though I told him years ago that they look ridiculous.

Didn't you hear me, world? I said I didn't want to talk to anyone but LumberLegs. Stephen-the-Leaver is definitely not LumberLegs.

"What the hell are you doing here?" I ask as I kick off my soaking-wet Converses. It's not a halfling day. He shouldn't be here. "And what the hell were you doing at my school?"

He sighs and runs his hand over his fade. "Don't swear, please."

"You can't tell me not to swear. You're not my dad." Not any-more. I ignore his disgruntled face and push past him toward the stairs. Disgruntled is a great word. I should use it more often. I wonder if you can be just gruntled. I should get a baby pig as a pet and call it Gruntle.

"Meg! Wait! I—your mom said you bought tickets to LotSCON already. On her credit card." There's a touch of amusement in his otherwise serious voice, like he thinks it's hilarious that I bought tickets to something that of course I had no hope of actually getting to. Because plane tickets cost approximately one million dollars. And because of course I'd never win something school-related. And I'm obviously not actually going to poison anyone with peanuts. Which means I'm not going.

"Yeah, so what?" I start up the stairs and don't look back. "I already did my time for that. Ask Mom."

"So I want to take you."

I pause, midstep, the water in my socks probably seeping into the carpet. "Take me where?" I don't turn around.

"To LotSCON. In Toronto. I've got enough points to fly us both out. I thought we could make a weekend of it. You could even take the Friday off school. Nolan's always talking about that You-Tuber you like—LumberLegs, right? I think he's going to be there."

I spin around to face him. "Let me get this straight: you want to go to LotSCON with me. For an entire weekend." *When you haven't spent any time with me for months and months. And months.*

He runs his hand over his bristly head again. "Yes, like those trips we used to take. We don't have to spend the whole time together. I could skip all the panels or events or whatever else you do at these things, and we could just have supper together each evening or something."

I don't know why he looks so hopeful. He doesn't want me. He hasn't even tried to call me for months.

Except I blocked him.

But whether he's been calling or not doesn't matter. If he wanted me in his life, he should have said that to the judge, should have said that to me. And he didn't. He said I wasn't his. I should just storm off upstairs and never speak to him again.

But it's LotSCON.

And I don't turn down gifts from Stephen-the-Leaver. Hating him doesn't mean I should deprive myself. Like with the tablet he gave me for Christmas last year. Or my skateboard.

For some reason, though, this feels more like the stuffed polar bear. I clench my fists just thinking of that stupid bear.

But—LotSCON. I can't turn down LotSCON. I just can't. Not when Legs'll be there.

"I want my own room," I say.

"Of course," he says immediately, like he's already thought of that.

"And Kat gets to come."

His dark eyebrows dip at that one.

"Kat gets to come or I don't go," I say, before he can protest.

Creases spread out across his forehead. "Kat your science partner?"

"Kat my best friend."

He hesitates. "She'll have to pay for her own flight."

"Fine," I say. Some tension flies away out of my shoulders. If Kat comes with me, that changes everything. "But if you even try to talk to me throughout the weekend, I'll scream as loudly as I can for the police."

"Meg!" Mom says, popping her head out of the kitchen. I don't know what she's been doing in there all this time. Probably Stephen-the-Leaver begged her for a few minutes alone with me, and she's finally run out of ways to say no.

I turn and start up the stairs again, taking them two at a time. "Fine, no police yell," I say over my shoulder. "But I want a Lumber-Legs T-shirt." And then I'm at the top of the stairs and down the hall and in my room, where I slam the door behind me and sink onto the floor, leaning uncomfortably against my bed frame.

I run my fingers over the carpet, feeling its fuzzy softness and a tiny bit of stickiness where I must have spilled something and never cleaned it up.

LotSCON.

I am going to LotSCON.

I feel like I just ate bacon.

Except the bacon came from Gruntle the pig.

I'm sorry, Gruntle.

I lean forward and wiggle my phone out of my back pocket. Time to call Kat and tell her the good news.

KAT

"MEG! ARE YOU OKAY? I'VE BEEN CALLING YOU NONSTOP!" I CLAMP MY PHONE in place with my shoulder and disentangle myself from my computer keyboard, which had been balancing on my lap.

"Oh my gosh, guess what?" she says, ignoring my question. "We're going to LotSCON!"

My stomach twists. "Did you poison Sunil or something?" That's totally something she would think of.

"What? No. That's bananas. Stephen is taking us." Her voice is a few decibels too high-pitched, like she's acting out the happy ending of a children's TV show.

"Your stepdad?" She can't be right about this. She doesn't even talk to him.

"*Ex*-stepdad."

"But you hate him."

"Doesn't mean he can't fly us across the country. Would you refuse to accept a million dollars from Osama bin Laden just because he's Osama bin Laden?"

"He died. Years ago. But yes, I would."

"Shut up. The point is we're going to LotSCON. To see Legs!"

I think she means it. I think Stephen-the-Leaver has actually offered to take us. My stomach doesn't know whether to twist or untwist. Because here's the thing: Meg hasn't figured out some harebrained way to convince the school to send us to the fair, so I still don't have to fly or even refuse to fly. Which is a relief. But here's the other thing: now I have to tell Meg about the sold-out tickets.

One it's over . . . two bad news . . .

"Meg . . ." I pause, preparing myself to rip off the Band-Aid. *I'm sorry, Meg.* "They're sold out. LotSCON. The tickets are all gone."

"Dude, I bought us tickets like a million years ago. Didn't I tell you? I'm sure I told you!"

"I—what? No, you definitely didn't tell me! You—" I break off as bile rises in my throat. I thought I was home free. How am I supposed to explain to Meg that I don't fly—that I never planned on flying? There's got to be another way out of this.

"Oh, well, I'm telling you now then. I have a ticket for you! Surprise! And you can stay in my hotel room, so all you have to pay for is the flight."

Pay for the flight. That's my answer. There's no way I can afford a ticket myself, so I'll have to ask Mom, and she'll say no, and then it won't be my fault.

Before I can say anything, Meg snaps, "Why aren't you excited about this? You're supposed to be excited about this!"

"Sorry, I just—I'll have to ask my parents." They'll say no. They have to. But what if they don't? *Seven metal death trap . . . eight defying gravity . . .*

There's a long pause. Then, "Okay." She sighs. "Just let me know as soon as you can. We have to book flights."

After she hangs up, her words hang in the air. *We have to book flights.* My chest tightens like Hulk is holding it in a death grip.

Twelve green monster . . . thirteen aviation . . .

Would it be so bad to go?

Because here's the thing: it's not LotSCON that I'm scared of. I mean, I don't love the idea of being surrounded by thousands of people. But it wouldn't just be people, it'd be thousands of video-game nerds, which makes it mostly okay.

And Dan will be there. Hulk tightens his grip on my chest. But Meg would be there, too. With me. Hulk's grip loosens a little.

But here's the other thing: I don't fly. I just don't.

I pull up a map app on my phone and type in Toronto. Thirty-three hours by car. So that's not happening. One hundred and ninety-two hours by bike. Definitely not happening.

Three hours and thirty-five minutes by plane.

Three hours and thirty-five minutes hovering thousands of feet above the earth.

Three hours and thirty-five minutes in a metal box I can't escape.

I love LotS, but I don't love it that much.

Mom will give me an out. She's my only hope.

I close the map app, hop off the chair, and rush upstairs. Mom's rolling out a pie crust in the kitchen. She swipes a loose hair back, leaving a streak of flour across her face. Then she sees me and smiles. "I'm making coconut cream pie. Your favorite. I thought we'd celebrate your win."

"It was just second place," I say.

"And you should be very proud of that." She beams at me.

She's not going to say no. She's in too good of a mood. She'd probably give me anything I asked for.

Including an excuse. An excuse that would allow me to lie to Meg. Lie. To Meg. Is that what I've already been doing?

Mom stops rolling and glances at her pie dish, then at me. "Did you want something, love?"

If I ask Mom for an excuse, I'll be asking her to lie to Meg, too. I can't ask her that. I bite my lip. "Just . . . can I go over to Meg's? Just for a little bit. I'll be home for supper."

"Of course, sweetheart," Mom says cheerily, and I know that not asking her was the right choice.

Meg's mom answers the door. "Kat! Congratulations on second place!"

"Thank you. Is Meg home?"

Her forehead crinkles. "She's downstairs. Head on down."

My heart thumps with every step down the stairs.

Meg's lying on the concrete floor, skateboard across her stomach like a plank.

"Hi," I say as I reach the bottom step.

She hops to her feet, skateboard thudding against the ground. "What'd they say? They said yes, right?"

She looks so hopeful. A frantic sort of hopeful.

I take a deep breath, letting the air fill my lungs and stretch them into my stomach. Ease it back out again. I could still lie to her. Tell her they said no. Make it their fault, not mine.

But of course, I wouldn't. Couldn't. I don't lie to Meg. I

should have told her a long time ago. "I . . . I didn't ask."

"Why not? Is it the money? I'm pretty sure I can get Stephen-the-Leaver to pay for it. He—"

"Meg, no. It's not that." I just have to tell her. *One gravity . . . two fiery death . . .* "It's the planes, okay? Flying freaks me out. All that metal just hovering in the air. Just thinking about it gives me an ulcer. I don't think I can do it. I know I can't do it."

She blinks at me for a long moment, and I wait for the deadness to enter her eyes. But they don't die, just droop a little, like her shoulders. She tugs at one of her curls. "Is this like the party?" she asks.

I nod.

She gives her skateboard a little absentminded kick, and it rolls across the room, bouncing off the couch. "Okay," she says. "You have to help me decide what to wear, though."

That's all it takes, apparently. But I shouldn't be surprised. Meg gets me. And she'll be fine on her own, won't she? She's always fine on her own. I wait for the tension in my shoulders to relax, but it doesn't. "So you're still going to go?" I ask. "With Stephen?"

"Look, it's not like I've never spent time with him before. We've gone loads of places together. Of course, all of those times we were talking, and this time I'm not talking to him for even a second." She follows the skateboard across the room and collapses onto the couch. "And yeah, there are like seven billion people on the earth I'd rather go with than him, but seven billion people aren't offering, are they? So I'm going with him, and I'm going to meet LumberLegs, and it is going to be magical."

"Well, good," is all I can think to say. I walk across the room and settle onto the couch beside her.

She rolls the skateboard back and forth with her foot. "Because I'm going to date LumberLegs, you know."

"I know," I say.

She stops rolling the board. "Hey, what were you going to do if we won?"

I shrug. "I was just hoping we wouldn't." It's surprisingly easy to admit, though I really shouldn't be surprised. Meg's my best friend. Of course I can tell her anything.

"You worked really hard, though," she says.

Not as hard as you, I think, and guilt ripples through me like a shiver. Meg will be fine, though. Meg is always fine.

"Yeah, well, I still wanted an A," I say.

Meg laughs. It's not a dead laugh, but it's not entirely alive, either.

22

MY BLUE POLKA-DOT SHIRT HAS ARMPIT STAINS. I'VE NEVER NOTICED THAT before. Are they recent, or have I accidentally worn it this way? I yank it off and toss it at the garbage can. It hits the rim and slides down to the floor.

I've had two whole weeks to figure out what to wear, but nothing says quite what I want it to, which is, "LumberLegs! See how hot and awesome I am? Now, ask me on a date." And since LumberLegs announced he's doing a whole Q & A and signing on Friday night to kick the convention off, and since Friday night is *tomorrow*, I need to conjure up a brilliant outfit stat.

As I stare into my stripped-bare closet, there's a knock on the door. "Come in!" I shout.

The door creaks open, then immediately slams shut. "Meg!" Kat's muffled voice floats in from behind it. "Put some clothes on! Honestly, I thought you said I could come in."

I march over to the door and yank it open. "It's not like I'm naked. I'm wearing underwear. Just pretend it's a bathing suit and get in here. Can't you see I'm in distress?"

Kat steps inside, not looking at me. She leans against the wall and surveys the heaps of clothes—on my bed, on my chair, on the floor. "Dude," she says, "what's wrong with what I told you to wear?"

"What did you tell me to wear?"

She steps over a pair of leopard-print tights and starts weeding through the pile on the bed, laying the odd item over her arm like a store clerk. When she finishes with the bed and starts searching the floor, I climb onto the bed and push the heap to the end to use as a pillow. Something sharp pokes my arm, and I pull out a belt and throw it on the floor.

Kat should be packing her bags too, to come with me, but if she can't, she can't. I don't have it in me to fight it.

After an eternity, Kat hands me a small bundle. I spread the items across my lap, one by one. Short patterned skirt. My Pizza and Winglings T-shirt, with its cartoon of winglings sharing a pizza. Plain navy leggings. Sweater blazer.

"Geek chic," she says.

"No leggings," I say, tossing them on the floor. "I have to show off my legs. But yeah, it's good otherwise. Thanks." It's perfect, really. Sexy in a commitment, long-term-relationship, I-want-to-play-LotS-with-this-girl kind of way.

She settles onto the bed beside me, close enough that her shoulder bumps into mine. Apparently, she's gotten over the fact that I'm still not wearing any clothes. She takes the outfit from my lap and folds each piece neatly. "Are you okay?" she asks.

"Okay?" I stand up. "I'm amazing. Tomorrow I'm going to meet LumberLegs and he's going to ask me on a date and then we're going to live happily ever after." I grab a random shirt from the floor and pull it over my head.

"Okay, but what if it doesn't go that way?"

I grab a pair of jeans off the floor. "It has to. I have it all planned out. Right after the Q & A, he has an autograph signing. I'll be one of the first ones to show up at his table, and I'll remind him about the turtle email he sent me, and he'll remember me, and when he does, we'll chat for a bit, and then I'll tell him that LotS joke I made up, the one about the wereboar, except I'll stop just short of the punch line and he'll be all like, 'What? What did the wereboar say?' and I'll be like, 'Call me later if you want to know,' and then I'll leave him my number and slip away, and the joke—and my charm and sexiness, of course—will play through his head all evening so he'll have to come find me later, and I'll tell him, and he'll laugh really hard in that hyena way he does, and then we'll leave together. Or something like that."

"Good plan," she says, then throws me a pair of socks. I wasn't even going to bother with socks, except now that I'm holding them, my feet do feel a little cold. I start to pull them on. "Hey, you don't actually—" Kat says, then breaks off, patting the neat pile of clothes in her lap a couple of times before continuing. "I mean, this is just like your LumberLegs wedding fantasy, right?"

I laugh. Turquoise dresses, beach in Maui, photos at sunset— it's going to be amazing! "Exactly like that," I say.

"Okay, just checking. Well, sounds romantic," she says. She strides to the corner of the room and places the folded stack of clothes in the suitcase I've thrown open. Then she starts plucking a few other things off the floor—my favorite pair of jeans, a knit sweater, pajamas—and folds them into the suitcase. "Have you packed underwear?"

I yank open a drawer, grab a random handful of undies, and drop them into the suitcase. "Done. Now what poster should I take?"

"You're taking a poster?"

"Yeah, for Legs to sign."

"Won't there be things there for him to sign? Like postcards and stuff?"

I shrug. "I'm not risking it. Besides, getting him to sign one of my posters is cooler. So which one?"

Kat looks around at my walls, then points to the one above my bed with Legs's cartoony head and "BE AWESOME" in big bubble letters.

"That is the correct choice," I say, then hop up onto my bed and pull it carefully off the wall.

"How are you going to pack it?" she asks.

Lizard balls. I didn't think of that. "Maybe if I roll it . . ."

"Wait here." Kat hops off the bed and disappears out the door. Her footsteps clomp down the stairs, fade away, then clomp back up again. When she returns, her hands are full of cardboard, probably from our recycling bin in the kitchen.

As I roll up the poster, Kat rolls up some cardboard. It takes a few tries to find a piece that's rollable, but once she does and secures it with some tape, I hand the poster to her, and she slides it into the cardboard shell. "Perfect," she says, handing it back to me.

"Awesome," I say, then give the thing a quick hug before dropping it into my suitcase.

When I look up, Kat's studying me. "Are you sure you're okay?" she asks.

She's been asking that since the science fair. It's starting to drive me bananas. I got another B on my last math test, the snow has melted enough that I can skateboard outside, Mom is so happy about my math marks and the A+ on our science project that she's letting me miss an entire day of school to fly to LotSCON, and tomorrow I start dating LumberLegs. How could I be anything but okay?

I scrunch my face up at her.

"Okay, okay," she says. "Sorry. I'll stop asking. Just have fun tomorrow, okay?"

"Well, duh," I say.

．　．　．

When Stephen comes to pick me up the next morning, I leave my suitcase on the porch for him to carry—screw feminism; he's not getting away with less work—and climb into the backseat of his car. It smells like sweat and wood shavings, just like it always used to. I roll down the window and stick my nose out into the wet air.

Stephen lowers my suitcase into the trunk, then slams it shut. Mom doesn't have to be at her office until eleven, so she's on the sidewalk to see us off. She hands a folded sheet of paper to Stephen, which he sticks into the front pocket of his shorts, and then waves at me. I duck my head back into the car.

When Stephen climbs into the driver's seat, I expect him to tell me to get into the empty front seat, but he doesn't—just turns on the car and pulls out of the driveway. He doesn't say anything at all, except, "Got your passport?" Which I do. Mom made me check before I went out the door.

He flicks on the radio to a station I wish I hated, and some mellow song, which I know all the words to but can't remember who sings it, bursts out of the speakers behind my head. He taps his fingers on the steering wheel, not quite to the beat. His hairy dad-legs stick out from his khaki shorts. In this moment, I could almost forgive him.

"What did my mom give you?"

He turns the radio down. "What?"

"The paper. She handed you a paper."

"Oh, just a consent form. To make sure you can travel with me."

Right. Because he gave up all rights to me. "Turn the music back up, please," I say. Then I don't say a single word to him for the rest of the drive, the check-in at the airport, or the entire flight.

KAT

I WISH MEG WOULD TEXT ME, JUST ONCE, TO LET ME KNOW SHE'S OKAY. But of course, I don't really want her to text me, because she's on a plane and it's possible cell phones really do interfere with the plane's instruments, and when you're defying gravity and sitting in a heap of metal thousands of feet above the earth, there are some things you don't take chances on.

"Are you practicing to be in the Queen's Guard?" Granddad's question floats through the kitchen door behind me.

Then Mom's: "Shouldn't you be in school? I thought you didn't get out until two on early-dismissal days."

I've been standing, frozen, at the kitchen table, one hand resting on my math textbook, the other clenching my message-less phone, for I'm not sure how long. Five minutes? Ten?

I turn around. Mom and Granddad stare at me from the kitchen door. I didn't even hear them come in. I swear Granddad used to be taller than Mom, but hunched over his cane, he's more than a foot shorter. Behind him, Mom holds out one arm as if ready to catch him if he falls.

"English teacher didn't show up for class," I explain. "So I came home."

Last time that happened, in Ontario, I sat in the empty classroom for the entire period, working on my homework and worrying about whether the teacher was in a car accident or had a heart attack or hit her head and was wandering around somewhere with amnesia. This time, I just got up and left with everyone else.

Granddad shuffles into the room. He has managed to get movement back in his left leg after the stroke, but the foot still drags a little, like it's full of rocks nobody's thought to remove.

"Well, that's great," Mom says. "You can watch your granddad while I go out and run a few errands."

"I don't need a babysitter," he says as he inches across the room.

"I know, Dad. That's not what I meant." She picks up a huge stack of papers—a textbook proof, probably—from the kitchen counter. "I'll be home in time for supper. Pizza okay?"

I nod, and Granddad just grunts, and then she's gone.

Despite his foot full of rocks, Granddad has made it over to the kitchen table. He pulls out a chair and lowers himself into it. He sets his hands on the table, causing his bony shoulders to rise up as if his saggy-skinned turtle neck is receding back into its turtle shell.

"So, why the long face?" he asks.

"I don't—"

"You look worried. Is it school? Math test? Boys?" He says all three with a straight face, though his eyes do twinkle just a little at the last one.

I unclench my fingers and set my phone down on the table. "It's Meg, I guess." I can't think of any reason not to tell him.

"Your short, chatty friend?" he asks, as if I have oodles of friends over all the time and he can't keep them straight, though of course, he knows exactly who she is. "She has spunk. I like her."

I nod. Clench, then unclench my fists again.

"So, what's the problem?" Granddad asks.

Where do I even start? How do I explain why it worries me that the science project made her so manic about school that she actually started passing? Or that she still hasn't told me why she and Grayson broke up? Or that she hasn't spoken to her ex-stepdad for months but went on a trip with him anyways? Or that sometimes, when she talks about dating LumberLegs, I think she might not be joking?

"I don't know," I say. "It's like—it's like she's standing on the edge of a cliff, ready to leap and soar and show off her bright, feathery wings. Except she doesn't have wings. She just has arms. And I can't tell her that. How am I supposed to tell her she doesn't have wings?"

Granddad nods his turtle head, as if my rambling actually makes sense. "But if you don't tell her . . ."

"She plummets to her death." I sigh and pull out a chair,

leaning on the seat with one knee.

Granddad's forehead creases. "This is just a metaphor, right? Meg's not actually leaping? Or dying?"

"Right."

"Great. I love metaphors."

I straighten my phone and my textbook so they're perfectly aligned. "So, what should I do?"

He taps the fingers of his good hand on the table. "Well, you're going to have to tell her. About the wings, don't you think? Or maybe not even about the wings. Just whatever she needs to hear to keep from jumping."

I settle fully into the chair, slumping against its hard back. "That's the problem. I think she already jumped."

Granddad massages his deadened left hand with his right one. I wonder, if I took his left hand between my own, would he feel it? He says it's getting better, but I'm not sure what that means. He looks up at me, straight on, his blue eyes shining.

"Well, then—can you catch her?"

Up in my room, I lean against the icy window, staring blankly out at the straggling piles of snow that just won't go away. Granddad's words echo in my ears, and ideas flutter through my head before realizing that they, too, lack wings and can only plummet and die.

Meg is the ideas person. The brainstormer. She is cantaloupe thrown from roofs and speed runs for science. I am questionnaires and control factors.

Maybe I can buy her a nice card. Or bake a cake. Maybe a sleepover when she gets back late Sunday night, even though it'll be a school night?

I wander over to my bed and settle onto it. Pick up Meg's purple button—the one from the hospital—off my nightstand and twirl it between my fingers. Run my thumb over its waxy smoothness. Clutch it tightly in my fist, the way I did when Meg shoved me through that hospital door. When I walked through that hospital door.

I bolt to my feet and down the stairs. "Granddad!" I shout. "Granddad!"

I know what I have to do.

23

---------------------------------- MEG ----------------------------------

BY THE TIME OUR PLANE LANDS, MY BRAIN LITERALLY HURTS FROM concentrating on not talking, so when our hotel shuttle arrives at the airport, I climb into the front seat and start chatting with the shuttle driver. He has a heavy accent and I only understand about half of what he says—something about his son or maybe the sun or maybe he got shunned and that's why he moved here—but he listens while I tell him that this was my first time flying and the plane was smaller than I expected—no middle row like you see in the movies—and those recliner seats really don't recline much, and they asked me to choose between cookies and pretzels, but apparently I stumbled upon a magical secret, because when I said I wanted both, I got both.

When we arrive at the hotel, I've gotten it all out of my system, and I manage to return to stony silence while Stephen-the-Leaver checks us in, then carries our luggage up to our rooms. When he suggests the hotel restaurant for supper, I just shrug.

At the restaurant, I hide behind my menu and watch the couple at the next table. They hold hands right up until their food comes, and then she trades half her chicken for part of his steak. After tonight, that's going to be me and LumberLegs. Except I'm ordering the steak, because *steak*.

After we place our order, the waiter takes away our menus, and with nothing to hide behind any longer, Stephen-the-Leaver and I are forced to stare at each other. His deep-brown face is the same as it always was, and yet it's different. His dark hair's dotted with gray at the temples, and there are extra creases around his eyes. Probably laugh lines now that he doesn't have to worry about raising a teenager anymore. At least not until Nolan and Kenzie grow up, which, let's be honest, is probably never going to happen.

I wonder what other people think of us sitting here, both with the same shade of skin. We probably just look like a dad and his kid, but we're not. We're so very not.

"So, how's school?" Stephen-the-Leaver asks.

"That's it?!" I want to yell at him. "You've had this entire day of silence to think of an interesting, probing question about my life, and that's the best you can come up with?!" Except I guess he doesn't actually care about my life, not anymore. Maybe not ever.

"Fine," I say. I'm not letting him ruin my evening. Tonight, I meet LumberLegs and my happily ever after starts. I don't need Grayson or Stephen or any guy at all except LumberLegs.

"Meg, I don't want to push this," he says, pausing to chew on the insides of his cheeks like he always used to do whenever we kids were driving him bananas. "I'm not going to force you to spend every minute with me. The convention center is connected to the hotel, and I'm not going to follow you about, as long as you don't leave the property and you're back in your room by eleven. Okay?"

I shrug. "That's fine." By tomorrow, LumberLegs and I will probably have eloped anyways, and I'll be long gone.

We spend the rest of the meal in silence. When I finish scarfing down my macaroni—because I had a brain fart while ordering and chose the three-cheese macaroni over a delicious steak—I stand up. "I'm going to the LumberLegs Q & A tonight," I say. "I have to get ready."

He nods, pulls out his wallet, and hands me two twenties. "You can't buy my love, mister," I want to say. Instead, I snatch them from his hand.

"Remember, be back in your room by eleven," he says, which is my cue to leave.

It takes me forever to get ready, because my curls puff out in Ontario's wetter air and I have to rake in way more styler than usual. Plus, my shirt is wrinkled and there's no ironing board, only an iron, so I have to lug a chair over to the outlet and iron on that. By the time I get to the LumberLegs thing, carrying my Legs poster in its cardboard shell, I'm only half an hour early, and the line winds all the way out of the building and partway around the block.

Maybe a tenth of the people in line are in costume. Some are simple—purchased LotS swords, or elf ears and a cloak—but there's one guy who's gone full dragonlord, with scaly gold skin, retractable wings, and red armor painted with a black shadow-dragon. "Dude, that looks amazing," I say to him as I pass, and he does a dance that's a perfect imitation of the dance Sythlight's dragonlord does in game.

I tried texting Syth, but he won't be at the con until tomorrow, so I take my place in line alone.

A white girl ahead of me in line by about twenty people is wearing the same shirt as me, but she's just wearing jeans, while I have this super-adorable skirt and my silky-smooth legs. The snow's all melted here, but a not-very-springlike wind zips down the street, commanding an army of goose bumps on my legs to stand at attention. But that doesn't matter, because by the time I talk to Legs after the Q & A, I'll be inside, warm, cozy, and de-goose-bumped.

Kat printed my ticket and pinned it to the inside of my sweater blazer pocket so I wouldn't lose it—"What if I lose my sweater blazer?" I asked her, but she ignored me—so when a guy comes along the line to collect tickets, I rip it out and hand it to him, exchanging it for a wristband.

Not long after that, they open the doors and the line starts moving forward, thank Her Majesty the Queen, because I didn't bring a coat and I'm pretty sure the goose bumps have spread to my arms and maybe even my stomach.

The doors open into the front of the room, beside the make-shift stage. The front several rows are already filling, but I spot a single seat in the third row that's empty, which is the one upside of being here all by myself. I beeline toward it, holding my poster tube close to me so it doesn't get crushed, weaving around a whole pack of white girls all wearing matching LumberLegs T-shirts. Then stop.

"Hey, watch it," says someone behind me, and I sidestep out of their way. But not into the row. Because Grayson is sitting next to the empty seat.

Not Grayson, obviously.

Just someone who looks kind of like him, with the same shaggy brown hair, same eyebrows, same slouchy way of sitting. He looks up, and he really doesn't look like Grayson at all— different nose, different eyes, different scrunch to his forehead— but all I can think of is Grayson's bare chest against mine, his hand on my leg, his breath in my hair.

I leave the empty seat and let the crowd push me farther back into the room, where I file into a row somewhere in the middle and plop into a seat right behind a guy who's a million feet taller than me. Crap on a stick. But the rows behind me are already filling in, and I'm not going to move and risk ending up way at the back. I slip off my shoes and tuck my feet under my butt on the chair, raising myself by a few inches. Thank goodness there's a stage, or even my natural booster seat wouldn't be enough.

I set just one end of my Legs poster tube on the floor, leaning the other against the chair, resting my hand on the top so I won't lose it.

There're still a few minutes before the Q & A is supposed to start. I could text Kat, but it seems unfair to remind her that she's not here for this, the night I meet my future husband in person for the first time.

I turn to the girl next to me. She's white, too. I thought there might be more black girls here, but so far every girl I've seen has been white or Asian—though now that I'm specifically looking, I spot a couple. "What's your favorite Legs video?" I ask the girl.

She blinks at me through her heavy black eyelashes, like either she's surprised I'm talking to her or she's put on so much mascara she can't see properly. She shrugs. "I'm just here because of him." She points to the guy next to her, who's looking at the con schedule on his phone, then turns away from me and stares at the phone, too, as if she finds it the most fascinating thing in the world, even though obviously she doesn't.

The guy on my other side is talking animatedly to his friends. They're all wearing track pants and look to be about twelve years old.

It's fine, though. I need to get in the autograph line as quickly as possible after Legs is done, and I can't have anyone distracting me.

I glance at my phone again and search through my email folder for the email Legs sent me. Sent *me*.

And then applause starts scattering through the room. I shove my phone into my sweater blazer pocket and sit up as tall as I can, leaning around the head of the guy in front of me.

Where is he?

The stage is still empty. And he's not at either of the entrance doors. He doesn't seem to be anywhere.

How did they know to clap? Did someone say something? Did I miss it? More and more people start clapping, and the noise fills the room like thunder, like a roaring waterfall, like the badlands tearing open into a rift. I join in, clapping as loud as I can. I should have brought a drum. With a drum, I could be the loudest. Louder than all these fools. Because everyone's clapping now. Clapping and leaning eagerly forward in their seats.

And then he's there. On the stage. Legs is on the stage! He scampers—no, scatters . . . no, saunters—across the stage to the table and mic in the center. He's tall and broad-shouldered and even more muscular than he looks in his vlogs, and his black hair is slicked back in an almost *Grease*-like puff. And I am going to hear his jokes and banter and advice *in person*.

"Woo, LumberLegs!" I shout. Mascara girl glances at me through her curtain of blackness, but I don't even care. LumberLegs is here. I am here. We're together in the same room.

As the applause finally dies down, LumberLegs leans toward the mic and says something. Someone in the front row laughs, but no one else does because none of us can hear him.

"No sound!" shouts someone off to the side.

"Fix the mic!" shouts someone else.

Even from my place a dozen rows back, I can see Legs's face turn bright red as he reaches forward and fumbles with the mic. Someone wearing a LotSCON polo shirt scurries across the stage, and they fiddle with it together.

An earsplitting screech echoes through the room as the microphone comes on, and everyone groans. The LotSCON staff member taps it, and the *thud thud* echoes through the room, so he falls back and LumberLegs tries again.

"Hi . . . I'm LumberLegs . . . I . . . play video games. For YouTube. On YouTube." He fiddles with the drawstring on his hoodie. He seems uncomfortable, like the technical problems made him forget what he was going to say, or like he's used to talking to people through a camera and seeing them in person is frightening, or like he's actually an alien who's been warped into LumberLegs's body and told he has to do this event even though he hates public speaking.

Whatever the reason, he doesn't look like the usual, confident Legs he is on camera. As his pause stretches into a full stop, discomfort ripples through the whole room, making people shift in their seats or play with their hair or fidget with their costumes.

Legs can feel it, I can tell. I want to hug him.

Instead, I cup my hands around my mouth and shout as loudly as I can, "To the rift!"

For a terribly long moment, the room is so silent, I can hear my words echoing off the concrete walls. But then a chorus of voices in the front shouts it out, too. "To the rift!" And then half the room is shouting it, and everyone is laughing, and Legs is rolling his eyes and saying, "You guys!" But his shoulders relax, and as his eyes roam over the crowd he's grinning, and then for just a moment he's grinning right at me.

He knows that it was me. Knows that I fixed it. We're a team now. No more stupid Grayson—third row look-alike or real thing. It's me and Legs forever.

And then he goes into his material, talking about how he got into YouTubing, how his Speed Run Fails videos went viral and propelled both him and the speed runs mod into fame, how his life has changed because of it—mostly for the better. People laugh a lot, because now that he's gotten over his initial nerves, he's just as funny in person as he is online. He's just as perfect in person as he is online.

Partway through, Legs announces that he's going to answer some questions, and I sit up, ready to hear the question I submitted to the Q & A's online form about his ideal first date. I mean, it would be with me, obviously, but I want to know what we'll *do*.

He starts off answering a bunch of questions I already know the answer to, since I've watched pretty much every one of his videos—multiple times. Which I get. Not everyone's as big a fan as me, so it makes sense to start with the basics. What did he do before YouTube? Cooking school. What's his most embarrassing moment? Vomiting in front of his crush in grade six.

Then a couple of silly ones he's never answered before. Like what LotS baddie he'd be in real life: filthworm. Or where he'd live if he could live anywhere: Mars.

He has to be getting to mine soon.

But the next question asks for advice about how to decide what to do with your life. He rambles a bit about education and dreams and passion. "So just figure out what you're passionate about. Something you can do because you love it, not because you expect someone to pay you for it," Legs concludes. "Oh, and be awesome."

And then he stands and says, "Thanks, everyone!" and then everyone's standing and applauding, and Legs is walking off the stage, and my question hasn't been answered, but LotSCON shirt guy is explaining that autographs will happen out in the hallway where they have a table set up, and I have to get there first, so I don't have time to worry about what it means that he didn't answer mine. I grab my poster and dart through the crowd, past mascara girl and her boyfriend, around the dragonlord, through a group of kids who are way too young to appreciate LumberLegs's brilliance, and into the hallway.

Where the line is already stretching down the hall.

Lizard balls. I thought I was quick.

Once again, I take my place at the end of the line. I shift from foot to foot as I wait, my only encouragement the thought that Legs is probably finding this line just as boring as I am—until he meets me, of course.

I take my poster out of its cardboard sleeve so it's ready to go. I watch more people in costume go by. An elf. Another dragonlord. A surprisingly accurate mutant rabbit.

And then, suddenly, I'm at the front of the line, and Legs is there with his perfect jaw and shining eyes. I wait for him to say that he recognizes me, but he probably doesn't want to make the people behind me feel left out, because all he says is, "Hi."

"Hi," I say. "I'm Meg. I'm your biggest fan. You might think it's one of these other dweebs, but it's not, it's me."

His sharp green eyes meet mine, and he grins his handsome grin, and for one long, perfect moment, my insides are melting and everything in the world is exactly as it should be.

Then he frowns, tiredly, reaches out to take my poster, and unfurls it onto the table just enough to reveal a small place to write. "What did you say your name was?" he asks without looking at me.

"Meg. With the turtle? I didn't put him out in the snow, don't worry." Legs nods without looking at me and lifts his Sharpie. "And I just love your Speed Run Fails series." I'm speaking so quickly it comes out as *speedrnfls*. "I practically pee myself laughing every time I watch it."

He scribbles something on the poster, then rolls it back up and hands it to me. "I'm glad you enjoy them. I hope you have a good evening." His gaze barely even pauses on my face before it shifts to the next person in line.

"Wait, don't you remember—" I start to say, but the people behind me in line have already pushed forward and are telling Legs their names.

I should tell him my joke. I would tell him my joke if he'd just look up at me again. But he doesn't. Doesn't glance my way even once.

That's it. My time with him is done. He's on to the next fan. And then the next. I scan down the line, which has grown at least ten times longer. There are so many of them. With Legs's face right in front of mine on my laptop or TV screen, it always feels like it's just me and him, but it's not. It's me and him and his millions of other fans.

I step away from the table, fading into the crowd, just another fangirl among hundreds of other fangirls. Unless—I glance down at the poster in my hand. Did he give me his number? I unfurl the thin paper and find his Sharpie scrawl, hoping for numbers. A phone number.

There are no numbers. Of course there are no numbers.

Instead, right below the bubble-lettered "BE AWESOME," he's written:

Meg,
Be Awesome.
—Legs

Be awesome. Be. Awesome. How am I supposed to be awesome when I can't even be noticed?

I want out of here. I push my way out of the crowd to the nearest door, then shove it open and burst out of the place.

I expect to step into icy winds and streetlights and passing cars, but the exit spits me out into a dingy, darkened hallway. The door closes behind me, muffling but not muting the happy chatter of all the stupid LumberLegs fans.

My phone reads 9:52. I'd planned to stay out past eleven just to tick Stephen off. I'd planned to stay out past eleven with Lumber-Legs. Maybe everyone here had the exact same plan.

Now, all I want is to be back in my hotel room, with some very loud music and maybe a bottle of expensive red wine. I wonder if room service would deliver it without carding me if I told them that my mom had just stepped out and would be right back.

If I ever even find my way back there. I trudge down the ugly, dark hallway, which probably leads to Mordor. *Be awesome be awesome be awesome.* The words pound through my head with every heavy step. If I was awesome, people wouldn't keep leaving me. My friends. Brad. Brad's friends. My birth dad. Stephen-the-Leaver. Grayson.

I turn a corner and go through a door and find myself at the edge of the hotel lobby. Which should be a relief, but every step feels like a slog as I hike through the lobby, past the front-desk clerks, who don't even seem to notice me, to the elevators.

It's this poster. This stupid, meaningless, very-not-awesome poster. It's weighing me down with its epic blah-ness. A garbage can sits beside the elevators, and as the elevator dings its arrival, I scrunch up the poster and shove it deep into the trash, where it belongs.

The elevator doors open, and I step inside the gloomy, empty cube and stand by myself in the center of the dingy square of carpet. I am not awesome. If I was awesome, I wouldn't be so miserably alone.

The doors open again, and I begin my trek down the just-as-gloomy, empty hallway to my room.

Except the hallway's not empty. Outside a hotel room door—my hotel room door—someone is sitting on the carpet, back against the wall, knees pulled to her chest.

Kat.

She looks up at me as I draw near. Her winter coat is spread out under her like a picnic blanket, and a bulging backpack sits beside her. A strand of hair has slipped out of her ponytail to hang over her shoulder.

"Hi," she says shyly, as if we've just met.

"What are you—why—how did you get here?" I slide down the wall, dropping into place beside her.

"Granddad," she says. "And Luke. Oh, and this." She holds

out her fist and opens it to reveal a purple button. My button. The one I gave her the night of Granddad's stroke.

"I'm so glad you're here," I say. And then I lean into her shoulder and start bawling like a baby.

24

KAT

MEG SOBS INTO MY SHOULDER FOR A LONG TIME. TEARS AND PROBABLY SNOT seep through my shirt and press hot against my skin.

It was actually worth it. The puking in the airport bathroom. The three thousand breaths I counted on the plane before finally falling asleep for the rest of the flight. The long, creepy forever-ness of this hallway after Luke dropped me here so he could go to some party. It didn't feel like it at the time—it felt like I was foolish and irrational—but now it feels like nothing. Because it *was* nothing if it got me to Meg when she needed me. I wrap my arm around her shoulders and squeeze.

When she finally stops shuddering, I search through my backpack. I find a single probably-not-used Kleenex and offer it to her. She blows her nose, then pats at her makeup-streaked cheeks with the snot-drenched tissue.

"Let's go inside," I tell her, gesturing toward her hotel room with my head. I've sat in this hallway long enough. I've counted every faded gold swirl in this bloodred carpet, have imagined every person who might be behind every door and what they might try to say to me if they found me here, looking homeless and out of place in this hallway. I stand, offer my hand to Meg, and haul her to her feet. As she opens the hotel room door, I grab my backpack and Meg's discarded Kleenex from the floor—I can wash my hands afterward—then follow Meg inside.

Meg stops just inside the room, shoulders slumped. Her eyes are red-rimmed, and a black smear of mascara cuts across her cheek like a battle scar.

"I had sex with him," she blurts out.

"LumberLegs?" There's no way. Her bizarre plan can't possibly have worked.

"No, Grayson."

"Oh," I say. Then, "Oh!" It all makes sense. The mood swings, the panic, her obsession with marrying LumberLegs. "Are you pregnant?"

"Why? Because I'm black? Seriously, Kat? We used protection."

"No, I—" I break off, catching myself. I want to tell Meg that it has nothing to do with her being black and everything to do with the fact that even though I know in theory that lots of kids in our grade are having it, the word immediately makes me think about health class and signs at the doctor's office and the terrible things that happen in books like *Cider House Rules*. But we learned in social studies that people can be racist without even realizing it, and besides, this isn't about me, it's about Meg. And if I've made her feel like a stereotype, I feel terrible. So instead of asking if they used two different forms of protection, like they taught us in health, I say, "Well, that's good, then."

"I guess." She marches over to the far bed and pitches herself backward onto it, landing with a grunt. She spreads her arms and legs out like a star and stares unblinkingly up at the ceiling.

I'm so incredibly out of my depth here. How are people supposed to feel after they've done the *s* word with someone— ecstatic? swoony? broken? terrified? I've never really thought about the emotions side of it, just the pregnancy and STDs and other scariness side.

I snatch the blanket off the other bed. "Here," I say, spreading it over her. "Make a cocoon." Cocoons are the best. Warmth, safety—a soft, fuzzy shield.

She blinks at me for a minute, seemingly confused, even though she's seen me cocoon half a dozen times. Then the haze clears from her eyes. "Yes," she says simply. She grabs the edges of both blankets, holding them tight against her body. Then she rolls over once, twice, three times, and tumbles off the edge of the bed with a thud.

"Meg! Are you okay?" I leap onto the bed and peer over the edge. She lies facedown on the ground, blanket still wrapped tight around her, face smushed into the grimy carpet, shoulders shaking—with laughter, I hope. "Are you okay?" I ask again.

"Can you roll me over?" she says into the floor. She's definitely laughing.

I clamber around her, grab an edge of the cocoon, and pull.

Meg blinks up at me, arms pinned to her sides inside the blanket.

"Do you want out?" I ask.

She shakes her head, sliding her hair back and forth along the floor. She looks like she hasn't slept in days.

"Ugh, what is wrong with me?" she asks the ceiling.

"There's nothing wrong with you!"

"Then why doesn't anyone like me? Guys . . . friends . . . Grayson . . ."

"He liked you enough to . . . well, you know." I sit in the nearby armchair.

"Sure. And then broke up with me right after."

"He did *what*?"

"I mean, he didn't explicitly. But he wanted to, I could tell. And so I left, and he didn't call me again, ever, so that's basically breaking up with me, right? And it was kind of my fault, but still, I—"

And then she's sobbing again.

I slide to the floor, rest my hand where I think hers is under the blankets, then lie down beside her on the germy carpet, tilting my head until it presses against hers.

When her shoulders stop shuddering, she sniffs, then cranes her neck forward and wipes her nose along the edge of the blanket. Then her head drops back with a thud.

"Even my own dad doesn't want me," she says.

"He died. That doesn't mean he didn't want you."

"No, not—I meant Stephen. I mean, I know he's not my bio dad, but he was there for like seven years. And then he didn't want custody of me. Didn't even ask for visitation time. I saw the court papers." She kicks her feet, trying to loosen the straitjacket blankets. "I mean, am I super annoying or something?" Kick. Kick. "Do I have bad breath?" Kick. "Is it an ADHD thing?" Kick. "Maybe I'm too forgetful. Or that other thing. Immunity. No. Imbecile. No. You know, it starts with an *i* and means I make bad decisions." Kick. Kick. Kick. Kick. "Ugh, I hate when I can't think of words. Maybe other people hate that, too. Maybe that's why everyone leaves me." Kick-kick-kickkickkick.

"Meg, stop! Meg!" I grab at her flailing legs, which are only tangling her up further and further in the mess of blankets, and pin them to the ground. "You are not annoying." I find the edge of one of the blankets under her knee and pull it out. "And I'd tell you if you had bad breath. Lift your shoulder, please. You are amazing. And your other knee. I mean it. You're smart, and you're so brave. For my entire flight here, I kept feeling for your purple button in my pocket, and I thought over and over that if that button held even just the tiniest fraction of your bravery, that would be enough."

Meg sits up, shaking off the last bit of her blanket prison. She stares at me with big puppy-dog eyes.

I stare right back. "Meg . . . you inspire me."

Her eyes narrow. "Really?"

"Really," I say.

"Then why did he leave? Stephen, I mean. Why did he tell the judge I'm not his real daughter?" She leans back against the bed, shoulders sagging. She loved him as her dad—that much is obvious. Which means the next part is obvious, too.

"Because he's an idiot," I say. "And a jerk. You don't deserve to be treated like that."

She stands abruptly. "You're right. I'm going to tell him that."

"What, now?"

"Yes, now." She strides toward the door.

I pull the purple button from my pocket. "Do you want—" But she's already out the door. Which is fine. Because Meg doesn't need a button to be brave. She just is.

MEG

I POUND ON THE DOOR. THEN POUND AGAIN. AND AGAIN.

After about a million knocks, it finally clicks open. Stephen-the-Leaver stands in the doorway in his plaid pajama pants and oversized T-shirt, lines from the sheets etched into his cheek as if he was already sleeping. Which he probably was. He always went to bed idiotically early.

"Oh, you're back," he says, then yawns and turns to look at the bedside clock. "It's not even eleven yet."

Turned sideways, he no longer fills the doorframe, and I push past him into the room. As the door clicks shut, we turn to face each other like we're about to duel. "You left!" I shout. "How could you do that to me? How could you leave like that?"

"I thought you didn't want me to come to—oh, not that You-Tuber thing." He wipes the sleep out of his eye and studies me. "You mean the divorce. Meg, you're old enough to understand how these things work. Your mom and I, we just didn't love—"

"No, not Mom. I mean me. How could you leave me like that? You didn't leave the halflings. You pick them up all those weekends, and on Wednesdays and special occasions, and I was just supposed to—what did you say, call you whenever I wanted? For like the first six months, you never even tried to call me."

He runs his hand over his scalp. "You were so angry. I thought you just needed some—"

"What, because a girl's never been mad at her dad before?"

My cheeks flush hot, and I wish I could take the *d* word back. He doesn't think of me like that—not anymore, and apparently not ever. He was my dad, but I was not his daughter. My eyes brim with tears, but I blink them back. I've cried enough tonight. I am not going to cry in front of him.

I stand as tall and straight as I can. "I didn't deserve that. I didn't deserve to be treated that way. I might have ADHD and be annoying sometimes and have trouble holding on to friends and not understand math, but I'm brave and funny and . . . inspiring, even. You may never have thought of me as your daughter, but you still shouldn't have treated me like that."

"Meg." He takes a step toward me, rubs his eye again. "Is that what you think? That I didn't think of you as my daughter?"

"That's what you told the judge."

His brow furrows. "Did your mother tell you that?"

"No! Don't bring Mom into this. I read it. In the court documents. They were in Mom's desk." I've pictured it so many times—how he must have stood there, in the courtroom, saying those awful words. "How could you say that? How could you say it in front of Mom and the judge and everybody?"

His face falls. "Oh, Meg. I hate that you had to read that. Those were just legal arguments. I didn't even go to court, my lawyer did. I would have had to pay way more money for child support than your mom needs, and my lawyer suggested— Never mind, I just— You and I were so close. I thought we could sort it out ourselves, without any court order. Just you and me. I didn't mean to hurt you." He closes the distance between us and crushes me to him. I don't hug him back, just stand up straight, blinking and blinking away even the thought of tears. I refuse to cry.

Am I really supposed to believe that? Am I supposed to believe he'd tell a judge—or let his lawyer tell a judge or whatever—that I wasn't his kid if he didn't fully, deeply believe it?

He releases me and takes a half step back. "Meg, I'm sorry. I shouldn't have made it about the money. I should have known that might hurt you, and you're so much more important than money.

"And I'm so sorry I took so long to call you after your mom and I split up. I told your mom you could call me anytime, and when I didn't hear from you, I thought you were just taking your mom's side. She was so angry with me. I thought with a bit of time, you'd come around and we could start figuring out time to spend together, maybe plan some trips together. I didn't realize waiting would make it feel like I didn't want to spend time with you at all. I should have asked you, should have talked to you right away. I'm sorry."

I shove my hands into my blazer pockets. "It's fine. I get it. I'm not your kid."

"You are, though. How can I—I just—I want to—" He pauses, wordless, unable to argue further because there's no further argument he can make. Then he reaches over to the side table and grabs a black wallet with fraying lime-green trim. "Look," he says, "when people ask me about my kids, this is what I show them." He holds it out to me. "Open it."

Open it? I can tell just by looking at it that it's the one I gave him for Christmas a few years ago, but that proves nothing; I use his gifts all the time, and I still hate him.

I rip open the Velcro clasp. If he wants to try to bribe me with money, that's better than nothing. I think.

The wallet opens like a book. One about the halflings. Because there's Nolan on the left, serious and worried, glasses slightly askew—his most recent school photo—and Kenzie on the right, with her goofball grin and more plastic ponies than she should be able to hold clutched to her chest. Kenzie and I look more like Stephen than Nolan does, but they're his blood and I'm not, and that's the only thing that matters, apparently.

I snap the wallet closed and shove it back at him.

"No," he says. "Not that." He opens it again, to credit cards this time, then flips past bank cards and memberships, back to Nolan and Kenzie at the front. Then one more flip, to the very first page.

It's me, beaming, mid-laugh. Behind me, a swimming polar bear clings to a floating barrel. It's from that day at the zoo. I'm wearing the faded yellow T-shirt I still have tucked away in the back of my closet, even though it hasn't fit me in years.

I look happy.

"Your mom gave me this year's school photos," he says, "but I like this one best." He closes the wallet and taps it against his palm. "This is what I show people when they ask about my kids. All three of you.

"Meg, I've been trying to connect with you. I've been calling, texting, asking your mom to have you call me. I've got a bedroom for you all set up at my place that I keep hoping you'll use."

"You do?" I'm not sure what to say to that. Has he had a

bedroom for me this whole time? Kenzie and Nolan have never mentioned it. Maybe he just means a guest room. I can't bring myself to ask.

The blankets on the bed behind him are thrown back. A sleeping mask and earplugs lie abandoned on the nightstand. He was definitely sleeping. The fluorescent red letters on the clock read *10:59*.

It's true that he's been calling. Or at least, he was before I blocked him. So maybe it's true that he tells people I'm his kid. Maybe I do have a bedroom—a place where I belong—at his house. Or maybe he's lying.

Or maybe he's not.

He's never lied to me before, but even if he's not lying, is any of that enough?

The numbers on the clock transform to *11:00*, and an obnoxious beeping blares out of it.

"My alarm," Stephen says sheepishly as he strides over to it, "to get up and make sure you were back." He smacks the button on top, silencing it. I tug at one of my curls, then catch myself and stop. He said I had to be back by eleven, but I didn't think it actually mattered to him. I didn't think he cared. He turns back to me. "You *are* inspiring," he says once he reaches me. "You are witty and adventurous and brilliant, and you make every minute of life interesting. But I need you to understand something." He takes me by the shoulders again, stares straight into my eyes.

"Even if you weren't—if you were obnoxious and conceited and the most boring blob of nothingness to sit on the face of this earth—I would still love you as my daughter."

"Shut up," I say, though I'm not entirely sure whether I actually want him to. He's giving me the words I need to hear, and they feel like a gift—though I'm not sure yet whether they're more like the tablet or the skateboard or the polar bear or something else entirely.

"Meg, the fact that I've missed out on almost two years of your life is the saddest thing in mine," he says, then wraps me in another hug.

I still don't hug him back; I'm still not sure how I feel. But this time, when the tears come, I let them.

25

—————— KAT ——————

THE CONVENTION CENTER SWARMS WITH PEOPLE, BUT IT'S OKAY BECAUSE they're all nerds like me, and because Meg has her arm through mine, so it's pretty much impossible to get separated and lost. (Universe, please don't take that as a challenge.)

We stayed up late last night—talking, and watching *Friends* reruns, and eating salt-and-vinegar chips and Rolos and Kit Kats from the vending machine—but I don't feel tired. I am at LotSCON. In Toronto. With my best friend. Who looks more alive than she has in months. Her eyes are still red-rimmed from all the crying, but whatever powerless darkness kept trying to

347

move in there is completely gone.

"What do you want to do first?" I ask. "We could go to the vendors' hall or the play-testing area, or go line up for that panel."

"Are you kidding? You know Syth is here, right? You have to go meet him!"

"Uh, no, that's okay. Maybe if there's time later. Let's just go to—"

"Dude! You went to the airport and rode on a plane and found my hotel room and sat in a dark hallway for hours all by yourself. You can definitely manage to say two words to a guy you've already talked to about a million times."

One heart attack . . . two be brave . . .

"Okay," I say. "Okay. I'll send him an email." I pull out my phone before I can lose my nerve. "No guarantees that he'll get it in time, though. What should I tell him? I could meet him somewhere tomorrow. Maybe at two, after the cosplay contest?"

Three I can do this . . . four I can—

"I already texted him. I told him you'd meet him at the food court at eleven."

"Oh. Okay. Um. Okay." I lock my phone, stick it back in my pocket. "Wait, eleven today?"

"Correct. Let's go." She steps away from me and gestures for me to follow her like I'm a small child.

"Meg, that's in like ten minutes!" Whatever bravado I felt a moment ago is gone. My hands are instantly clammy. *Five stutter . . . six awkward silence . . . seven I can't do this . . .*

Meg grabs my arm and pulls me through the convention center. My feet move as if they're disconnected from my brain. Because my brain is saying, "No, abort, abort! Stop! Don't move!" But as Meg guides me along, my feet just keep moving.

Then we're at the food court. I don't know how we got here, because I didn't see the vendors' hall or the information booths or the bathrooms, or anything other than the hazy outline of my ballet flats. I force myself to look around.

It's not even really lunchtime yet, but the food court is already buzzing with people.

Eleven I can't do this . . . twelve overcooked pizza . . . thirteen I can't do this . . .

"How're we supposed to even find him?" I ask, a little more frantically than I would like. "I don't even know what he looks like."

"I sent him your picture like a million years ago. He'll find us."

"You *what?*"

"There. See?" She points.

A lone guy in jeans and a blue knit sweater is winding his way through the crowd, only a few tables away. I can feel Meg stepping away from me. "Don't leave me," I whisper, but when I look over my shoulder, she's grinning at me in a way that makes me think, just for a moment, that I actually can do this.

Then she's gone.

And then he's here.

He's tall, and scrawny thin, with white skin, blond hair, and a spattering of freckles across his nose. Behind his thick-framed glasses, his brown eyes are warm. He's cute, in a nerdy sort of way.

"Kat?" he asks.

"Dan?"

He holds out his hand, and we shake, like we're having a business meeting, which for some reason calms me a little.

He pushes his glasses up with one finger. "I thought you weren't coming to this." It's strange hearing a voice I know so well coming out of a stranger's mouth. We've never used video chat. I worried that he'd be too handsome and I'd be terrified to talk to him. And sometimes, on days I'm not so proud of, I worried that he'd be too ugly. But he's neither.

"It was a last-minute thing," I say.

"You haven't been online in a while. I was starting to worry. Is everything okay? Like, with Meg?"

I've been so busy worrying about Meg lately that I've barely had time to play. "Yeah, I think it is now. Thanks."

We talk for a few minutes about nothing—about the convention, about the friends he came with who are off at some panel, about the weather—and as we do, the voice starts to fit better and better with his face, like when you're staring at a Magic Eye and you finally get your eyes to relax, and suddenly the 3D picture pops into view.

"Hey," he says, pushing his glasses up again, "I didn't get a chance to tell you my good news."

"Good news?" I parrot.

"Yeah." He puts his hands on his hips, then into his pockets, like he's not quite sure what to do with them. "I got accepted to the University of Alberta. In Edmonton."

My heart and my throat and my stomach all constrict at once. If he came out to Edmonton, then he'd probably want to meet in person again. Which would be okay, I guess, but then what if we started dating, and he liked me, but then he stopped liking me, and then we stopped dating, and then he was stuck in the endless winter of Alberta with no family nearby for four whole years and it was all my fault?

"I mean, I wouldn't come out there just 'cause of you or anything, of course," he says quickly, as if he can read my mind. "But, you know, they're the only ones who've offered me a scholarship so far, so, um, it's the obvious choice."

I don't mean to frown. I don't mean to feel sad at all, but I do, suddenly. He's coming out for the scholarship, not for me. I look down at my feet. "That's cool."

"But Kat?"

I look up at him. His eyes are so deliciously, perfectly warm, like hot fudge. "Yeah?"

"If I did come out there—I mean, to Alberta—I mean, to go to school and stuff—would you, um, would you go on a date with me?"

I bite my lip, then stop. Meg is always telling me to stop that.

One balloons . . . two rainbows and lollipops . . . three newborn kittens . . .

"I—yeah, I would. If you asked me."

He grins. His smile is a little crooked, the kind of imperfection that only makes him more adorable.

I've talked to Dan for hours at a time on VoiceChat, but suddenly, I can't think of a single thing to say.

Meg bumps into my side, coming out of nowhere. "Hey, Syth," she says.

"Meg, hey." He's still grinning.

"We were going to go to the Wereboars versus Mutant Rabbits panel," Meg says. "Want to join us?"

"Sure. If that's okay." He looks to me for confirmation, and I nod.

Meg loops her arm through mine, and then we're off, with Dan trotting along after us. The conference room's already filling up when we arrive, but we manage to find three empty seats in the fourth row from the back, and we file in—Meg, then me, then Dan. His knee bumps against mine as he sits down next to me.

As the panel starts, Meg leans toward me and whispers in my ear. "Dude, why are you smiling?"

"Oh, shut up." I elbow her in the ribs. She just winks at me.

But I am smiling. I'm smiling because my best friend is beside me, because I'm at a super-nerd convention, because I survived a deathly plane ride to get here, and because, as the panelists begin to debate whether a wereboar or a mutant rabbit would win in a fight, Dan slips his slightly trembling hand into mine.

MEG

WEEKENDS ARE WAY TOO SHORT. LIKE, SERIOUSLY, THEY SHOULD PASS A LAW to make them longer, because who likes them that short, really?

Sunday evening, Kat and I are in the airport, waiting for our flight in the deathly boring seating area at our gate. All they have is chairs and a television too quiet to hear. Whoop-de-do. Would it kill them to maybe bring in some musicians or dancers? I'd even settle for a magician.

Kat doesn't look bored. She's just staring off into the distance, grinning stupidly. It's better than her thinking about the flight, though. She already puked once this morning thinking about having to fly back alone, but after some negotiating at the check-in counter, complete with some particularly charming arguments from yours truly, we managed to switch the flights around so Stephen took her spot and she could fly back with me, and she's been better since then. Less white face, more googly eyes.

When we saw Stephen—Dad? I haven't decided if I should go back to calling him that—off at his gate, I let him hug me again, and that was okay. He still smells of sweat and wood, even after being away from the shop for an entire weekend. I don't know how he does it. Maybe next time I'll hug him back. Maybe.

I texted Grayson yesterday. Nothing rambly. Just, I'm sorry about before. I thought he wasn't going to respond, but this morning my phone chirped with his reply. Me too.

Kat's still grinning. I elbow her for like the hundredth time.

"Shut up," she says, for like the hundredth time. Then she sits up straight. "Oh my gosh, Meg, look. Over there."

I try to follow her finger, but the airport is busy with people. A middle-aged East Indian man buying a newspaper and a chocolate bar. Two young white kids running up and down the enormous hallway, shrieking with laughter as they chase each other in a seemingly lawless game of tag. A young white woman knitting a fuzzy orange scarf without even looking at her needles. I have no idea where Kat wants me to be looking.

"Come on." Kat hops up and hurries away. I grab my bag and hurry after her. She weaves through the shrieking children, loops around a Starbucks kiosk, and marches toward another gate, stopping just short of the last row of chairs. She looks down at the guy sitting in the final seat. His legs stretch out less than a foot away from her.

It's LumberLegs. Holy bananas, it's *LumberLegs*.

His slick black hair practically sparkles with gel as he looks up at Kat and me, who are just standing there, staring at him. "Um, hi?" he says.

Kat's mouth clamps shut. The muscle or whatever it is under her chin moves, as if she's trying ventriloquism. Trying and failing. She looks at me, wide-eyed, as if to say, "Dude, it's the world's most hilarious video-game player, LumberLegs, our idol, remember? You're the voice of this operation. Hurry up and say something before he thinks we're a couple of creepy, mute stalkers and calls the police." Or something close to that.

I put on my toothpaste-commercial-iest grin. "Hi," I say. "We are big fans. Like, the biggest. Can we get a picture with you?"

He shrugs. "Sure." He gets to his feet, shoving his duffel bag under his chair. I pull out my phone and recruit the curvy white woman two seats down, who's watching us with a grin, to take a picture.

She has to back up to get us all in the shot. As she does, Legs turns to me. "Hey," he says, "weren't you at my autograph signing Friday night?"

It's all I can do to keep from squealing. He remembers me.

I shake my head. "Nope. Wasn't me."

"Say cheese," says the woman with the phone. Legs puts his arms around each of our shoulders, and all three of us—me and Kat and LumberLegs!—say, "Cheeeeese."

The woman hands the phone back to me. "I snapped a couple," she says.

"Thanks," I say. Then to LumberLegs, "Thanks so much."

He nods. "No problem." He lowers himself back into his seat, checks for his duffel bag, then, almost as an afterthought, flicks us a two-fingered salute. "Be awesome."

"We will be," Kat says, finding her voice.

"We *are*," I say. Then I take hold of my best friend's arm, and together we cross the airport to board a plane back home.

ACKNOWLEDGMENTS

This is the part of the book where I thank only a small fraction of the multitudes of people I'm grateful for, simultaneously making me feel like a jerk and like one of the luckiest people alive. If I don't explicitly name you here, don't think that you don't make my heart beat with gratitude every day.

I am certain I hit the jackpot and won the editor lottery, because my editor, Stephanie Stein, has been nothing short of perfection. Stephanie, thank you for embracing the nerd in Kat and Meg, for your notes that always made me wonder why I hadn't done it that way in the first place, and for always pushing me to dive deeper and go farther. Thank you to everyone at HarperCollins who's touched *Kat and Meg* in big or small ways, especially copy editor Renée Cafiero, who helps save me from making too much of a fool of myself, Stephanie Hoover in publicity, Tyler Breitfeller in marketing, and the fabulously talented Michelle Taormina and Alison Donalty in design.

Thank you to my agent, Lauren Abramo at Dystel, Goderich & Bourret, who has been equal parts agent, therapist, and friend. Lauren, you are better than a freshly baked chocolate chip cookie with lactose-free milk. Thanks to the entire team at DG&B, including Mike Hoogland and Kemi Faderin, who make magic happen with numbers and money, and Sharon Pelletier, who social medias all the things.

Thank you to my family. To Mom, who loved Kat and Meg from the beginning like they were her own blood. To Em, who is my blood, but who I would choose as a friend. To Dad, Will, Anyu, Dan, Bear, Monkey, and the rest of my immediate and extended family, who send all their love and support to me from basically across the world.

I am so grateful to my critique group. I owe pretty much everything I know about writing novels to the years we've spent together. Leann Orris, you always saw what I was trying to do and helped me get there. Kat and Meg are as much yours as they are mine. Terri Bruce, thank you for all your tough-love pep talks. And Aimee, Teresa, Jeremy, Beth, and Sean, I am thankful for all your feedback and support.

To the Kats to my Meg and the Megs to my Kat, thank you thank you thank you. Katelyn Larson, you are the Sam to my Frodo. Laura Geddes, thank you for every friendship date we've had and for every one to come. Emily Bain Murphy, you are the heart on the crook of my elbow. I love you all dearly.

Sometimes I wonder how I'm possibly still standing, and then I look down and see all the people holding me up. Bree Barton, Caitie Flum, Chelsea Sedoti, Erin and Chris Dawson, Isabel Van Wyk, Jilly Gagnon, Kayla Olson, Keira Drake, Nic Stone—thank you for keeping me from falling into the abyss.

Thank you to my writer family, including K, Greggles, Morgan, Rachel, Jo, Josh, Katie, Jess, LL, Carrie, Tasha, Jason, and others already mentioned. You are my team, my strength, my cheerleaders, my silliness, my happiness.

Thanks to Allisha Ena Short, who let me steal the fine details of her life and give them to Meg. I am so grateful for my early readers, Dhonielle Clayton, Leah Henderson, Rebecca Barrow, Brianne Hoines, and Monica Bellous, without whom Kat and Meg would be stuck in just two dimensions, when they belong in at least seven.

Thank you to my fab swankies and electrics and sixteeners and Twitter peeps and every other beautiful soul I've met in this writerverse. Nothing can convince me that there are fewer of you than there are stars in the sky, because even when it's dark, I feel surrounded by light.

To YouTubers VintageBeef, Guude, Aurcylian, and the rest of the current and former Mindcrackers. Thank you for providing years of entertainment, suspense, personality, and laughs for my obsessive fangirl enjoyment.

And to my rock, Lorne. Thank you for sticking with me even when I'm a workaholic, exhausted, nervous wreck. More than that, thank you for supporting me and loving me and helping me know that everything will be okay. Oh, and thank you for the turtle. I love you.

Finally, thanks to God—for everything, forever and always.